CLIPPERTON

A Novel

CLIPPERTON

KARL BERGER

A Novel

HH
HARBOR
HOUSE
AUGUSTA

CLIPPERTON
By Karl Berger
A Harbor House Book/2006

Copyright © 2006 by Karl Berger

Harbor House
111 Tenth St.
Augusta, GA 30901
www.harborhousebooks.com

Cover design by Renee Conaway
Book design by Nathan Elliott

Library of Congress Cataloging-in-Publication Data
Berger, Karl, 1941-
  Clipperton : a novel / Karl Berger.
     p. cm.
  ISBN 1-891799-68-1 (trade pbk.)
  1. Clipperton Island--Fiction. I. Title.
  PS3602.E7543C55 2006
  813'.6--dc22
                            2006028218

Printed in the U.S.A.

10 9 8 7 6 5 4 3 2 1

The novel is dedicated to my wife Denise,
"The Cat Whisperer."

ACKNOWLEDGEMENTS

My thanks and gratitude go to Pamela Painter who decades ago taught me the first steps, to Sharon Stark who guided me through the finer points of short story writing and helped me struggle with the demands of a full-length novel, and to Elayne Masters who corrected and deftly chiseled my prose.

I also received guidance with technical aspects of the story: B. Gen. R.R. Porter U.S.M.C. (Ret.) helped me with military questions, Georgia Wahl from the Phipps Conservatory with details of orchids, and Byron Custer, my longtime flying teacher, with aeronautical advice.

Thanks also to my friend Maynard Witherell with whom I exchanged many thoughts, thus sharpening my perception of what this novel is all about.

"But he didn't see Auschwitz and despair.
He despaired as a way of not seeing Auschwitz."
—Adam Gopnik about French writer M. Cioran,
The New Yorker

BAVARIAN BURIAL

THE ROAD FROM WEILHEIM TO TUTZING winds between rolling hills. It meanders and snakes. It lulls you as it cradles itself into the small valleys. You don't suspect the drop to the lake. You drive across the rim. You fall into the chute. A straight run of half a mile directly toward the lake and a sharp turn at the bottom.

Hans Herrmann knew the road, but on that evening in April 1961 his Volkswagen ran off the track where the road turned away from the water. The car became airborne and plunged into the lake. There were no brake marks. Nobody witnessed the accident although somebody reported that the Volkswagen had briefly stopped on top of the hill before proceeding down the road.

They pulled him out of the water the next morning when a fisherman detected the vehicle. It was upright, and no signs of a struggle to exit the car were evident. During the night most of the orchids that had been carried on the backseat of the car had ascended through the half-open window and had floated to the surface where the fisherman spotted a carpet of yellow blossoms.

They buried him two days later, his body seamed by the very orchids that had ascended to the surface during the night of his death. Herrmann was married but had no relatives, no sister nor brother, and whoever might have been related had been killed in the war or scattered across Europe. Hans' parents had burnt to death during the Dresden bombings. And he had been a loner, secretive and brooding. A muted man sapped by hidden forces.

Rick, Hans Herrmann's brother-in-law, had flown in from the States on short notice. There were but a dozen people when the coffin was lowered into the earth. It was raining and the few colleagues from the BMW factory where Hans Herrmann had

11

worked as an engineer turned down their faces and pulled up the collars of their coats, then trudged away.

Although Frank was ten years old when his father died, he would never remember the burial well, but for weeks after his father's death, he would wake during the night and throw his hands into the air to hold on to a dreamscape of orchids as if they had the power to lift him up from the depth.

Had the life of frank's father been rooted locally, they might have given him a Bavarian wake, the way it might be done even today as a secret custom in some corners of the Isar region, only a faint copy of how it had been done say a hundred years ago, publicly, hysterically, with all the people of the village waiting in the local beer restaurant for the four church bells to be rung, at which time the taps would be hastily closed, the beer steins taken off the tables, and everybody would gather in the low-ceilinged kitchen of the departed and then take turns stepping into the living room, where the elders had put the deceased up in an open coffin.

There would have been candles in shallow plates and rows of candles on long boards and tall candles that looked like cattails and candles as stumpy as doorknobs. The elders would have stayed all night, their knotted stubbly faces rendered gaunt in the wash of light. There would have been children scurrying between the candles kicking up pulsing flickers, furtively blowing at them as if to challenge the lights, and they would have gently been reprimanded and told to dampen their voices so as not to disturb the peace of the departed.

There would have been coffee in the wee hours of the morning when the children would all have fallen asleep on the floor and the mumbling voices of the adults would not have been more than the lapping in a sea of dreams.

And if the departed had come from a long line of local ancestors, the priest would have given permission to take out the family's skulls as they had been preserved for hundreds of years in the parochial church, where the worshippers on their way to receive the Eucharist would pass the narrow alcove in which they were displayed, thus reminding the worshippers of their mortality, a thought never strange to the worshippers' minds during times when death at home was common and people knew houses by the names of those who died in them. The skulls would have been placed in a line and seamed with candles, and the mourners would pass the skulls and read the dates of birth and death that had been inscribed across the foreheads, and if the departed had been well known, somebody might have painted a wreath onto the skull and inscribed the names and dates of deaths and births of those preceding in death so that one might have read on some skulls that the departed had been the son of such and such who had died in the year of the Lord, an effort to hold up the chain of life against the void and the darkness that, now that the light of the candles was flattening, had begun to thicken the black inside the eye sockets and came reaching for the living. And then would come about the wee hour of the morning when candles would not be relit and one flickering light after the other would convulse and shrink and give way to the morning light.

But as long as there was the light of candles, the bereaved would sit and tell stories and rekindle memories. They would begin with recent events, then trace back timelines, and when the morning light came seeping through the windows they would end the night by retelling the story of the departed's birth and thus, in a way, his life would have appeared still ahead of him. And as they would have finished that last story, the eldest son of the departed would close the coffin and open the windows and thank the mourners, who now that they had told the stories would file out through the door, leaving the departed to the forces of nature and the feeble efforts of those trying to give death a meaning. For those elders knew that the real consolation lay in stories told backward in time, that this was the only force of resurrection that lay in the hands of mortals. They cultivated those stories and grew them and watered them like plants, for they were the only living traces that remained of the departed. Man had not fallen mum in the face of death.

It seems befitting then to weave stories backward into a conventional narrative, because we often do stop and reach back and reshuffle our steps and reconsider, and it is not unheard of that a person will splice those diverse stories together in the last of days. Such is the draw of the past. Because stories told backward have power and at certain times it seems right, even in the life or the death of a nation, to unravel a collective story back to its darker headwaters, and if one would write down such a story it would be tempting to reverse the numbering of the pages such that the story of the headwater, where it all started, would appear on the last page.

It was to be in the year 1989 that Frank would begin to travel back to the headwater. Not that he understood it so from the beginning. He had left Bavaria in 1961 when he was eleven years old. There never had been much of a family, as all bonds had been ruptured by war, nor did his father have a long line of ancestors. There never was to be a line of adorned skulls, neither in the village church nor in one of the many bone houses that to this date dot the landscape of Bavaria. But maybe it is more befitting to remain silent and leave ancient rites to the past because there are stories that burden you with a grief no wake can ever muzzle.

1

IN 1989, Frank's mother died suddenly and unexpectedly from a brain hemorrhage. Frank had barely kept any contact. So it was her brother, Rick, who received a letter from Munich just a few weeks after her death, which stated that several personal items had been found in the attic of the house she and Hans Herrmann had been living in until 1961. Some people in the neighborhood still remembered Herrmann and his American wife and provided the address. (In the postwar years American soldiers would commonly marry Fräuleins, but that a female American private would marry a German always had seemed odd).

Rick asked Frank to fly to Munich to sort things out. Frank looked forward to the trip, but he couldn't shake a feeling that Rick expected him to find something specific, and the undertone in Rick's voice made him anxious, even suspicious. Rick would rather have traveled himself, but he had cirrhosis of the liver and was waiting for a transplant.

As Frank walked down the old familiar street and the house slid into view from behind the tall pines, he found himself crossing the street to push the sight back into obscurity, to hold off the encounter. A bleary-eyed teenager let him into the house. She wasn't eager to talk, so he went right up to the attic. He cupped his hand over the doorknob and slowly turned. Everything seemed strangely disconnected. As he entered, his weight tipped the floorboards and dust burst from the crevices as if rising from underground fires. But he was relieved that even after thirty years the attic still felt familiar. He found the chimney crimps that led up to the loft, rusted thin now, and the

15

hooks from which his father had strung lines to dry tobacco leaves after the war.

As a child he had spent hours under the red clay shingles beneath the hip-end roof, his body wedged in the crawl space beside the centered chimney from where he could watch the street through ventilation slits, and sometimes at night he would lift a shingle and open the sky. His mother used to call him for dinner in a scratchy voice he could still hear, and when he appeared in the kitchen, his father would look up from his Münchner Merkur saying, "I can't figure where you're hiding." Winking one eye. Let's keep the secret.

The teenage girl entered the attic behind him. "We kept a tarp over it," she explained.

Frank was not sure if he smelled alcohol on her breath. It was Sunday morning and there was a plastic tray with beer bottles in front of her apartment. Frank crouched so as not to hit the rafters and slowly pulled the tarp, uncovering what looked like a briefcase and two cloth bags, items his mother had left behind when she moved after her husband's death in 1961.

"Where did she go to?"

"America." The tight space of the attic muffled the sounds but the word had kept its freshness. Amerika, the German spelling—a land of roads stretched like bands made of steel.

"Your uncle wrote from Pennsylvania. Sorry, I had forgotten.

"My mother died a month ago."

The teenager dropped her head. "Yes! In the letter," she said with a shuttered voice as if trying to knock herself out of a daze.

"Would you mind if I look at my old room?"

"It's a mess." She stepped backward through the attic door, rubbing her nose, and left.

After he'd taken the briefcase and the two bags, Frank passed her apartment on his way down; her door was closed. He stopped, his knuckles already touching the wood, but then hesitated, turned and left the house. He threw the bags and the briefcase into the trunk of his rented BMW and walked back through the fence gate into the small garden in the back of the house. The plum tree was still standing; the fruits had fallen off weeks ago. Its gnarled limbs, old enough to give a measure of time to Frank's life, showed wide gashes. He leaned against the tree and wedged his hand into the fork where the limbs branched away from the trunk. He remembered the routine: First jump to reach the lowest branch, then walk your feet up the trunk and hook them across a higher limb until you hang upside down, then work your shoulder over the lowest limb and roll on it.

It felt like yesterday though it had been twenty-eight years since he last climbed this tree. He found himself gripping the lowest branch with both hands. He needed to feel its heft again, the firmness it could send throughout his body, and he tensed his muscle for a short try but then let go and rubbed his hands to shake off some flaky bark that clung to his hands.

He was wearing dress shoes and slacks, my God! He looked up into the crown that long ago was his kingdom of late summer when the branches were bent by the weight of clusters of plums. He would roll them between his fingers to remove the fine white dust, bite them open, then push the broken pulp against his teeth. He remembered the sadness of that season, the smell of herbs and moldy grass, the dry stalks of wildflowers brittle and pale.

Frank walked away from the tree and started looking for traces of the glass house in which his father had spent most of his free time nursing his beloved orchids, but all Frank could see was a nubbin of the warm-water pipe now overgrown with weeds. He bent down and lifted some of the still-leveled soil. The frost would have killed the seeds; winters were cold in Munich.

Back at the airport he bought *Der Spiegel*, which was full of news about East Germans flooding across the border into Czechoslovakia and from there, by way of Prague, into West Germany. The Iron Curtain suddenly had been torn, and a mood of festive anticipation had spread across Germany.

There were demonstrations in Dresden and Magdeburg; candles were lit in windows and the newspapers showed pictures of young women lifting flowers to hands stretched toward them from the trains. But all that left him so strangely untouched that he was alarmed. He had lived his first ten years in Germany with a German-born father and an American mother and during those years he had crossed the Atlantic several times in propeller planes, which then still refueled in Iceland. He remembered languid summer days spent at the Starnberger See, his first skis slicing through the firn of late spring, the long walks to school . But all he felt now was a vacuous longing and a pained indifference as if all these memories carried a secret burden.

He flew back to New York City, arriving late Sunday evening. He called his house from JFK airport, waking Lucienne.

"I'm going to be busy at the college tomorrow," she said.

Before she hung up she asked if he found anything interesting. "Nothing unexpected," Frank said.

At home In Chappaqua he placed a gift box with chocolate-covered ginger sticks, Lucienne's favorites, on the kitchen table. He sat down and had two beers, but memories kept spinning through his head. He decided to call Rick.

"Did I wake you?"

"No. I'm still listening to the scanner for accidents," Rick said.

"Lots of guys crash at this hour," Frank said. He fought a chill. His uncle was on the list for liver transplants and the wait had narrowed his life into one single obsession.

"Did you know it's easier to get a liver if you live in the central time zone?"

Frank cleared his voice. "I just came back from Munich. Not much to report. I found his briefcase, his First Communion candle, some worthless ribbons from the war, a few notes and photographs . . . books, of course. . . . that's about it. "He paused to let the words settle in. If Rick had taken on the role of the family's historian, he should have some comment now.

"You'll show it to me. Will you?"

"Sure. I'll visit you soon."

"Nobody in this family will ever settle." Rick's voice had

become nagging.

"Lucienne and me—we've been living in Chappaqua for years."

"But you're trying to move, am I right? And my son, I don't even know what continent he's on right now."

"Jim sent a card from Nairobi," Frank said. He looked at his watch. One o'clock.

"Last thing," Frank added.

"What?"

"Are you looking for something specific?"

"You know so few things about your father," Rick said.

The remark stung Frank, but the jet lag had begun to numb him. Back in Munich they had already had coffee and Semmeln.

"I'll visit before the snow falls," he said.

The following Wednesday Frank found the time to examine his father's briefcase closely. It was cut from deer hide, very spacious in the front, its back divided and expandable. The leather was chafed and worn but a couple of oil rubs would take care of that. The front flap closed with two antlers fit into loops. This was unusual. He wondered if they had already invented zippers when this briefcase was crafted, and for a second he felt disoriented and dizzy as if cotton had been stuffed under his feet. Though he never cared about the past and didn't like briefcases, well, this one would be exceptional as it was one of the few things left by his father. Wiping the inside of the briefcase, he saw that one of the dividers had become unglued. At the bottom of it something white had become stuck. He took a pocket knife, inserted it into the gap and pulled out two crumpled photo prints. The first picture showed a World War II submarine in a harbor; the second a group of soldiers wearing German military uniforms. He recognized his father's face only with the help of a magnifying glass and only because somebody had circled his head; otherwise, the faces were washed out and wide cracks baring white paper ran through them. On the back of the submarine photo a few German words were written in pale blue ink:

Dear Herrmann

See you on the Egg Islands with Requin. Japanese. Heil Hitler.

He'd better keep this to himself, Frank decided, but as he hastened to put the magnifying glass down, ready to slip the prints into his pocket, Lucienne walked in. She spotted them right away. "This photo here was taken some time between 1940 and 1944 because one of the signs reads '*Etat Vichy*,'" she commented after she had closely examined them.

"What could this submarine have to do with my father?" Frank asked.

"You told me he flew for the German *Luftwaffe*."

"Exactly!"

"Except that the words on the back address him by name." She paused. "What did he actually do during the war?" She sat down and lit a cigarette.

"I know that he flew long-distance missions. Later in the war he was working at BMW – something to do with jet engines. According to him, that got him his job in postwar Germany. He built an egg-shaped two-seater car, which had a motorcycle engine sixteen horsepower strong. The door of this car—they called it the Isetta—swung toward the front, moving the steering wheel out of the way. You can imagine what an odd thing that was; it nearly ruined the company."

"Do you know more?"

"I can show you pictures."

"I mean do you know what he did during the war."

"What does my generation know about their fathers? They went to war, returned home if they were lucky, made babies, then told their children a couple of stories."

He knew she would look right through that. He'd never asked questions. Suddenly he felt gummed up inside.

"We should take this briefcase apart," she said. He was reluctant but didn't want to say no, and after they found nothing further he felt vaguely reassured.

The next day, Thursday, was Lucienne's day off from her teaching job, and she had time to research in the White Plains Public Library. She found out that the submarine in the photograph, a Requin class submarine, had been built in France in the 1920s. Some of the nine Requin class U-boats had been captured by the Axis forces, and it appeared that the Germans had moored one or two in Genoa harbor to reload batteries, not using them properly in view of the fact that Requin class boats were oceangoing double-hull boats with a range of more than seven thousand miles. Information as to what eventually happened to these boats was sketchy and poorly documented. It was presumed that the Requin, Dauphin and Espadon had been scuttled in September 1943 by Axis forces.

At least there was now information about the submarines, but her efforts to locate the Egg Islands were fruitless. There was an Egg Island on Hawaii and an Egg Island in a remote Canadian lake, all of which didn't add up.

Secretly he resented her finding out all this. In some ways, it was as if she had shaken the balance of a ship, tipped the ballast close to the bilges.

They spent the evening checking their financial statement and Frank looked only briefly at the photocopied material from the library. There were issues more pressing. Tomorrow they would try again to find a bank willing to finance the purchase of the house.

"This is going nowhere," Frank said. He took one of the folders from the kitchen table and slapped it onto the floor.

"Your payment for the airplane is one problem."

"So what's the other?"

"Get off your high horse and accept Joel's offer to co-sign."

"Not from that scumbag."

Joel, whom Frank's mother had married after Frank's father had died in 1961, had swiftly sold every single item he'd inherited when she passed. He had already cashed in her life insurance, sold his paper factory and bought shares in an exclusive Sarasota country club.

"God forgive me, I'm actually trying to change your mind," Lucienne said, sliding her hands off the table.

"I guess."

"You're not a player."

He knew she would get back at him. He felt like repeating it all, trying to convince her again, pouring out his heart.

Why had his mother allowed Joel to sidle into her life, silent like an eel, sly and slick?

Joel had been a high school acquaintance from way back on Long Island. He happened to be in Germany learning about packing techniques when Frank's father died. Frank had hated him at first sight. He called him "carton man" because Joel had an obsession with folding cartons. The foldable moving-van box was just the beginning, he once told Frank, with an air of reminiscence floating across his fat face as if such a box had ended up on the register of historic treasures. There was a whole universe of origami in his head.

For him the future was shower stalls that fit in the trunk of a car, complete walk-in closets, vacation homes that would unfold from a flatbed truck. What crap! Quite in step with the capitalistic method, he aimed to use as few materials as possible. Spongy wafers could replace solid panels: more air, less substance. Carton Man had always been a most genial manipulator of the void.

But Frank understood that Joel held the one card his mother couldn't resist: return to the States, a life of luxury, a life idling away in the oak-paneled dining rooms of country clubs.

"No! When it comes to Joel, I am not a player," he said.

"We haven't applied at Consolidated Bank before." She snipped the ash from her cigarette.

"What's his name?"

"Paxton." She looked at the business card.

Loan Specialist. Consolidations. Refinancing. Daily hours 9 to 4. Saturdays 9 to 12. Sunday by appointment.

Mr. Paxton was in his forties. He had an extensive rash that poured out of his sleeves and rose up from his collar like some bloody mush. Frank could almost feel the itch. He started to scratch himself but saw the comedy of scratching himself in front of a man who suffered itch day and night. The book of Job, wasn't that the part? Barely paying attention to what was going on, he lost his thought trying to remember the name of this condition . . . psoriasis.

"It comes down to additional equity." Mr. Paxton said.

"Count my plane as equity."

"Sorry. Bank policy. You know the FAA. Litigations related to planes are notoriously difficult to resolve."

"We would have to sell the plane," Lucienne said.

Mr. Paxton nodded in agreement. "I am not suggesting this, of course, and there's no hurry. Think it over."

On the way back from the bank, they didn't talk. Frank opened the moon roof. The rush of air was masking the silence between them.

Frank and Lucienne had been living in Chappaqua for several years. They rented the house from a retired psychiatrist who had offered it repeatedly at a reasonable price. Besides a few colleagues from college, mostly English teachers Lucienne had befriended in her function as French teacher, they knew few people. Everybody here looked for privacy, and if the men didn't meet while doing their lawns or picking up mail, there was no contact. The landscape had swamps and boulders and small cliffs. The houses were nestled far away from the winding small roads, small castles in the green.

Mr. Lipschitz was Frank and Lucienne's neighbor. Once a year he would give a garden party. This year the gathering was on the Saturday following their visit to the bank. Lucienne had bought a tight cocktail dress weeks prior to the invitation and had slowly starved herself into it. "Nothing works better for weight control than a high school reunion or a Lipschitz party," she'd say.

And on that Saturday afternoon, she did look great. It was one of those moments when Frank felt that he had to catch up with time, that he had lost out on some pleasures that were right in front of him. Her reddish hair was flowing across her shoulders just enough tousled to hint at carnal passion and those eyes could look so deep and perplexed. Oh, yes, she was aware of it—circling her hand on her flat belly, sliding her leg forward to make the long cocktail dress cling to her thighs. Yet still it was as if he preferred to stifle the sexual tension that had begun to build up between them, and he slowly walked toward a group of men standing in the corner. They were talking about the stock market and the fine points of BMW cars, holding their cocktail glasses, drinking for numbness, aloofness and ways of separation.

"My father built the first BMW car after the war," Frank said.

"What's that?" somebody asked.

"A two-seater."

They barely looked at him. "That's exactly how my new Beamer feels," a tall man in denim slacks and a pink shirt said, and everybody started a short, embarrassed laugh. The relief of having deflected an intruder, Frank thought.

He was glad to feel Lucienne's hand on his shoulder. "Mr. Lipschitz wants you to see his collection," she whispered.

They walked into a large study where Mr. Lipschitz was already addressing a small group of couples. He was pointing at one of the dozen metal contraptions set on small tables that were draped with the kind of black velvet cloth used for jewelry displays.

"This is a charred harp. Where the fire was hottest the strings sintered together," he explained. Then, turning, "And this is a molten TV chassis."

"What fire was that?"

"One of the L.A. wildfires two years ago. The L.A. police have authenticated the art pieces. The date is inscribed and the general location and on some pieces even the address."

"Anything from Europe?" somebody asked.

Lipschitz smiled politely. Maybe it was an apology for the

remnants of fire having become business but Frank could not see it that way. He remembered that his father had told him about the firestorm in Dresden in February of 1945 . . . how Frank's grandparents died in a shelter. They felt safe in it, but the firestorm raged so intensely the earth cover above the railroad ties pulverized, then blew away, and the heat of burning beams charred them to death.

Mr. Lipschitz said, "Later this evening we'll hold a silent auction. If you want to see more, please visit my gallery in Soho."

Back in the large living room Mr. Lipschitz walked over to Lucienne and Frank. He put his hand on Frank's shoulder and gave him a light shake.

"How's the writing coming along? I like your piece in *Architectural Digest*. I'm watching you, Frank!" Mr. Lipschitz was a towering man, all presence and confidence, a man you wanted to have on your side.

Though Frank didn't like the patronizing gesture, he still felt flattered by the personal attention.

"I'm looking for a change," Frank said.

"Continuous adaptation, the essence of business."

"The job market is tight right now."

"I know what you mean and it's worse right here. Our garbage man has a Ph.D. in environmental science."

"I teach French to students with double BAs," Lucienne said.

He turned toward her, leaving his hand on Frank's shoulder. "Can you finally buy your house?"

"We are still renting," she said.

Mr. Lipschitz turned back to Frank. "Go out there. Pull your strings!" He took his hand off Frank and pivoted his arm as if he were driving a golf ball. "Shyness doesn't pay in Westchester County." He tapped Frank's shoulder with the ball of his hand.

"You should listen," Lucienne said. Frank hated that social grin on her.

After the party Lucienne brewed herself some tea to soothe

her stomach. "A classic Lipschitz cream cheese attack," she said, rubbing her belly. Frank was sitting at the kitchen table. For a second he felt the urge to circle his fingers across her belly the way he'd done it years ago.

"Stay out of the woods," she'd say, pointing at her pubic hair, and he would widen his circles until he felt her shiver ever so slightly and they would make love right on the floor.

He looked down. The tiles appeared cold. He noticed the cracked caulking.

"You didn't have to agree with Mr. Lipschitz," Frank said. "He's making money from other people's bad luck and, by the way, I didn't believe this certification baloney one bit. He's probably melting that stuff in a burning chamber, probably has a good deal going with an undertaker. He's an overbearing crook, and you stand just there and tell me to listen."

Lucienne set her teacup on the table. "Why do you make it so difficult for yourself? Why can't you separate what's good about the man and what's questionable? He's so much better a businessman than you are, so take his advice, to hell with the rest."

"Go ahead! Bring up Joel again." Frank felt a tightening in his chest.

She sipped from the tea. For a moment her hair fell across the rim of the cup, blotting it out. "You always take the moral high road. And your world always seems to split into good or bad, damned or saved and nothing in between. But that keeps you from playing the game."

He heard derision in her voice now. She looked at him, searching his eyes. The words had nettled him but he held back, weighing what damage a bitter argument could do, deciding against it. In a week he planned to fly Lucienne to Biddeford to see her mother, stepfather and sister, and her decision to come flying with him had been shaky at best. They seemed to have different notions what to do with their lives.

That night he stayed downstairs mindlessly clicking through TV channels while Lucienne was upstairs sleeping. He was good in making a case against himself; it was the old Catholic way. But it had been his cousin Jim who in strange ways seemed to know him better than he knew himself.

Jim once told him, "You're afraid to be bad because you know you wouldn't have fun. Too bad you're not having fun being good either."

Frank went to bed. Nobody can stand memories like that at two in the morning.

2

FRANK WOKE UP when the *New York Times* Sunday edition landed on the front porch with the familiar thump. As he walked downstairs, he smelled freshly brewed coffee; he poured himself a cup, and after putting on a sweatshirt and jeans, stepped out on the porch and sat down. The October sun felt good.

Lucienne was already working in the garden to thin out the matted stalks of her favorite wildflowers. Her sister Leila had been trying to make her change the lawn into a wildflower garden. Eventually she had agreed, but not to appear being talked into it too easily, she went about the preparatory tilling slowly. And, as a snub to Leila, she let her plant only a thin row of the seeds Leila had been stripping from sage grasses that sprouted close to gravestones and thus had never been mowed. It was an ingenious method to culture grasses from a time before weed killers and lawn mowers. Ingenious maybe, but Lucienne didn't want to hear of it.

She put her hands into the small of her back, then wiped her forehead with her shirtsleeve. Frank felt relieved to see her gardening. He knew she loved to dig, her hands wrapped in thick gloves, her feet encased in clay-covered boots, and he knew working with flowers would ease her disappointment about the recent loan rejections.

This house reminded Lucienne of the farmhouse in Montpellier in the south of France where she had spent much of her childhood. She liked its chalked walls framed by ivy, its trellised vines, and the slatted light the sun ran across its oak floors. A country house like this was hard to find.

Frank propped his feet on the railing and slouched into

the lawn chair. Rick's remark "you know so few things about your father" still stuck in his mind. He wondered if he might have dreamed about his father last night and didn't remember. Tugged by history, his mind slipped back in time.

Frank's mother had been a private first class in the American occupation forces in Munich. She had arrived during the hunger year of 1947, and after 1948 witnessed the 'German economy-miracle.' She spoke German fluently, and as she was well liked by the locals around the Chiemsee where she was stationed as a secretary, she befriended many Germans. But falling in love with a German? And marrying him? That raised some eyebrows.

Frank's mother had never talked much about her courtship and as the years passed she turned even more secretive. "That one should leave things untouched" was her favorite saying.

It never had been a happy marriage, and the clots of clay on his father's coffin had barely dried when she returned to the United States.

The day in April 1961 when the police pulled his father from the submersed Volkswagen changed everything. Frank was taken out of the German *Volkschule* and sent to Pittsburgh where he was enrolled in a private Catholic school. From then on he would see his mother infrequently, and it was Rick who became close to him.

In the 1960s Rick was healthy, though alcohol already had begun to overshadow his life. In 1989, however, his time was running out. Frank needed to visit Rick soon, show him the two photos, and question him about his father whose past had begun to appear murky. He suddenly felt unhinged. It was as if these sepia prints had bared a hidden pain.

Lucienne came walking up the steps from the garden. She sat down on the railing beside Frank's feet, stretched her arms and lifted her gloves covered with black soil. Her heavy boots had left a trace of clay on the porch. Frank noted her clunky walk, so unlike her sister's glide and tilt. As usual he conjured up Leila's image.

He closed his eyes.

"Get your boots and give me a hand. Get out of your rut!"

"You saw the pile of papers on my table," he said. She dropped her head and bit her lips.

"Are you telling me they aren't important?" He glared at her.

"Why keep that job? You keep publishing in good journals and still there's no reward."

"I do my best," he said. He took his feet off the railing.

"It would save money if you'd stop flying," she said.

"The old argument again!"

"I'm doing you a favor by going to Maine." She looked straight at him. There was an angry green light in her eyes.

"In what way?"

"You know." She slapped her work gloves together releasing a small rain of dirt onto the floorboards, then jumped off the railing. She turned. "Do your goddamn paper work!"

Frank was alarmed. He wondered if all this was one of Lucienne's quick stabs at her sister, who always called when she wasn't home, who'd take over Lucienne's garden tomorrow if she'd let her, who would dress as if she was available to just about any male biped coming down the street. Wasn't that obvious to Frank? And it didn't help that Leila was a few years younger and more lithe and less bookish.

Frank screwed his eyes into the ground and slinked off into the living room where he sat down at the word processor to crank out yet another essay about architecture. This was how he seemed to spend most of his Sundays these days: trying to publish in the hope to become better known. But it was more than that. He was trying to rekindle the excitement of the years when he had been studying under the architect Christopher Alexander at Berkeley, years that instilled in him a view of architecture as a presentation of a beauty innate in nature.

It had been Christopher Alexander's book, *A Pattern Language,* which codified this knowledge through clear and somewhat rigid guidelines. It had grown into a Bible of sorts, but now postmodernism with its deliberate and strained playfulness had taken over the land, and Christopher Alexander had run into controversy at Berkeley. Architecture had been drained of any philosophical notions and merely was to be a stage for human play far removed from nature.

Frank, however, had kept his convictions, although he had worked with Christopher Alexander only a few times in recent years: during the Mexicali project in 1976 and, in 1980, the Linz-café project in Austria. Apart from this, he had done only a few site visits and a few drawings for houses in California when Christopher Alexander had been away in Japan. His main source of income had been his job as an architectural editor for the Readers Forum. This association, so he had hoped, would give him a chance to become published in well-known architectural journals. However, not much had come of all those photo trips and all those sunny afternoons spent rummaging through dusty tomes in public libraries, and when Frank would hand in one of his essays, his editor would just glance at it with a cheesy smile and say something like, "Interesting, but," and the buts came in all variations.

Frank, he would stress, made too much of organic growth. (we are not talking of plants); and bad architecture making one sick (Leave that up to the doctors); and the suggestion of individuals actually designing their houses and even changing the layout. Wouldn't that throw everything into chaos? (Who's the architect here?)

But Frank did not quit. He had not given up hope. He knew of New York's cutthroat competition, but also that the Big Apple had always been the yeast for change. And a revolution it would be! The time would come when Christopher Alexander's ideas would flourish. People would finally see that space itself was alive. Form and space would reaffirm themselves and beauty would reign.

Frank typed for an hour. The workspace they shared was crammed with two desks, two swivel chairs and a typewriter hidden by columns of stacked books, piles of manuscripts, half-open journals and neatly tied bundles of students' essays that needed to be corrected. There also was Frank's tilt table, a wooden model of Frank Lloyd Wright's Falling Waters, a gift from Rick; a clutter of pencils and compasses; and blue prints and photographs. A creative chaos necessary to shake up reality just enough to make art—that's how Frank wanted to look at it, but there were many days when he saw how contrived it all was.

Frank picked up a half-open book, Camus' notebooks, which Lucienne was teaching in her French language class. She had underlined a sentence in bold red: "An architect is always superior to a simple student, because he is obliged to consider things as they are; otherwise the house will fall on his head."

Frank put the book down. As often as Lucienne might vent her frustration, she did have ways to let him know her appreciation. His cousin Jim had no insight into this, he thought. The intellectual life had its rewards.

Walking back out on the porch he took in the smell of musty leaves. Lucienne was sitting in her oversized rocking chair looking down on the tangle of wildflowers which she had been thinning out. "Smell my hands." He bent toward her. "I rubbed open hundreds of seed pods today."

"I like that sentence in Camus' book," he said.

She kept looking at the stand of flowers. Though it was fall and most colors had wilted away, there were still some Cosmos sticking their pink petals above drab-looking stalks. She seemed to be satisfied with her work. They sat quietly side-by-side and listened to the hoarse song of the grasshoppers, tree frogs, and crickets, and she seemed comfortable wearing her muddy boots. For a while she dozed in the sun, and Frank went into the kitchen and made fresh coffee. When he joined her again, she had taken off her boots.

"I hope Jim won't be his usual condescending self when we visit Biddeford," she said.

"I'll handle him." But even without looking at her he knew she was thinking, "What crap!"

"I kindly decline to comment," she said.

A scene from the past flashed through his mind: Jim wrestling him to the ground, locking his calves around his neck, rendering him utterly helpless, and for endless minutes bending him whatever way he wanted. For a second Frank felt as if there was no space to breathe.

"He makes a lot of people feel like dirt," Lucienne said. "That should help you feel a little bit better."

"I know," Frank said.

"For one thing, he can't stand you talking literature or philosophy with Leila, can he?" Frank sensed slippery ground. He took a sip of coffee and closed his eyes. He inhaled deeply, trying to pull in all the vexation.

"It is bothering you, but you don't talk about it. I rather wish you would." She joined her hands behind her neck, tipping the rocking chair backward.

She's ready to get into it, Frank thought. It was time to change the topic. "Jim and Leila might have ideas where to search for those Egg Islands," he said.

"I always think that Rick knows a lot and doesn't say."

"When I called Rick he was in a bad way. I'm worried he's going to die soon. His sister's death really shook him up."

"Visit him in two weeks when I'll be busy during the parents' campus weekend. You need to go back to your roots. I always missed that in you." She said all this gently. Then she tilted the rocking chair forward and touched his arm, and he sensed her deep deference to the natural flow of things.

3

THE WEATHER FOR THE TRIP to Maine turned out pleasant; only a few clouds hung in the sky like fringed scarves. The flight was uneventful until Frank, surprised by a sudden gust, bounced the single-engine Cessna several times at touchdown at the Biddeford airport. Jim and Leila were standing at the small FBO building, watching. They had traveled from afar. Leila had been working at the Scripps Institute in San Diego; Jim had been on assignment in Africa. Not having seen them for months made Frank feel anxious.

Leila and Lucienne embraced awkwardly until Jim put his arms around the two sisters and pulled them together in jest. "Come on! Where's that tenderhearted sisterly touch?" He shook Frank's hand. "Your landings need work."

"There was wind shear," Frank said haltingly.

"You'll get there eventually," Jim retorted, patting Frank's shoulder.

Leila poked Jim with her elbow, then hugged Frank. "Don't take this guy seriously," she said. Her smile hadn't changed. It was gentle, promising in a subtle way, and as he looked into Leila's eyes, he noted their deep green color again. Pond eyes he'd called them and once, years ago, in a teasing mood he'd told her they had the color of pond scum, which made her laugh.

On the way to Biddeford Jim gave a running account of his adventures in Africa—floating across the Serengeti in a hot-air balloon at treetop level, camera clicking like crazy until Leila interrupted, "What's new in your life, Frank?"

"New plumbing in the bathroom."

"You're not funny," Lucienne said. There was a sudden halt

34

in their talk and they all stared out the window.

Leila eventually broke the silence to tell her sister about their mother's deteriorating mental state. "You haven't seen her for a couple of months. I couldn't bear to tell you on the phone she's now permanently in a wheelchair and must be fed through a tube; she might not even recognize you. Pierre built a ramp leading into the garden and there's a nurse on duty most of the day. The nurse is very caring but there's not much talk between the two because Mother keeps mumbling in French."

It was sad that, after a life during which she had shown so much courage, Celine was now drifting into oblivion. In 1961 she had followed her husband, a colonel with the French paratroopers, to Algiers. He was killed on patrol in the outskirts of Oran leaving Celine widowed with four-year-old Lucienne and pregnant with Leila. Still hoping that her nursing skills would make a difference to the maimed and wounded, Celine stayed in Algiers. Yet exile was unavoidable. In 1964 Celine had to board a ship for Montpellier in the south of France, where she would raise her two daughters. It was her marriage to Pierre, a Canadian landscape artist, which eventually brought the family to the States.

Frank and Lucienne moved their luggage to the third floor, down the hallway from Leila and Jim. They freshened up, then everybody met in the kitchen.

"Let's take Mother for a ride to the beach," Leila proposed. "I'll drive."

"I wanted to say just that," Lucienne seconded, so the men rolled Celine's wheelchair up the ramp onto the flatbed of Pierre's old red truck and they all crowded around her. It was a pleasant ride. The wind had settled, bringing out the gossamer warmth of fall when the brittle beauty has the quality of pushing ever so slightly against one's throat. Crossing the center of town, the truck bounced over cobblestones, swirling dry leaves across the street; people walking the sidewalks stopped and waved at the lady being jolted in the wheelchair.

They crossed horse country, white fences to their right,

flats of sages and low-knotted brushwork to their left and at the horizon, dunes. Leila turned the truck onto a barely visible path of deep-rutted sand that made the truck sink and heave like a ship in stormy waters. They stopped behind the dunes, lifted the wheelchair off the flatbed and pulled the old woman to the crest to see the ocean. Undaunted by the bumpy ride, Celine kept looking around and smiling. When Leila wet her mother's lips with pastis liquor, Celine's face lit up.

"She told me that every glass of pastis she drank made me kick inside her womb," Leila reminisced.

"It was Dad who gave me my first taste of pastis," Lucienne said.

"Can't be. You were too young."

"No! I wasn't."

Leila gave her a questioning look.

"Whatever," she snapped back.

"What about that story of the pie man and his stamps?" Frank was trying to ease Leila's irritation.

"The one on the beach near Agde? He had collected postcards from all over the world with the original stamps still pasted on," Leila said.

"They smelled like garlic," Lucienne interrupted.

"Not only the postcards."

"Even the pies he sold had a garlic taste."

"Yes! And he kept them under a glass splattered with flies."

"Where was that?" Jim asked. He had joined them.

"One place you haven't been," Lucienne quipped. A sudden insecurity flickered over Jim's face.

"Get along, you two!" Leila said. She turned and started to walk back across the dune, then stopped and waved at Frank. "I need you to help with the rest of the stuff."

Soon they were crossing a field of rust-colored sages in the lee of the dune.

"I think Jim's burnt out from all that traveling," Leila said.

"Where does he get his energy from?"

Leila shook her head as if to dispel a thought. They sat down on the rear bumper of Pierre's truck, a 1950s Ford with a wide grille and wheel covers curved like fish tails.

"I doubt that he ever makes an effort to understand the people. He just visits and takes pictures." Leila paused. "I believe you can find peace in spaces as small as the palm of your hand."

She bent down and slowly pulled a stem of beach grass out of the sand. "Ammophilia," she said. "The more sand you pile on it, the faster it grows. It has a sense of destiny. It yearns for light."

There was an expression of expectation on her face. Frank pulled his knees up and breathed in the salty air. From the moment they had left the beach, a painful memory had been tugging at his heart.

"We were here together before," he said. He suddenly realized how much courage he needed to say it; a cramping fear had seized him.

Leila smiled. Against the red of the truck, her auburn hair looked strangely colorless. "This is the dune we visited that summer." She gave it a pause. "So you do remember."

"We were on bikes that day."

"1981. I was twenty."

Backward in time, against the stream, toward the headwaters and back into the eddies. And with it the burning sense of failure and the sting of missed opportunities.

Frank met Leila in 1980. Immediately attracted to her, he fell in love but never had the courage to tell her how he felt. He hadn't dared to compete with Jim and settled for Lucienne. They were the runner-up couple.

Frank struggled with his regrets.

There had been too many paths in his life he hadn't chosen, too many chances he hadn't taken, too many moments of indecision that would haunt him.

That afternoon on the beach in 1981, Lucienne stepped into a barbed wire and Jim volunteered to drive her to the hospital.

Frank and Leila stayed back at the beach. They sat halfway up the dune and she laid a stem of beach grass across her palm.

"I dream of making love in the dunes," she told him, grazing his arm with her fingertips. The urge to pour out his feelings cut into him like a blade.

"I am not sure about Lucienne and me," he'd told her.

She had burrowed her hands into the sand and flicked a few grains at the sun, staring at them as if she wanted to blur her vision.

"It's not going so well between Jim and me," she responded. "Once we have returned from separate trips and unloaded the news, there doesn't seem much left to talk about."

Why had he not told her then? She was the one he loved.

That day in 1981 he saw a red speck in the periphery of his vision and a flag of dust, and he suddenly knew it was the truck with Lucienne returning. Leila, too, had spotted it. She stood on the crest of this very dune with one hand sheltering her eyes against the reality, and for a moment she turned to the beach as if to race down the dune and deliver herself to the water. Instead she followed the approach of the truck with her eyes. Frank would never forget the expression of defeated expectations on Leila's face.

Dunes do not stay the same; they only seem to. One does not enter the same river twice. Nothing could change the fact that Frank's courage had shriveled in the face of truth.

As it turned out, Lucienne had changed her mind, suddenly found medical attention unnecessary and, putting up quite a scene, made Jim drive her back to the beach.

"I shouldn't have brought up old times," Leila said. She dropped the blade of beach grass into the sand.

"I keep thinking of that day," he said.

Leila got up from the bumper. Frank opened the car door; she took the basket from the passenger's side. Her words: "So you do remember" still rang in his head.

"I wonder, too, if my life could have run differently," she said.

She knew. Yet he still couldn't tell her.

She kept looking at him with an inviting expression on her face, but he was choked up and couldn't say a word.

Eventually she handed Frank the basket. "Put in the wine bottles," she added hastily, giving Frank an apologetic smile. They walked up the back of the dune and, for a moment, Frank had the illusion that they were alone, that they would cross the crest of the dune and see the ocean spread out before them and all the forking paths of their lives would have taken a circular course.

As they reached the top, Lucienne came running up the dune's face, rotating her arms like a windmill's. "Where have you been? We're hungry."

Jim had rolled Celine close to the water. When Lucienne called to him, he turned the wheelchair and started back up the dune. Celine's face was tilted into the southerly breeze that blew strong enough to tousle her hair.

Jim, Leila, and Pierre had prepared a French picnic with tomatoes, baguettes, Camembert and Pierre's two favorite pâtés that Lucienne had brought up from Tarrytown. They spread a large cloth and leaned against the scarp of the dune, toasting the occasion with red wine decanted into crystal glasses.

"Your father would enjoy it," Pierre said to Jim.

"In that case we'd run out of booze," Lucienne remarked.

Everybody suddenly was chewing silently. Jim pushed his elbow into Frank just forcefully enough to make him topple ever so slightly.

"Why don't you say something in his favor, Frank?"

"I," Frank began.

"Well, Frank! Isn't he your guru?" Jim's voice was clipped.

"And your father." Leila cut in, looking at Jim with a gleam of anger in her eyes.

"He always did so much more for Frank," Jim snapped.

Everybody shrank into silence listening to the waves with bent heads until Lucienne said in a shaking voice, "I'm sorry. I shouldn't have said that."

Frank was startled by her uneasiness. Was she afraid that the conversation would escalate into an argument and Jim would humiliate him?

Jim glared at Frank, then stood up. "I have some firewood in the truck," he snarled and stumped back up the dune. Frank got up too, stepped across to Lucienne and gently laid his hand on her neck, but she merely shrugged her shoulders.

"I didn't like what Jim made of my sister's remark," Leila said.

"It's true that Rick drank far too much, but that's in the past, and now he's fighting for his life. We have to give him credit," Pierre said.

They kept eating, not saying much until Jim returned. When the sunlight weakened and the wind felt chillier, they arranged the wood into a low tepee and soon were seated around a small fire. "Wrestling will warm you up," Jim told Frank. He knelt down and locked his arm around Frank's neck. Frank felt Jim's muscles carve into his neck and a sudden fear flamed through him. He'll rub my face in the sand and there's nothing I can do nothing, he thought

"Stop it!" Leila hissed. But Jim still kept hazing Frank, who tried to make himself as limp as possible. Eventually Pierre stood up and said, "You heard her, didn't you?"

"Fine. I'll let you go this time," Jim said and threw his hands up.

The incident had brought on a sober mood. When they rolled Celine close to the fire, covering her with a blanket, she still kept shivering, so they decided to leave. Just as Frank began to cover the embers with sand, Lucienne pulled on his arm and said, "It frightens me."

But before Frank could question her, Leila asked them to stand and join hands and observe a minute of quiet. "This is a precious moment," she said. They stood around the embers, heads bent, in the gathering dark of fall. Frank felt a tugging sadness.

On the drive back they placed Celine on the seat between Jim and Leila; Frank, Pierre and Lucienne huddled together on the truck's flatbed beside the folded wheelchair.

"What did you mean when you said 'It frightens me?'" Frank asked. He held his mouth close to Lucienne's ear, cupping his hand against the rush of air.

"Whatever! Don't we all fear death some time?" she said. The truck had slowed down, and the dense fall air smelled like a mixture of musty leaves and mud. For a moment Frank slid into a weightless indifference.

After Celine had been washed and put to bed by the nurse, Pierre joined them in the kitchen. He heated a dozen chicken wings, piled them on a big plate, uncorked two bottles of Cabernet and filled their glasses from a decanter. A vague feeling of awkwardness still lingered on though nobody left. It was as if they waited for somebody else to dispel it. The chicken wings went fast and so did the wine. Pierre uncorked two more bottles, leaving them on the table before he retired to his bedroom above the garden house.

"Why did you keep Jim from wrestling?" Lucienne asked her sister.

Leila took a chicken wing and snapped it apart so hastily the two pieces flew out of her hands. Lucienne stiffened.

"We wrestled each other in high school," Jim explained.

Lucienne glanced at Frank and Jim. "So?"

"Once or twice." Frank lowered his head, realizing too late it was a sign of surrender. He felt the chair push into his legs. All of a sudden everything was heavy. Lucienne kept staring at Frank but eventually looked away. She tapped the table with her fingers and slid them across to lift her glass.

"We could shoot paper wads at each other. Frank and I used to do it all the time on my father's farm," Jim suggested.

"Yes! I remember." Frank held down his voice so as not to show his relief about changing the subject.

"Well! Act stupid! Go ahead, shoot each other," Lucienne said.

"I'm in," Leila said.

"No, you're not!"

"Yes, I am!" Leila blurted out with a tipsy voice. Lucienne emptied her glass and refilled it. She was gulping her drink fast, absentmindedly, as if to demonstrate a small space of defiance before she nodded to indicate that she would be part of the battle too.

"Honor system. Any hit counts. Three lives per person and no teams and no lights," Jim explained. He already started to roll wads from strips of newspaper he had sprinkled with water. "I still know the tricks," he said.

Pierre's house had three stories centered by a foyer with a wide curved stairway and several landings; the kitchen was to the side on the ground floor. They would start on the third floor and work their way down to fetch a spoon in the kitchen and bring it back up to the two bedrooms that lay on opposite sides of the third floor. There would be two minutes in the dark before the shooting could start.

Frank started out cowering on the third floor, waiting to crawl down to a landing where he had seen two cupboards that stood far enough apart to allow him to squeeze in between. Off and on the whipping sound of a wad broke the breathing silence. Just as he reached the cupboards, a wad hit his neck. It had to be Jim's because the shot came from somewhere above. Frank squeezed in between the cupboards. He briefly spotted Leila who was lying flat on the stairs scooting down backward. He couldn't hit her because of the railing in between. He waited, then made a run for the second floor and continued down to the lower level.

Two wads whipped by his head without hitting. This gave him a strange jolt, as if the near miss had proven him invulnerable. He kicked the kitchen door open and scooted under the table just in time to turn around and shoot Jim who was trying to enter. They know I'm in the kitchen, he thought. Quick now! He reached up to the drawer and took a spoon. Then he remembered that there was a second exit to the porch, that, assuming the door had not been locked, would open to the hallway. He took his chance, ran out on the porch and crawled back into the empty hallway the very moment Jim's legs disappeared through the kitchen's main entrance.

Frank hurried alongside the wall, caught his breath, then pushed the kitchen door open; Jim's body was outlined against the window. Neither of the two made a sound. Once Jim's wad whizzed by, Frank threw himself onto the floor behind the door and shot off two wads before Jim could reach cover. One wad hit Jim's body with a strangely stifled sound.

Later, when he had time to reflect, Frank wondered they hadn't said a word or even displayed a sign of surprise, and he remembered the indifference in their silence. Years ago he had grunted as he struggled to prevent Jim from pinning him to the mat.

He slid out backward, kicked the door shut and ran back to the stairway, where he folded himself into a small space to wait below the bottom stairs. He shot Leila as she came around the corner, but she continued running up the stairs. How could she possibly have made it to the kitchen before him? In the commotion he made a run for the third floor. A wad whizzed by close to his ear. As he reached the upstairs landing, he threw himself down, hastily crawled into the hallway toward the bedroom and pushed the door open.

"I'm still alive." Leila's voice came from somewhere inside.

"Oops!" Frank said.

"Under the bed!" she said with a low voice.

He crawled beside her; they lay cheek by jowl, still breathing heavily from the chase. They kept silent but Frank felt her breath. Her firm breasts touched his ribs; her hair brushed across his nose, and he felt her lips graze his neck. He turned his head slowly, feeling his breath being curved into the mold of her earlobe. He sensed an almost imperceptible shiver, a thickening of her breathing. There was a gentle grunt in her exhalation, the way a word might signal its formation before anybody can hear it, a signal before all signals, still folded inside the raw of their nerves. And all he could think was: Let everybody go away; let us have this moment.

After the light had gone on and the paper battle had ended, Jim opened a bottle of Merlot. Tired as they were, they might have simply slouched toward their beds, except that Jim couldn't help talking about how Frank got into the wrong bedroom. There was a hint of derision in Jim's behavior, but the more raw his voice became, the more Leila seemed to fold herself into her seat and retreat into a sheltered reverie where Jim could not reach her. Frank gave her furtive glances.

"You're telling me that while I was waiting alone in my bedroom Frank was with Leila under the box spring?" Lucienne eventually asked.

"Well! The first thing they did when I entered the room was shoot me," Jim said.

"The whole thing was stupid," she said quickly, her voice raw with emotion.

"It's just a game." Leila lifted her head for the first time.

Lucienne gave her a sharp glance.

"God! I was just joking about Frank and Leila under the bed. Jim put his hand on Lucienne's shoulder but she didn't seem to notice.

Lucienne had become so drunk that Frank had to support her as they were walking back to their room. "It was my fault," Frank said. She sat down on her bed and rubbed her eyes, wiping off tears.

"Did you enjoy it?" she asked. "While I was sitting alone on this bed waiting for the idiotic game to end?"

"I'm sorry," Frank said.

She let herself fall back into the pillows and turned away. "All I want is sleep."

Frank switched off the light and lay down. He kept listening to the silence around him. Jim and Leila had disappeared into their guest room at the end of the hallway; it was quiet in the large house. Frank kept listening to the wood creaking as the house was cooling. Simple physical processes, he told himself, all driven by the laws that had been providing him the indifference that he had sought for, but now he was restless. Maybe it was the alcohol.

Frank quietly slipped out of bed. He slouched into one of the deep cushioned chairs in the alcove that separated the two bedroom wings. A full moon cut into the sky, and the bare branches in front of the window cast a dizzying pattern onto the oak floor. He conjured up Leila's scent, her breast rubbing his chest. Why earlier that afternoon had she turned off the main road into the same grass covered, rutted path they had taken that day in 1981? Why did she ask him if he remembered?

Thinking of the return to Chappaqua made him wistful as if time had run out again as it had that day on the beach so many years ago. He knew that something had to be settled. He drifted into a sullen mood until he became aware he was intensely listening to subtle noises coming from the room in which Leila and Jim were sleeping. There were vibrations now, creaks, and then it was as if their bed had thumped against a wall. Frank's breath quickened and so did the creaking noises; then they subsided. Frank suddenly felt sweaty.

Somebody at the end of the hallway opened the door. Frank felt a draft and then he smelled marijuana. Leila and Jim sitting on the doorstop sharing a joint, he thought. He crouched deep into the chair, tensing his muscles as if ready to jump up and run over to the room and yell something.

The draft abated and Frank heard the gentle thump of a door closing. The noises started again, this time faster. Frank felt drawn into the dark rhythm, and he kept listening until it was gone. Even after that he kept on sensing vibrations, though soon he recognized that it was he who was shivering. He slouched into the armchair as if folding himself inside a womb to feel again that strangely pleasant sense of paralysis. Eventually he went back to bed, where he lay listening to the quiet and oppressive night.

Leila's scent was still on his mind, the feel of his hipbone tracing her flat stomach. The smoldering sensation now flared to a burn. Wide awake he contemplated why he felt cut off, why he didn't participate in life. He was confused but at the same time strangely fulfilled, as if the cacophony in his mind were a relief of the emptiness he feared most. The lull of the wine made him eventually drift into sleep.

The next morning everybody rose late and had breakfast at the large kitchen table. Pierre bought croissants and Leila and Lucienne threw together some eggs. They looked like friendly sisters again, giggling out of control when Leila tossed up an egg and with a knife's blade held in midair split it open and made it burst right into Lucienne's lap. She seemed to be in good humor again; she didn't refer to last evening and only once complained about a headache.

Jim burst through the kitchen door sweaty from a morning jog just as Frank set the platter of eggs on the table. He had tried to entice Frank to join him, but Frank had obeyed Lucienne's warning glance that seemed to say: "Don't try to match him!"

Frank had been sensing for some time that Lucienne was attracted to Jim's strength, his energy, even his restlessness she claimed to detest. On languid summer weekends spent at the beach Jim occasionally would surprise Lucienne; he would overcome his aversion to deep water—he had almost drowned twice in the Juniata—and carry her into the ocean, and the two would get into some horseplay that eventually plunged them into the surf.

"I like to be scooped up and swept away," she'd say, and Frank would feel deficient and inferior. Once she told Frank jokingly that Jim had a grip nobody could escape from, and Frank had paled at the intense childhood memories of helplessness.

That morning they all went their own ways, but drawn by a lingering indecision, each one of them eventually circled back into the kitchen to sit on one of the stools and fill up another plate of food or pour another cup of coffee. Huge as he was, Pierre had himself placed onto two stools and was eating yet another string of sausage links.

"What should I do with that oversized kitchen?" he asked Frank, who was sitting beside him.

"If you remodel the kitchen, don't change the flow of light! You know I always liked this kitchen because it draws light from three directions," Frank responded.

"This morning I marveled at the light seeping in from the porch. How it strengthened and reached across the floor."

His study of architecture had taught Frank to look for patterns—transitions, borders, confinements, and openings— but above all it taught him to see the light.

"Do you still draw inspiration from *A Pattern Language*?" Pierre asked.

"I am still searching for the quality without a name," Frank said wistfully. He felt a strong urge to reread the book that had sustained his inspiration.

"The book is still Rick's favorite," Pierre said. "I should have pulled him away from his woods more often."

Lucienne came to the table carrying a clasp envelope. "You forgot something."

Frank hesitated, but eventually he slid his elbows across the table to make some space between paper plates, mugs of coffees and bread crumbs. He spread out several blowups of the two documents he had found in his father's briefcase in Munich.

"I just came back from Munich. Rick wanted me to bring back my father's briefcase, which my mother must have left in the attic," he began. "I found two interesting photographs stuck inside a divider. Looking at all that material, I believe it possible that in 1944, at the end of World War II, my father was aboard a German U-boat heading for some island."

"Why would my father send you to Munich in the first place? What's he up to?" Jim asked.

"Your father didn't tell you about my trip?"

"I was out of the country."

Frank bent across the table and began to explain the prints and what was written on their backs. Everybody looked closely, holding the prints up to the light, except for Jim, who kept his hands crossed behind his neck, rocking to and fro as if blunting a seething anger. Frank could see his muscles.

Frank felt himself shrink inside as the thought flashed through his mind: "He'll always be the stronger one!"

"What could this possibly be all about?" Leila asked.

"Maybe to smuggle something to the Japanese..." He hesitated.

"Go on!" Leila said.

"Some secret mission."

"The documents name the islands, Egg Islands. Don't they?"

"Where are these Egg islands?" Jim asked.

"They're part of the chicken archipelago," Leila responded.

"Don't joke. This is bothering Frank," Lucienne cut in.

Leila blushed.

Pierre shot his hands across the table. "Frank is asking for our help!" he said. Then, very slowly, he pulled his hands back off the table; he had their attention now. Turning to Frank. "What did you find out?"

"Lucienne and I searched the New York Public Library, all the card indices we could find on campus and a dozen encyclopedias. Egg Islands do exist but none among them is a group of islands."

"You're sure there's a plural 'S' written after island," Leila interjected.

Frank continued, "I am sure! One island lies off New Jersey, one is in a remote Canadian lake and one is near Hawaii.

"It does not make sense."

"It's Frank's story that doesn't make any sense," Jim said.

Pierre seemed irritated by Jim's brush-off. "This is about Frank's father," he said, and after a pause, "We'll help him and look for the Egg islands . . . and now we'd better clean the kitchen." Pierre could be very firm. The discussion fizzled.

After clearing the table, they rolled Celine in her wheelchair to the porch railing, then slumped into the wicker chairs. Leila placed herself beside Frank. She had piled on pillows and slouched sideways, draping her long, limber legs across the arms of the chair.

"Egg Islands translates into French as, '*Iles d'oef*', and it seems to me that I've seen the name but can't figure where," she said.

They lounged until early afternoon. Lucienne had to struggle to pull herself away from the people and the house that meant so much to her. And although Frank was eager to leave—Flight Service forecast showers that very evening—it still turned into a long goodbye. They formed a circle around Celine's wheelchair, hugged each other and kept touching her old leathery face that had seen so much of Africa's sun. Leila began to hum a song and everybody joined in with voices choked by emotion.

4

BECAUSE JIM AND LEILA INTENDED to stay a few more days, Pierre let Frank and Lucienne drive his truck to the airport where Jim and Leila could pick it up the next day.

As Frank and Lucienne drove down the driveway they kept waving back to the people on the porch, their ephemeral faces soon like wisps of cotton against the dark wood, and they kept waving even after the faces were gone until even the cut of the familiar roof had vanished into the trees. For a while they sank into the silence that follows reunions when the exhilaration caves in and the hollow of life pinches the mind.

Halfway to the airport Lucienne said, "I think Jim's into drugs."

"Just because he smokes pot occasionally?"

She shook her head. "Where is Jim most of the time? We really don't know, or do we?"

She glanced out of the window then added, "He supposedly was in Africa and, during the coming months, so Leila tells me, he'll develop a trekking path up to Machu Picchu, do photography at Angel Falls, and then fly ultralights into remote Andes valleys."

"Adventure. That's why Leila is attracted to him," he said.

"But my sister has her own life and, as far as I know, rarely travels with him," she said. "This time Leila showed me his postcards, miniature billboards of his superiority. And all those teasers, 'Must come here…Surfing the wave of the century. . . . The men are stiff as cardboard here but the women are great.' My God!"

"He's putting on a front. I know he keeps away from

water."

"You are right!" she interrupted. "He doesn't like swimming."

Didn't keep him from horsing around with you, Frank thought. But this was not the moment to bring it up.

"I wonder if he sleeps around a lot," Frank said.

"Well! Leila plays the game, too."

The game. He never had played it. Was it the Catholic resentment of the shriveled heart? For Christ's sake, those Catholics should have a Latin word for sucking the pith out of me, he thought. And here he was, stranded in eddies as the stream of life was passing. So what if Leila had her affairs? Of course she always had been a kind of a tease the way she would run her hand through her hair, turn her head, kick out her pelvis. She liked attention. During her teenage years in Montreal, she made the best of it sunbathing along the St. Lawrence River, wearing the tiniest bikinis, running with half-naked guys who spoke broken French. Nobody else dared to go as far as she, or made such a point of it. Leila flaunted herself as if to prove her rejection of the puritan culture's hate of the body.

Too much sorrow had suffused her childhood. The memories of veiled women, daggers sheathed in the folds of tunics, the rage that hung in those crowded alleys of the *Pieds-Noirs* ghetto of Montpellier. Leila escaped life's harsh cruelties by aligning herself with the same lightheartedness that prompted the Greeks to explain their world by imagining a multitude of fallible gods and demi-gods. What would the Greeks have conjured up if they had had Darwin among them? They might not have felt the sting of despair. Lacking a single organizing principle, not having conceived of the Christian God of exclusion, they would have laughed. Theirs was playfulness, not the anguish of Frank's world of religious convictions and deep principles. Given a choice between the play of Eros and the compulsion to reach finality, Leila would take Eros, reject depth and play the surface.

"Heads up!" Lucienne called out. "Speed bumps!"

They had arrived at the airport.

The sight of a runway always gave him a pinching sensation as if the bands of concrete were the runes of ancient civilizations.

"At the beach Leila used the same exit we took years ago," she said.

"Good memory."

"That day you stayed alone with Leila at the beach."

"You stepped onto some wire," he said, wiping his forehead and turning his head to look at the airport building. "I want to get into the air."

He parked the truck, hid the key, then quickly walked to the phone to get the latest weather information.

The airport's self-service fuel pump was broken, but Frank estimated he would have enough gas for the return flight. Getting off the ground as early as possible was important in order to arrive before nightfall and avoid the low ceilings Bangor Flight Service was predicting over Long Island. Frank took off as soon as he could and immediately turned into the southwesterly wind. He filed the instrument flight plan from the air to save time. Once the plane leveled off and the flight seemed to proceed routinely, Frank's thoughts drifted back to his past.

For a moment it was as if he could smell Jim's sweat on the wrestling mats again.

After his father's death, Frank's mother had not wasted any time sending him back to the States for schooling. "Popeye"O'Neill had been assistant principal of Catholic High located east of Pittsburgh. He was an Irish priest who looked cut right out of the potato famine, and it was rumored that in the 1950s, before joining the priesthood, he'd worked his way through some bare-knuckle Chicago joints. He had a scar nobody dared to inquire about. He wore double-pleated black pants, shoes that looked like boats that had taken on water, and always had a cut below his chin where the collar kept rubbing his Adam's apple.

The real world, he told his students, was conflict, battle and raw power. "At the banks of the Jabbok, Jacob wrestled with the angel and received the name of Israel," he told them, "and Enkidu wrestled Gilgamesh."

He promised that whoever qualified for wrestling didn't have to serve as altar boy at the morning mass, but rather could spend the first hour of the day in the cellar gym with coffee and Danish and all the freedom to roar and pant and throw. Frank performed average, barely making it on the team.

At one of the first meets with other high schools, he was scheduled to wrestle his cousin Jim, whom he had just visited during summer vacation at Uncle Rick's farm at the Juniata River.

Jim had acted hostile all summer, telling his friends his tear-jerking German cousin was visiting from priest school because Frank's mother had her own life now and preferred to unload the boy at her brother's farm in Pennsylvania.

Jim's parents had recently been divorced and even to Frank, who was twelve years old when he spent his first summer on Rick's farm, it was clear from the way his uncle was carrying on that this divorce must have been a nasty affair. Most of the time Jim lived with his mother. Even during the summers he spent on his father's farm, Jim would visit her on Sundays in their Johnstown family home along the Conemaugh River. These were the only times Frank was safe from his cousin, who would hide snails and garter snakes in Frank's bed and repeatedly pepper his underwear with the hairy fuzz you find inside quince buds, a coarse powder which was impossible to remove and caused a long-lasting itch.

The message was clear: Go home! And Frank would have left and put up with his mother's indifference and the Carton Man's rejection had it not been for those private Sundays with Uncle Rick. It was on those days that Frank found retribution, using the weapon that would serve him best: by letting Jim create his own hell.

Caught in the conflict of teenage angst and his parents' divorce, Jim rejected his father's ideals and, at the same time, craved his acceptance and approval. In contrast, Frank enjoyed his uncle's obsessions, perhaps because they reminded him in some way of his father's. And, since his own son had no interest, Rick loved sharing them with Frank. And Frank knew this was hurting Jim, and so, in his own oblique way, Frank could get back at Jim.

Frank would sit beside the table on which Rick had laid out blueprints for tree houses and draw designs of his own that sometimes surprised Rick, sometimes made him laugh. Then Frank would pull out another sheet of drawing paper, and in no time he'd create an even quirkier version.

"From whom do you get that?" Rick asked.

"Dad was a draftsman," Frank said.

"You got his talent, boy! And you aren't a bad map-reader either. Do you remember our drives on Long Island?" he asked, and Frank nodded.

During the fall of 1962, the last time Frank could remember staying with his mother, Rick had been visiting quite frequently. According to Frank's mother, her brother's mind had always had the tendency to flit from one project to the other, In the fall of 1962 he'd taken an interest in cultivating an obscure variety of black locust (*rectissima Raber*), also named ship-mast locust because its trunk grew tall and straight. But this variety had sparse flowering, and as far as Rick could ascertain, the last living stands could only be found in Roslyn near Washington's tavern and on some abandoned farms on Long Island. The easiest way to scout the area was to stay at his sister's house in Massapequa.

Rick returned every evening with a handful of saplings and small trees and would sit on the kitchen floor studying bark and pulp with a magnifier identifying which of the saplings were of the variety he was collecting. Often finding only a few, he would lovingly pack the roots in wet soil, and Frank would help him wrap the small trees in burlap. Intrigued by his uncle's outings, Frank would sometimes accompany Rick. They would drive through the morning fog to a bagel store, pick up breakfast, and then travel the Long Island Parkway outbound while thousands of commuters were crawling toward New York City, heading for another day of parking garages, elevators and anxious talk behind glazed windows. During these drives, Uncle Rick would tell Frank about high moors with flesh-eating plants and secret islands of prairie grass in the middle of Pennsylvania, and about the way settlers had cut fence posts from willows, and how the fences were long gone, as were the settlers, and all you could see now were miles of straight lines of willow trees.

"The fence posts were giving off shoots," Frank said.

Uncle Rick clicked his tongue. "Smart fellow. You should visit my farm more often."

And even back then he would talk about some obscure idea about tree houses. The summers of 1963, '64 and '65 when he suffered the slings of Jim's tricks and humiliation in front of Jim's friends, Frank took satisfaction in watching Jim squirm while he and his uncle drew plans and walked among the trees.

Jim's grades dropped to a bare C, and every time Jim's school report was in his hand, Rick would drop into a sullen mood. Jim became so defiant toward his father that Rick smacked him repeatedly in front of Frank. And after all of Jim's cruel pranks, Frank hardly felt sorry for him. He felt he was gaining some ground on Jim until the night of the wrestling match.

The teams met in the sports center of a small college town. It was rather large for the expected crowd, but the closer seats were filling up rapidly; it was the first meet of the season and one could feel an air of anticipation and pent up energy. In the passageway Frank and Jim were walking side by side just long enough for Jim to whisper into Frank's ear, "Today I'll make you quit wrestling."

Frank and Jim were to fight after two matches that had led to warnings for stalling; the crowd had begun to shout for action.

As they shook hands, Frank saw a caustic expression in Jim's face, an icy glare in his eyes. Seconds later they locked arms. By this time, Frank had lost all confidence.

Jim started pushing to keep him off balance then suddenly

ducked and went for Frank's legs, and Frank found himself on his knees struggling to support himself. He threw both his arms out in front and crawled toward the mat's border. Already, the first row was a blur of faces through his sweat. He kept struggling, but Jim managed to yank back his left arm and pull it through between his legs. Frank's upper left arm was now pinned to the mat. Jim used his right hand to push Frank's face down and rub it into the mat. He had already slung his legs around Frank's, and as much as Frank tossed about, he was unable to crawl even an inch. Frank threw his right arm backward to try to grab hold of Jim, but he might as well have drawn circles in the air.

Frank remembered a moaning in the crowd, a collective hum of ridicule. Some laughed. He kept throwing his right arm about, as it was the last part of his body that could move. Then Jim would even stop that. He pulled Frank's right arm back and twisted it, rendering him completely helpless.

Now he had all the time to prepare the pin. He kept bending Frank in every direction, lifting him and shoving him into the mat. Still, Frank could do nothing; his left arm was pulled through between his legs, his right arm bent behind his back. Jim had total control.

Slowly, very slowly, he would go for the pin, carefully preparing for the moment he might have to change his grip. He rolled Frank on his left side, twisting his head toward the ceiling inch by inch. The lights pained Frank. Jim's grip poured fire into his neck and, as he began to see the people on the benches, the pain of humiliation flooded over him. Jim kept bending Frank's body backward like a reed, firmly scissoring Frank's legs. He was at the mercy of Jim's relentless arms and legs. Convulsing into one last effort to escape, Frank twisted his body and tried to arch, but Jim had so much control that he hovered above Frank like a spider, a chilling grin on his face, calmly waiting until Frank's effort collapsed.

In the final agonizing seconds that seemed as long as a life, Jim held him with his left arm still bent behind him, separating his shoulders from the mat. It was as if Jim had decided to prolong Frank's agony. Somebody cheered. Then silence. Jim pulled Frank's arms out to the side and bent his shoulders into the mat as easily as if he'd laid down a baby.

Though it had happened years ago, Frank could still feel the humiliation.

Frank became suddenly aware that he was clutching the airplane's yoke as if still trying to arch away from Jim's domination. The radio transmission caught him unprepared. "Cherokee twelve, forty Uniform turn left heading one-five-zero for traffic. "

He acknowledged the call and turned the auto pilot pointer to one-five-zero.

Frank remembered that at the end of the fight he could barely get up, as if by lying there his defeat would go away. He remembered Jim releasing his grip, then the silence around him, and how his chest began to heave uncontrollably as tears lay heavy as stones on his eyes.

The wrestling match had taken place in November shortly after Frank had moved to his uncle's farm. Frank felt so completely humiliated he could barely face Jim and was ready to go back to his mother, come what may.

Then came the day of the chute toward the Juniata.

During the night the hill above the farm had been covered by an early frost in the high country. The land there had been fallow for years, and the grasses had been blown into cowlicks by winds that rushed from the mountains into the Juniata valley

At breakfast Jim called out, "Time for the ice run." Frank went along, deciding it would be the last thing they'd ever do together.

In the first morning light, Jim and Frank trudged up the hill leading away from the bluff above the river, dragging their plastic sleds behind them on long ropes. Small flags of frozen breath loomed in front of them, and the sun lit up the crowns of the maple trees in the valley, their trunks still in darkness. The grass, coated with melting ice and the crunch of crystals, slipped under their feet. Jim tied the two sleds together—maybe ten yards of rope between them.

"I'll be first," he said. "Don't be a coward!"

They sat down on the round plastic dishes, gripping the rims for the ride down to the river. Frank tried to hide his trembling. They let go. A sudden rush of cold air. Jim's sled in front whipped up a shower of ice crystals. Then the exhilaration of the chute kicked in. Through tearing eyes, Frank watched the trees along the gorge come closer and fill the horizon—his sled speeding up, his heels kicking into the icy grass. Jim spun around, face frozen in terror, became airborne above the valley and flew between trees, his coat a black sail. The ground below Frank dropped away, and he wheeled through the air. Suddenly everything stopped in midair, the churning water below Frank a scalloped rim of dirty ice stretched like a row of shields.

Clinging to the plastic sled, he yelled for Jim. From somewhere nearby Jim called out, "I'm right beside you."

Frank could see him now. Having shot across the bluff, they were tossed into the ravine in a free fall until the rope connecting the two sleds fell across a limb and snagged; suspended in midair above the icy river, they were held merely by a rope and the balance of their weights.

"I can't hold on," Jim yelled.

"Lock your elbows across the sled."

In the tree above them the wood was cracking. Frank felt it give and spotted a white splintering scar between the branches.

"Don't move!" Frank shouted when he realized that the slightest wiggle would cause the branch to give.

The reality of the situation hit Frank. If I let go of my sled, he will fall and die. I can make him die.

Frank glanced down at his boots and the tufts of wet grass still coiled around them, then beyond into the river and the floes of ice. Strung to each other and frozen with fear, their only chance was to scream for help. Finally they heard dogs barking and men calling out to them. Clutching the yellow and red ropes the men threw between the branches, they slid to safety.

The ice chute would glue Jim and Frank together with a

CLIPPERTON

strange force as if they were yin and yang, two principles symbiotically bonded together.

Frank jumped when Lucienne kicked him with her elbow. "Pay attention!"

"Cherokee twelve, forty Uniform, we have an amended clearance. Advise. Ready to copy?"

He scrambled for his pad and pencil.

"Ready to copy," Frank responded.

Boston Center ordered him on a new course that would not only lead him away from land but also cause a major delay.

"Read back not correct. CREAM intersection after Victor 34," Boston Center advised. Frank still didn't understand. "CREAM...CREAM," the voice said.

Lucienne looked at Frank with an anxious expression in her face. Frank fumbled for his map to identify the intersection.

"Do you have enough fuel?" Lucienne asked.

"I'll look into it once we're south of Boston," he said. "I might ask them for a cut toward land." He switched tanks.

"I smell gas," Leila said.

"That's what happens when you switch tanks. You should know that by now!" He was irritated.

"I don't trust small planes," she said.

Frank looked at his watch. Should he call Center now? The smell of gasoline was intense and lingering. His palms were sweaty.

But Frank decided to continue. Boston Center was busy. Having obtained his instrument license just recently, he was hesitant to cut into the flow of transmission. Soon they crossed the Block Island Navigation Aid and headed west. It was reassuring to cross the tip of Long Island, although with low overcast skies and dark coming fast, they could not see much land. Suddenly, at CREAM intersection, six thousand feet above water, the engine sputtered but picked up again when he switched the tank. The smell of gas overtook the cockpit.

In a panic, Frank called New York Center. "Cherokee twelve, forty Uniform. We're getting low on fuel, request vectors to New Haven."

"Are you declaring an emergency?" Center asked.

Frank tried not to overreact. "Negative. Just a bit low."

"We're losing gas," Lucienne cried out. "We have to land right now. Right now!" She held her hands up as if to grab the yoke.

"Calm down, damn!" He ripped her headphones off. She struggled to push them up again. Another stutter of the engine. Frank called Center. "Cherokee twelve, forty Uniform requesting vector to closest airport. Expect engine out."

"Forty Uniform, turn left heading two-three-zero. Cleared down to four thousand. We'll work on it."

Without an engine, Frank would need every foot of altitude to stretch the glide. With one word he could have denied the request: Negative. Instead of trusting his own judgment, he blindly obeyed and descended to four thousand feet.

Moments later the engine coughed; the propeller began to flutter. In a desperate frenzy, Frank kept switching fuel tanks, turning the fuel pump off and on and off and on. The plane shuttered.

"Cherokee forty, we have engine out."

"You are eighteen miles northeast of Calverton."

"Fifteen hundred, breaking through clouds."

Frank banked the plane. Looking through the side window, he saw nothing but water and haze stretched to the dark horizon. Lucienne sat still, frozen, her face cleaved by fear.

The Center advised, "Cherokee, radar contact lost. Advising coast guard."

"I'll ditch," he yelled.

Already he saw a swell of dark waves spiked with white foam. Pull the nose up, up! Stall.

Horn blaring...droplets racing across windshield... terrifying thump...plunge into darkness...a black wall in front of the windshield...glass bursting without a sound...water gushing in, thrusting into his throat...the acid taste of it.

Then a sudden lift. He glanced at Lucienne the moment the

cabin shot back out of the water into dim light. She threw herself against the door and pounded the glass with her fists. Somehow, it opened and she crawled onto the wing. Frank followed her.

At least the airplane was floating.

"Are you all right?"

"Get something to float on," she yelled. Lucienne was lying flat on the wing, her left arm reaching around the leading edge. There was blood on her right arm; it appeared limp. Frank crawled back into the cabin.

"I can't find anything," he yelled. He couldn't see. The water was above the seat cushions already. He crawled back out.

"Never mind," Lucienne said, "there's still daylight and the copter is coming."

They were lying side by side on the wing shivering in the cutting wind. The right wing was sinking slowly.

"I have to move to the other wing," Frank said.

"Don't leave. Stay here," she said.

"I have no choice," he said. "The plane is tilting."

She began to cry.

"No!" he said. He felt all the ice of the world sink into his soul. As he moved away, she reached for his hand and he felt her fingers scraping his palm, trying to hold on. But he let go. It was the last time he would touch her.

Frank climbed over the cabin to the other side and crawled onto the left wing where he lay shivering. He heard helicopters overhead but none ever came close. Off and on he could hear Lucienne calling, "I can see it." It never came. Minutes later the airplane sank below the surface. He swam toward Lucienne, who had begun to shiver violently. It was dark now. Somewhere Frank could see the beam of a lighthouse scraping the thin fog hovering over the Sound.

"I'll swim toward the light," he said

"Save me, Frank," she pleaded.

When he looked at her, she turned away. Something absolute was happening between them. It was as if his whole life emptied into this one turn of her face. She did not wave or call out as he swam away, and when he looked back he saw that her face was still turned away from him. Suddenly, it was as if they always had been apart.

5

A HELICOPTER PLUCKED FRANK from the Long Island Sound shortly after he had swum away from the plane, but although the Coast Guard called in additional units and continued to search all night, they were unable to find either Lucienne or the downed aircraft.

Leila, Jim and Lucienne's stepfather arrived in New York the next morning and stayed at Frank's house. Frank joined them after a short observation stay in a hospital. For days they would walk aimlessly through the living room waiting for the call that never came. Jim and Pierre rented a motorboat and crisscrossed the Long Island Sound. Later, after Jim had been called away by *National Geographic*, Frank went out with Pierre, but their search was futile.

Leila and Pierre left after several days. The vacantness of the house felt oppressive, but as if following a deranged logic, Frank had the urge to empty it even more. He cleaned out the counters and in a few days threw away more things than he had in years. For days he scoured the floor, scraped crusts off the kitchen tiles, scrubbed every corner. Giving in to a strange need to rearrange, he pushed the furniture onto the porch. Then, as if to guard himself against the excesses of purging, he locked the door to Lucienne's work studio and taped it shut.

After one week he went back to work, but, reminded of the accident each day at dusk, returning to the empty house in the evenings was difficult. On these long evenings he often phoned Leila, listening for any inflections in her voice that might give away her anger. But Leila kept saying, "It is not for me to judge. You looked for help. You didn't abandon her."

He felt better after these calls but only for a short time.

Frank existed on canned soups. He slept fitfully. In the mornings he went downstairs and spooned instant coffee onto hot water and watched the grains spread like pollen dust on the surface. He jabbed them down, stirred and jabbed, stirred and jabbed.

December came with a constant drizzle and low clouds.

He started jogging again to ease the loneliness, but with each stride came the memory of swimming away from Lucienne in the Sound.

When it came to friends, it became obvious that all his friends had really been Lucienne's. Even his neighbors who right after the accident had brought over some dish of quiche or an apple pie and would sit down for five minutes of comforting talk were now busy with their lives. Lucienne's acquaintances from City College had drifted away, too, but one day in January, a former colleague from the Classics Department phoned and requested an essay Lucienne had been working on.

Frank refused. "Nothing will be touched until she is declared dead."

"You're being unreasonable," the woman said.

Although he knew she was right, he could not get himself to open Lucienne's studio. When the court finally issued the death certificate, Frank asked Leila to fly to New York and help him go through her sister's belongings.

The winter had been unusually mild. The afternoon Leila arrived, the heavy air smelled tart and fog drifted above the remaining patches of snow like thin gauze. They untaped the door to Lucienne's studio and a musty smell wafted out that choked him. He sat down at her desk, elbows on his knees, and rubbed his eyes with the balls of his hands to stem back the tears. Leila entered behind him and laid her head on his shoulder. He felt her body shaking, her tears dampening his shirt. Eventually she knelt down on the floor and began sorting her sister's letters in silence. She held up an envelope, turned it upside down and shook out what looked like tiny flakes of dried blossoms that drifted to the floor like snow.

"I sent these from California," she said. "I wanted her to move there."

"She loved this house," Frank said.

She took his hand. "It's good that you can cry."

"I cry while jogging. All the world can see is a wet, sweaty face."

"Oh, you men!" Leila hugged him.

They silently sorted Lucienne's letters and notes until Frank handed Leila a folder from the top of a chest of drawers. "She was working on this," he explained. Leila, seated on the floor, legs crossed, began to thumb through the pages. "It's a translation of a Camus short story, 'Death in the Soul,'" she said. Frank looked at her and all he wanted was to pry this moment away from the flow of time, to preserve it forever, sensing that something in her, something keen yet calm, had the power to pull him back to life.

"*Une lumière naissait. Je le sais maintenant: j'étais prêt pour le bonheur.*" She looked up. "*The birth of a light. I know now that I was ready for happiness.* It was the last sentence she ever translated."

Her hands were shaking.

"You both liked Camus," Frank said after a pause.

"It was the Mediterranean culture," Leila said. "The taste for life, the weight of the sun and that peculiar sense of boredom that is the art of anticipation."

After they left Lucienne's room, they sat on the landing, not quite ready to go downstairs to the distractions of television, the telephone and all the clutter of life.

Later, Frank started to prepare the guest room. He draped towels neatly over a chair, gave the flowers fresh water and stashed chocolates into the folds of her pillow. Uneasily aware of Leila's presence across the hall, Frank had trouble falling asleep that night. How alive she was. How he yearned for that quality in himself!

He thought back to the gray winter morning in 1981 when he

woke up in Lucienne's Brooklyn apartment and found himself wrapped in clammy bed sheets beside her. He sat down on the floor of the apartment, drank black coffee and waited for her to wake up, waited for the courage to tell her he was not sure, that Leila was on his mind. He'd always known that Leila was the one who could make him live. Why had he been so indecisive?

Was it because he knew in the depths of his soul that he would fall short? A phrase from the Book of Revelation came to his mind, the message from the angel to the town of Laodicea: Because you are lukewarm, and neither hot nor cold, I will spit you out of my mouth.

These dark words unhinged him.

Next morning at the breakfast table, Leila commented on Frank being a good host. "I felt like I slept in the Hilton," she said.

"Your night light was on until midnight."

"Are you spying on me?" Leila looked at him with a knowing smile in her face. "I kept browsing through your books."

"They're all over the place," Frank said.

"I wouldn't mind." She sipped coffee then folded her leg lithely onto the chair. With a notch of intensity in her voice, she said, "Jim lives without books. Did you discuss books with my sister?"

"We liked the same writers."

She started flicking her fingertips against the sugar bowl. "Come out to San Diego."

"I'll visit," he promised.

"I mean for good." She looked up. "I have a swimming pool."

Frank suddenly felt insecure. "Things do kind of drag on here," he said.

"I might be able to do something for you, " she said. " I know quite a few people."

She set her fingers on the tablecloth and looked at her watch. It was time to leave for the airport.

Leila went upstairs to gather her belongings. At the door,

she put down her luggage and asked for a quiet moment alone. Frank walked out to the garden. After a while she came out and Frank watched her walk slowly among the wilted flowers, gently parting the barren stalks. Her wet coat already covered with the white fuzz of seedpods, Leila sat down one last time amidst the grasses and stayed there for several minutes. It was the way she wanted to say good-bye to her sister.

At the airport they talked a few more minutes.

"I am still puzzled by those Egg Islands," she said.

"I sent copies of the photographs to Rick," Frank replied.

"And?"

"He doesn't know how my father could possibly have anything to do with it."

Leila looked at Frank. Her gaze was intent. "He knows more than he lets on. Your father and Rick were friends for some time. They knew each other well."

The boarding call interrupted her. At the flight gate she put her arms around Frank. "Don't wallow in the past," she said. "Surf's up." She kissed him on his cheek, and for a second her slightly parted lips slid across his mouth.

KARL BERGER

If Frank's father had been buried according to time-honored Bavarian customs, his loved ones would have had a wake, and during those long, languid hours before sunrise, they would have burrowed back into Hans Herrmann's past to create the story of his life. With the immediate circumstances of his death already having been told in hushed voices some time after the plates had been removed and the candles lit and the children put to bed, it would have been the proper time for Rick, Herrmann's brother-in-law, to tell his part.

Rick knew Hans Herrmann had been fighting depression for years and had asked him to take some time off and visit him in the States; Rick intended to get him away from his Nazi friends whom he suspected fueled his brother-in-law's despair, but Hans would always say no. Still, they remained friends until the events of January 1961. But who could have anticipated Hans' sickness of soul would ultimately lead to deception and betrayal?

In the winter of 1961, Hans' had invited Rick for a ski vacation in the Alps. He'd told him it would be interesting to ski across a frozen lake, the Königsee, which lies in the extreme southeast corner of Germany. To the west of this narrow band of cold water, seven miles long and half a mile wide, the sheer cliffs of the Watzmann rise five thousand feet tall. To the east and south are some of the highest mountains of the Austrian Alps. During winter, the lake freezes, forming an unfeeling eye amidst the mountains not visited by any living soul. Hundreds of years ago, an avalanche cut off the southern end of the Königsee damming off Obersee, a small and forlorn lake onto which the surrounding mountains would cast an eternal shadow. There, one can find patches of vegetation never touched by the sun's rays.

During summers, the Königsee is a tourist attraction. Boats carry visitors halfway down the lake to the hamlet of

St. Bartholomew, which has a church with two onion-shaped steeples, a small restaurant and a few farm buildings tucked between the lake and the wall of the Watzmann. On rare occasions, boats might venture farther south, but they always turn back before the visitor glimpses the Obersee because the waters at the southern end of the Königsee are treacherous, shallow and strewn with underwater boulders that tumble down from the icy mountains in winter. There is no road, no railroad track, not even a hiking trail. In December, before the lake freezes, boats evacuates St. Bartholomew and from then on, there will be no human for miles. Everything freezes into icy sleep.

That day in January of 1961, Herrmann told Rick they would ski across the lake with a third man named Heinrich, an experienced mountaineer with war experience. It was a last-minute change, he explained.

It was noon. Shredded clouds drifted along the cliffs. Nothing was moving except the three men skiing the frozen surface, heading south toward the Obersee. They advanced slowly, puffing small flags into the cold air. In the front was Heinrich, in the middle Rick and in the rear Hans Herrmann.

Besides the crunching of snow and the hissing of their breath, there was total silence. Rick's eyes clawed the endless white plane for some form or meaning. Ice crystals pricked his face and, despite the desolate whiteness around him, Rick sensed the walled mountains closing in on him. He wanted to return, but when they stopped at St. Bartholomew, Hans revealed the real reason for the trip: they were heading for two hidden bunkers that contained Hitler's last instructions, his testament, possibly treasures.

"We need you to blow these bunkers up so we can retrieve the stuff. After all, you're the one experienced with American fuses and TNT."

Rick started to speak, but Heinrich interrupted. "I know what you are going to say, 'We stole your material from the American Army.'"

He was grinning. His breath threw a flag of ice into the air.

Spitting with anger, Rick confronted Hans. "How could you lure me here under false pretense? You're my friend, my brother-in-law, for Christ's sake!"

Hans looked him squarely in the eyes and said, "The cause is greater than all of us. It's nothing personal; we need you. I do care for you. Rick, it's in your best interest to work with us for now."

Rick glared back, a sickening sensation in his stomach. "Who built those bunkers?"

"Hitler," Heinrich said.

"What are you looking for?"

"This was to be Hitler's last stand. There will be secret treasures."

"You're crazy," Rick shouted.

"We'll pay you well for blowing them up," Hans said.

Heinrich held a revolver. "You have no choice," he said.

A chill stabbed Rick's spine. They had been planning this for months. He avoided looking at Hans. Maybe he could talk them out of it. Heinrich took a flask out of his pocket, lifted it to his mouth and drank while keeping his eyes on Rick's face. Whenever he moved, his eyes pivoted like snake heads.

They skied into the cul-de-sac then crossed the gap that separates the Obersee from the Königsee. Here the icicled walls were no more than six hundred feet apart. The frozen surface of the Obersee looked strangely riffled like the skin of a white iguana. Rick did not spot the bunkers until Heinrich pointed out where they had been blasted into the western cliff. They didn't appear to be more than two slabs of concrete that barely protruded from the cliff out into the lake.

"They were absolutely safe from air attacks," Herrmann said.

"You lied," Rick snarled.

Heinrich started poking his arm then grabbed it. "*Ach du meine Güte!*" he said and laughed. "*Ach Du meine Güte!*" Rick felt Heinrich's grip tighten.

"You will blow them open, won't you?"

Rick pulled his arm away. The icy desolation around him spelled a grim death.

Heinrich ordered Rick to stay behind, and Hans and Heinrich left to look for supplies that had been stacked under white canvasses marked by small blue flags. Five hundred pounds of plastic explosives, underwater fuses, remote triggers, batteries —all scavenged from American Army supplies—and shovels, lamps, tents, ropes, ice picks and food for several days.

"There is a crack through the lower edge of the slab," Heinrich said once he was back. "We'll fix the dynamite there."

Rick's watch showed three o'clock. The light was fading fast; dark clouds were sinking down from the peaks.

"Tomorrow it will warm up over in the Watzmann, and like every year, mountaineers will use mortar charges to trigger small avalanches in order to prevent the real devastating ones, which means that our explosions will be just one of many blasts in these mountains," Heinrich said.

"You have planned this for some time," Rick said.

"I take that as a compliment."

Working in the dark, they tunneled into snowdrifts then slid into their sleeping bags. Inside his small cave, Rick watched the kerosene lamp melt a shallow hollow into the packed snow. It glistened like the water-dripping stalagmite caves of Pennsylvania. Everything here was glazed with cold death. He pictured the narrow tunnel that was his only access to the outside, the piles of snow, the rutted surface of the Obersee and then the immense length of the Königsee that he would have to cross before he would see another human being besides these two crazy Nazis.

The urge to run, to touch a tree or a branch or anything living gnawed at him. He crawled out of his tunnel into the cutting cold and stillness. The mountains were black, the snow was black—there was not enough light to see his own hand.

Rick fumbled around for his skis, but when he realizes they had been taken away, he crawled back into his cave and exhaled into the stillness. His breath settled back on his face like an icy fog. He relit the small kerosene lamp. Using his fingers, he scratched two dimples into the glistening snow wall, added a mouth and molded a nose into his wife's face. Lips that would remind him of split cherries, high cheekbones and eyes the color of prune pits. He felt a deep regret for his past, the burning rages in a drunken fog, his indifference. Lying awake in the ashes of stifling guilt, he tried to conjure up the line of maple and oak trees along the bluff of the Juniata. More than anything else, the image of this line of trees seemed to have been holding together his life in strange ways. He hadn't prayed for years, but he then did.

The next morning they made coffee. The day still dark but warmer now, they started wedging boxes with dynamite into a crack in the bunker. The first sunlight was touching a far peak. Rick molded in plastic explosives with several detonators. They worried about avalanches, but Heinrich said the mountains, surrounding the Obersee were too steep to hold snow. When the first mortar charges were going off in the surrounding mountains, they withdrew to the other side of the Obersee and Heinrich ordered Rick to trigger the explosives by remote. The pressure wave felt like a sudden dive into deep water. Snow bursts then settled, and rocks continued crashing onto the frozen lake smashing the ice and making water gush through holes that opened like black boils. The bunker had buckled and a wide gash had opened, but the major part had tilted into the lake and broken through the ice. Heinrich was furious. "You knew that," he yelled into Rick's face. Hans turned pale. He threw up onto the snow.

Heinrich climbed onto the slab, adjusted his headlights, then lowered a rope ladder through the blown out opening and entered the bunker. He stayed for several minutes. When he surfaced again his frozen face seemed tightened by an invisible coil.

"I knew this was to be the Führer's last stand," he said.

Rick knelt down by the opening and shined in a flashlight. The musty smell nauseated him. Whatever content there had been appeared to have sunk into a black muck at the bottom. Water continued pouring into the bunker. Some uniforms came floating to the surface, billowed across the cone of light then got sucked back.

There were pieces of wooden crates, but they, too, disappeared into the rising water. For a moment, a large poster of Hitler rose and spread out at the surface, as if all this were happening in a darkroom, and the print, ready to be lifted off the developing tray, seemed to come to life—but then it curled, turned and sank.

"We need divers," Heinrich says.

Rick turned away from the opening. "When do you finally give up?" he asked.

"Shut up!" Heinrich said.

"He will," Hans said. He was sitting on the slab, pushing his fists into his stomach to ease his cramps. He barely looked around. "It's over," he stammered.

"It never will be over," Heinrich said. He started singing: "It is spring without an end."

Although Hans felt weak, Heinrich insisted that they ski back the same night. They threw most of the remaining supplies into the lake. As they moved out, the evening gray turned dark and coarse as coffee grounds, but even in the dark, the immense snowfield across which the three skiers cut their tracks continued to stretch like a white sheet.

They passed St. Bartholomew. Rick kept looking up into the ice walls, frozen curtains ruptured by dark crags that flowed like ink toward the lake. Somewhere in the height of the peaks he heard strange pings, then a rumble like distant thunder. Heinrich, in the front, stopped, leaned into his ski poles and looked up into the wall.

"Snapping trees," Heinrich said. But the rumble became louder though the air was still. Suddenly, out from a hidden valley, they saw a wall of ice and rocks tumble toward the lake. The ice under their feet began to shudder. They threw themselves into their bindings and rushed toward the opposite shoreline. Somewhere behind them, boulders, trees and frozen walls crashed through the ice. Some smaller rocks riding atop the tangled mass were flung onto the ice and appeared to slither out of total darkness.

"Don't look back!" Rick yelled ahead to Hans. A man-sized rock tumbled by, passed Heinrich and crashed into the shore ahead. Something began to work under the ice, lifting it, cutting a spider pattern of lines that widened into cracks; then black water came boiling through the openings and spilled across the snow.

Slicing their skies through the spreading slush, they made it to the shoreline and threw themselves into the wall of icy rock, holding on to whatever brushwork and bare roots they could clutch. It was midnight. They were shivering from cold and exhaustion, feeling despondent as they realized they couldn't possibly climb onto this shore, and even if they could, there wouldn't be any trails. They returned onto the lake, never venturing more than a few feet away from shore. Carefully probing the ice ahead, they took the rest of the night to ski back to Berchtesgaden.

When they arrived, it was still dark; Heinrich disappeared in the streets.

A group of early skiers huddled at the desk of the pension where they stayed their first night. Frank's father made up a story to explain the slush that clung to their wet clothes, but by he had used up all his energy and collapsed into the bed. For the next two days Rick did not move from Hans' side except to buy soup in a restaurant across the street, carry it up to the room and spoon it into his mouth. They knew Heinrich wouldn't be back.

The mid-winter thaw hung on. Rick stared out the window and watched rain splash the white facades of the clustered building, pedestrians meander between brown piles of crusted snow, and drunken skiers stumble and bawl songs he couldn't understand.

Off and on he looked back to the bed where Hans had been sleeping for days and wondered what dreams this man was dreaming, this man who had his own devil and no God. He drank their beer, which coated his mouth with a tart taste. He lined the empty bottles on the window sill. Most of the time he wanted his mind to go blank, forget Germany, forget the look of floor boards tramped on by nailed shoes, forget the sour smell of beer spilled under tables where dogs licked it, forget the bloated eyes of the drunks in the soft light of lamp shades.

Eventually, Hans gained his strength back. Shortly before they boarded the train back to Munich, Rick asked, "Why did you want me in on this? "

"I didn't know it would turn out this way," Frank's father said. "I needed you. I didn't think you'd mind helping me."

"Blow up some goddamn Nazi bunker?"

"Don't tell your sister."

"That's all you have to say?"

Hans kept staring at the floor, rubbing the balls of his hands against his temples. He sat down and began to rock slowly to and fro and then he began pounding the side of his head.

"You are insane," Rick said.

6

THAT WINTER OF 1989-90 the snows came and went. Some days Frank felt a yearning so dense it tugged on his eardrums. There were days when he avoided any human contact for fear of falling back into the habit of comparing himself to everybody else and coming up short. Unable to forget the image of Lucienne's white face floating in brown waters, he abhorred thinking of the moment she gave up and looked away from him, thinking of how he had abandoned her.

His colleagues talked to him but their words sounded hollow and, when smiling back at them, Frank felt as if his lips were sliding off his face.

One day, carrying Lucienne's leather folder, Frank's eyes fell on a slit pocket in the back cover from which he eventually recovered a dog-eared photograph. It showed French soldiers on an army truck and beside it, several corpses lying in the dust. The dead men's cheeks had been cut open wide. *La sourire*, he suddenly remembered! Lucienne had told him about it—the grin the Algerian rebels would cut into French soldiers' faces by slicing open their cheeks so wide it made their back teeth show. Reluctant to intrude further, Frank turned his eyes away. Later the thought came to him that one of the soldiers lying in the dust might have been Lucienne's father. She had rarely talked about her father's death, and neither had Leila.

In February, Jim called from JFK on short notice. He was back from Kenya, passing through, and wanted to visit.

"Better say yes," he said. "I can help you keep your head up."

You never could, Frank felt like saying, but not being quick

76

with evasions, he agreed.

The next evening Frank was waiting for Jim at the Chappaqua railroad station. Though it was almost dark, anybody could have picked Jim out from the sea of bobbing ties that spilled from the automatic doors. There had been another thaw, almost a glimpse of spring in mid-February, and Jim wore baggy pants and a faded khaki jacket opened in front showing a rough-textured blue shirt and a tanned neck.

The commotion around him didn't seem to faze him. He had crossed the dusty plains of Africa; getting picked up at a suburban train station would not daunt him. He brought with him the lure of terra incognita and a certain aloofness that seemed to render him invulnerable to the fidgety clutter of life.

Frank drove Jim to his house. The air felt so mellow, Frank threw some steaks on the grill outside. They put on pullovers and sat on the porch, taking in the unseasonable smell of rotting leaves.

"It must be difficult living in the house," Jim said.

Frank flipped the steaks. "Well done?"

"Oh! You remember."

Jim got up, put his hands on Frank's shoulders and looked into his eyes. "Listen . . . you didn't kill Lucienne and I said so to Leila. The worst anyone one can say is that you made a bad judgment; but in your situation, I might have done the same thing."

He walked away, leaning against the railing, his silence giving weight to what he just had said. Frank thought back to the painful interrogations by FAA inspectors, the court hearings, and the suspension of his license.

"You must fly again," Jim finally said. "Stop brooding over religion and all that philosophical stuff. The only way to deal with sadness is by pressing on with life."

Pressing on. What was it that drove Jim? It struck Frank that all his life, more than anything, he'd yearned to be filled with the denseness of direct experience. Maybe they weren't that much different after all.

"I'm ready for one of your stories from Africa, but I can't take more than one!" Frank said, trying to convey irony.

For a second Jim looked stunned, as if ready to ask, "Me? Overbearing?"

"Well. Here it is! In the Serengeti, I spent several nights up in the trees photographing rhinos at their water holes. I had the whole place wired with remote flashlights, but some asshole poachers tripped the wire and the rhinos got into a frenzy and scared the poachers shitless. They started to spray bullets in all directions, and one splintered the branch on which I was sitting. I fell and hung on my security line until my assistant got me out of there. And imagine, through all that, I kept thinking of the icy morning above the Juniata."

A gust of wind blew dead leaves across the porch. It was the first time either of them had ever brought the incident up.

Jim's face remained obscure in the shadows. In a strange way he reminded Frank of Lucienne; she would lean back against the railing the way Jim did.

Jim broke the silence. "What's Joel doing these days?"

"Dotting Sarasota with carton condominiums, I guess."

"I have some good pot," Jim said. "But it's a waste if nobody joins in."

"What the heck!" Frank said.

"Shit's good." Jim lit the joint, sucked some glow into it then handed it to Frank. They sat on the dark porch handing it off, creating points of light going from one to the other.

"Hell! We need some music."

Jim grinned when Frank hauled a boom box to the door and put in a tape of the Beach Boys. They slouched back in their chairs, listening in silence. Waiting for the feeling of riding a wave, of floating, Frank remembered lying beside Lucienne on the floor of her Brooklyn apartment listening to this very tape, blowing pot smoke into a window fan, giggling. Then that image faded, and he kept remembering a hill with sandy crests scraped into the flat landscape south of Munich. It had to be one of the German Volkschule excursions, maybe the last geology trip before his father's death.

Frank bent forward in his chair and looked at Jim's limber figure. A weak light from the living room slanted dark furrows into Jim's face.

"You haven't asked me about Leila," Jim suddenly said.

"I talk to her quite often."

"Didn't she visit you?"

"She helped me go through her sister's belongings."

"Before Biddeford you saw her hardly once a year."

"She wants me to leave for California."

"You're not cut out for California," Jim said. "Well, what I mean is you're one of those Easterners who wouldn't be happy there." He pulled back his feet, tapped the floor.

"California's where the future of architecture is going to be," Frank said.

"Where do you think you might be heading?"

"LA."

"I doubt you'll like it."

"And you?" Frank asked. "What are you heading for?"

"What's coming up now will be my last big job for a while. Some photo work on rope bridges in South America and then, who knows, I might just settle down…. Surprised?"

Frank nodded his head.

"Could be with Leila."

"I am surprised," Frank said. "Hard to give up a life like yours," he added.

"No boring desk job for me."

"We went different ways," Frank said.

The sudden silence was oppressive. Frank felt clammy.

"My father helped you a lot," Jim said.

"Yes."

"He paid your way into architecture school."

"Talking of architecture still makes him happy," Frank said.

"I hardly knew him as happy." Jim took a sip of wine, bit on the glass. "You don't know his dark side."

"You could have developed some interest, come toward him."

"Nope! Not me."

Frank felt as if Jim were peeling him raw. "I'm going to visit him," he said.

"I always wondered about those two."

"Who?"

"Your father and my father," Jim said.

The telephone rang. It was Leila. Jim started to get out of his seat but Frank waved him down. "It's for me." Then, after a few seconds, cupping the receiver with his palm, Frank announced, "Leila found the location of those Egg Islands."

Frank kept talking for several minutes in a low voice before he handed Jim the receiver.

When Jim hung up, Frank had already opened a map of the Eastern Pacific. He pointed at a dot about six hundred miles off the Pacific coast of Mexico.

"She's telling me Clipperton is an atoll barely four miles across. Nobody lives on it. She says the Egg Islands are part of it. No wonder nobody ever heard of them."

"How big are they?"

"Leila guesses they're thirty feet, each side."

"Ridiculous . . . how did she ever find out?"

"Leila's lab at Scripps is at the end of a hallway . . ."

"I know her office," Jim interrupted.

"Anyway, the Scripps has maps of remote islands hung in that hallway. Leila walks by those maps every day, but yesterday for the first time she had a close look, and there they wére, smack in the middle of the tiny Clipperton atoll: *Les Isles d'Oeuf.*"

"Why the French name?"

"Clipperton is French." Lifting his hand, "Don't ask!"

"Thirty feet . . . Why even name them?"

Frank shrugged his shoulders. "She's going to mail me a book."

"And how would that all tie in with submarines?"

"I still don't know, but Leila did find out that the U.S.

Navy occupied Clipperton Island in December 1944 to prevent Japanese submarines and airplanes from refueling there."

"It's going to be a dead end, Frank! Remember what Pierre said."

Frank put on a resigned expression to prevent Jim from knowing that his mind had been rolling ever since he had talked to Leila. She thought it possible: a U-boat mission with his father aboard, the transfer of Nazi technology to the Japanese—it all might fall into place.

They went to bed soon after, but Frank's thoughts kept spinning. He had worked so hard to maintain composure that evening for the sake of avoiding conflict. Here, alone with Jim, he knew he couldn't win an argument and he hated himself for allowing his cousin to intimidate him. But it was blatantly obvious Jim was trying to discourage him from pursuing the few hints about his father's life during World War II and, above all, from settling in L.A.

There had always been tension between the two couples, Lucienne's flirtation with Jim, her attraction to his bravado, which Frank so clearly lacked; of course Jim couldn't resist toying with her, watching her succumb to his charm.

Yet both of them seethed when Frank and Leila exchanged a furtive glance or engaged in deep conversation that excluded them. Perhaps they recognized that theirs could be a deep and real passion. Frank understood Lucienne's jealousy; in her own way, she did love both of them.

But Jim, saw Leila as one more conquest, a convenience that suited his wayfaring lifestyle. And now Jim sensed something developing between Leila and Frank, and his relationship with Leila was one more thing he could use to show dominance over Frank. He could fuck Leila every time he came back from who knows where, with timid Frank neatly tucked away in New York.

The thought ripped Frank. He left the bedroom, walked by the guest room where Jim was sleeping, went downstairs and sat down at the kitchen table. Drinking more of the Merlot dulled the impact of Jim's remarks, and Frank's thoughts slipped back into the past, memories of his father's funeral washing into his mind.

Spring of 1961: The fuzz of first leaves on the oak trees appeared like little torches lighting the way. Uncle Rick was driving a Beetle Volkswagen behind the black limousine that carried Hans Herrmann's coffin to the Army cemetery in Garmisch. Frank was in the back seat, his mother beside him. At one time they pulled into a rest stop on the Autobahn. The two men who drove the limousine came out of the toilet pulling their crotches. They had told each other jokes, and their laughs still lingered on their faces.

The drive took many hours. His mother fell asleep beside him. Her body began to tilt, then slumped against his shoulder. Her long black hair poured into his lap, as if to prepare a bed on which to rest her head. As they reached the mountains, the road began to curve. At times her head seemed almost weightless; other times it pushed into his thighs.

This was what he remembered most about his father's death, the weight of his mother's head on his lap, the limousine ahead, its taillights like hot coals in the night.

Family life had a stifling quality, and the happy times in his childhood appeared to him now like short bursts of fresh air. Frank was eight when he joined an Indian Scouts group. He loved the campfires on the lake, loved the lit circle of boys, their faces a rippled red in the play of shadow and fire. It was an intense summer. He made friends. And he remembered his father reading to him at bedtime from a book titled *Winnetou*. In Germany, every child knew Winnetou, the symbol of the good American Indian, created by Karl May at the end of the nineteenth century. And every child knew Old Shatterhand, the good white person, and wretched Salter, the money-hungry exploiter.

On these occasions his father sat down beside his bed, open the book and smoothed the pages with his fingers, as if he were stretching silk. His lips jumped into the vowels, and off and on his tongue snipped away a shred of tobacco. A lulling confidence came from him as he read the words, elbows on knees, fingers sliding confidently across the page, though at times his fleshy cheeks would quiver and his eyes would quicken.

Years later Frank wished he had known more of this father, the gentle man who read to his son. His father had dense eyebrows, a dark copse below the cliff of his forehead that snagged you and funneled you toward his eyes, which were strangely withdrawn.

After finishing the chapter, he would stand, put his lips on Frank's forehead, and turn off the light. Frank laid still and waited for the tingle left by his father's lips to slowly sink into his skin.

What Frank remembered most about the book was how its hero, Old Shatterhand, overcame pain with great stoicism. Once he was captured by the Indians and tied to the stake; they threw knives that sliced into his arms, and still, he didn't cry or move. The universe of pain riveted Frank, stories of wounds cut open with red hot knives, of amputated toes, of skin sliced to the raw.

Frank remembered his father talking about Russian winters so cold that merely touching steel gave you a cold blister. And there was the story of flying special transport planes to bring back molybdenum from Japanese-occupied Mongolia—modified diesel planes that took off at night, landed on some remote farm in Siberia way behind enemy lines where the pilots shot their way to diesel supplies, refueled and continued to Mongolia. His father told him proudly that the Russians knew they had to refuel on their return flight and still couldn't intercept them.

His father's war reports would bring on a sense of excitement strangely intensified by his growing anxiety about how he would measure up. He wanted his father to talk more about pain, the cold and deprivation. It was as if they shared the closeness of a secret fascination with death and the war. That's what men talked about when they whispered with their heads bent over. Seeking to share their experience, Frank would sometimes walk barefoot through the snow. One night he took a knife to bed and lay there pushing the blade hard against his arm. How much pain could he tolerate? Would he hold up as well as Old Shatterhand?

But it was clear he never could be his father's little soldier.

"You don't have what it takes," his father said. "You're not like me." Once, having fled a street fight, Frank came home humiliated, hammering his forehead with his fists to hide his tears, a chorus of voices pealing outside in the street, calling "Coward! Coward!" His father looked at him with an expression of disgust that speared his heart.

"I never ran," he said.

Then he stood up without looking at his son, pulled the newspaper from the kitchen table, and holding it like a shield, walked into the living room and slid into his chair. There he remained, immobile, except when tilting his head backward for a shot glass of schnapps.

Looking back, it was easy to see what alcohol eventually would do to their lives, but in the 1950s, life looked peaceful. On weekends the family would drive to the Chiemsee, south of Munich. His mother's U.S. citizenship gave them access to the Army's recreation area, but Frank's parents were looked upon as a couple "mixed the wrong way." They did not make any friends, although so many young German women were seen in the company of G.I.s that Frank's mother would often admonish her husband to get his roving eyes under control.

For a while they tried hard to be accepted, but as time progressed, Frank's father avoided those weekend visits and withdrew into cultivating orchids. With material that he took home from the BMW factory, he built a heated greenhouse adjacent to the garden, where he eventually spent most of his time tending to his orchids, drinking and reading into the night, his head bent over his favorite book, *The Marble Cliffs* by Ernst Jünger. More than once, he would read to Frank the part where two friars were searching the woods for the elusive orchid named the Red Forest Bird. The paragraph started in terse lyric language conjuring up a sense of nature as redemption until one of the friars happened to look up and cast his eyes on dozens of skulls nailed to the trees, and seeing the site of repression and shame. They had found the orchid, but they had found it amidst the slaughtered innocent.

As the years passed Frank's father spent more and more of his nights sleeping on a cot in the greenhouse. "Orchids give me peace," he would say. One frigid winter night when Hans was sleeping inside the house, the family woke to the sound of shattering glass; somebody had thrown rocks through the ceiling of the greenhouse. Several flasks with seedlings, fluorescent lights and trays with orchids had been smashed, but the heat escaping through the shattered ceiling was the most imminent threat; they had to move the orchids into the house immediately. For several weeks, Frank's father would tend to his plants in the living room and bedroom.

Frank remembered something strangely sensual about the way his father would lift the orchids' lips with his small finger as if by caressing them, he would receive some response, make their delicate heads nod and sway to some unspoken approval. And watching his father mix the agar gel, diligently sterilizing the pods with bleach and, after cutting them, pouring the seeds, Frank saw a gentleness in his father he had not recognized before.

It was to be a short interval of happiness only. After the orchids were moved back into the greenhouse, his father turned restless. He would sort things into numbered boxes and turn all the coat hangers in the same direction so that, in case of fire, he could more easily bunch the clothes together and throw them out the window. Fires were always on his mind, his own parents having died in the Dresden firestorm of 1945. But it was more than that....It was as if something kept threatening him. Like a man fearing he might be forced to suddenly leave and carry his belongings in a single suitcase, he would catalog things, discard old files and trim down his private possessions.

Yet from the outside, there was a deceptive smoothness to

their lives. Every morning Frank's father drove his blue Beetle Volkswagen to the BMW factory; every evening he came back at 5:20. Fathers who come home that early every day don't have important jobs, the brat up the street told Frank. That ruffled Frank, and he asked what his father did at work; but instead of taking him to visit the factory, he showed him pictures of the *Messerschmidt* jet fighter, the Me 262, always pointing out the two BMW jet engines below the wings.

"Top engineering. We were far ahead of everybody," he explained. "We could have produced them two years earlier and won the war."

Frank's imagination was taking off; he wanted to create brilliant ideas like his father. One evening he handed his father a sketch book with his own technical drawings and pointed out his innovation: a jet engine that looked like an oversized jalapeno pepper mounted above the cockpit of a fighter plane. Many wintry evenings he would lie on the carpet, surrounded by colored pencils, his legs stuck under his father's easy chair; with his father explaining things to him and seeming to draw pleasure from the way his boy picked up concepts like by-pass temperature, radar cross section or laminar flow. He would take Frank's sketchbook and add a line or run a quick drawing down the margin.

"Going to be quite an engineer," he'd say.

For young Frank, jet fighters were much more interesting than the miserly two-seated car his father was developing, a silly vehicle that he thought looked like an egg with a hunchback.

Years later, police divers pulled Frank's sketchbook from the Volkswagen with his father's body.

Later still, during a rare visit to his mother on Long Island, he asked about his father's past, but his mother merely would say, "I have a new life now; I have no stories."

Though he didn't dare press her, Frank ached to cry out: *But a man has only died if you forget his stories. I need to know my father; I need to know who I am.*

Sitting at the kitchen table that warm February night,

Frank kept losing himself in the Merlot and the memories of his childhood. He remembered quarreling voices, the clang of glass breaking, a door flung off its hinges at two in the morning, shreds of another truth.

"You have to quit drinking."

"The man hit first."

"You broke his jaw."

Frank went back to bed just before dawn. During the next morning's drive to the airport, Jim kept mum but did comment about the Egg Islands.

"I still can't believe that those islands on Leila's map would just so happen to be the ones mentioned on the back of the print."

"It's the best lead so far," Frank said.

"Lead to what?"

"There's a connection to my father."

Jim wrinkled his forehead. "Get real!" He bent forward and hit the radio search button. A breathless saxophone started wailing.

Frank turned off at the airport exit.

He had been trying to read Jim's face the same way he would his father's, every crag in it.

"I can't read his mood; Jim cows me," Frank thought. He hit the radio button. The saxophone fell silent.

"When are you heading to South America?" he asked.

"I'm going to stay with Leila a couple of days," Jim said. He sounded irritated but then seemed to come out of it. "A couple of hot days at the poolside . . . hobby-horsing Leila."

Frank stared at the road. Jim hit the radio button again and turned it loud enough to drown any further talk.

Frank stopped at the departure building and went around the car to unload Jim's two leather bags. They were parched by wind and sun. Ethiopian Airlines, the sticker read. Frank set them on the sidewalk.

"When will you be back from this next trip?" Frank asked.

Jim shook his hand briefly. "Not for several months."

"You're all over the globe."

"There's comfort in distance. Isn't there?" Jim lifted his bags, turned his head and walked through the glass door. This moment, more than ever before, Frank sensed the breech between them and wondered what dark power kept their lives entangled as if a thread had been spun between them that morning above the frozen Juniata.

On the way back he stopped at his regular coffee shop and took a seat at the counter. It was already after nine; most of the customers had left, and the usual fumes from the griddle had dispersed. His favorite waitress was leaning with her back against the side of the refrigerator blowing cigarette smoke through a small window. When Lizzy spotted him, she stubbed the butt into the windowsill and came over. It felt strangely comforting that Jim never had set foot here.

"You're late today," she said.

"The special with hash browns. Eggs over easy, rye," he said.

"Lots of people out with the flu," she said.

"I took the morning off." Frank looked through the front window at desolate chunks of dirty snow. The coffee shop felt like a refuge, though it hadn't always been that way. For weeks after Lucienne's death, Frank would have breakfast alone. He drank cup after cup of black coffee, pacing the kitchen until he could feel the lift of the caffeine and, with it, the courage to leave the house.

After she brought his plate, Lizzy set her elbows on the counter. Frank noticed her nipples lift a small tent into her shirt. "So what's up, stranger?"

"Just sent off my cousin to L.A.," he said.

"The photographer from Africa?" she asked.

"He leads quite an interesting life," he stated flatly.

"Probably walks through the jungle thinking how he could make his life more exciting," she said, grinning at Frank, whose mouth was too full to respond with anything more than a quizzical expression. "Look at the Wall Street tycoons. Stinky rich, but all they can think of is making more money."

"That's different," Frank said.

"It's the same old game of one-upping the next guy."

"Everybody does it." Feeling clammy and irritable, Frank forked the last piece of sausage link from the plate.

"It's written in the Bible: Do not compare yourself," she said

"I forgot; you're a Baptist's daughter," he said.

Wiping her forehead with a paper towel, Lizzy came forward and leaned over the counter to give Frank a look from the side. "Didn't you tell me you were a Jesuit?"

"Close," he said. Almost a Jesuit, almost a physicist.

"They teach you how to think," she said.

"And take the pith out of you while they're doing it."

She shrugged.

Frank shrugged back, slid two dollars under his plate and hurried to the register. As he walked to his car, he felt stupid for spilling out his feelings. Withdrawing from human contact provided him with a hidden comfort of which he was ashamed, though it invariably brought relief. The car door slammed shut, locking him into a safe womb of isolation. He thought back to night walks at the ocean, the water dark and endless, bereft of all meaning, demanding nothing. The secret relief of being empty and hopeless.

He contemplated asking Lizzy for a date, maybe dinner. After an hour or two of looking at her young face and listening to her fresh laugh, he might get the courage to work his hands under her shirt and rub her breasts. Then a thought stung him: could it be he liked her because she would know how to handle Jim? He laid his head on the steering wheel, trying to edge away from the confusion that had befallen him. He started the engine. By the time he got home, his mood had lightened.

That morning, Frank decided to start flying again. Something could be learned from Jim, he told himself. Hadn't his cousin overcome his fear of water, as long as he was on a boat, a fear Jim blamed on having nearly drowned in the Juniata years ago?

Frank had to admit grudgingly that Jim had proven to be a decent seaman in addition to being an excellent pilot.

Frank called San Diego. Leila's voice sounded muffled.

"Did you have breakfast already?" he asked.

"I never was an early riser."

"Jim flew out two hours ago," he said.

"He better remember I'm not going to pick him up at the airport."

"I made a decision to get back into flying." *I sound like a student announcing he's on the honor roll*, he thought.

"Good!" Her voice finally cleared. "Clipperton is giving me a thousand ideas. I didn't tell you yesterday that I talked with my section chief . . ." and she proceeded to tell him that there had been a Scripps exploration of Clipperton back in 1958, and that her supervisor was interested in her proposal to conduct a new study of the island's fauna.

"I could fly you there," Frank burst out.

God! Was he crazy? He'd just activated his license again. And the necessary supplies—how could he transport them to the island? He'd need a cargo plane. But Leila reacted as if she had anticipated it all.

"The Scripps has tremendous pull with the Navy," she explained "And the Navy is considering using land-based planes to air drop a pallet of supplies onto Clipperton Island. The catch is that they can't fly anything with two legs onto the island because Clipperton International Airport hasn't opened yet."

"Wow . . . I mean . . . that's great. Of course."

"I trust your flying." Her voice was calm, matter of fact. Silence.

"Are you there?"

"Do they use parachutes?" he asked.

"No. They overfly the island at fifty feet altitude and drop the pallet from the rear cargo door. The colonel told me they reliably hit anything larger than my bikini bottoms."

"Must be confident!"

"Just kidding. I trust you . . . .Okay?"

"Okay," he finally said. "You know Jim will be in South America?"

"I guess so, but you know more about his schedule than I do right now."

"It's hard to figure Jim's schedule."

"To change the topic, I handed your cover letter and journal articles to my friend at the *L.A. Times*. He seems interested."

"My boss at Reader's Forum keeps avoiding me. After he gave me that lukewarm promise about the Waterford article, he hasn't said a word about publishing my work."

"Your ideas are terrific. Think about the potential changes if architectural students designed public housing. Every house would be different. Every house would have soul."

"I would start from scratch, use the most efficient materials and throw away anything superfluous, but at the same time fill the house with passion."

"Michael Graves working with a tin can and a pile of third-grade lumber," she said.

"Right on," Frank said.

"Hey! It's time to make a move."

"How is your job?"

"The Valdez oil spill keeps us busy here. For months the Exxon Company has been airlifting mussels down to San Diego for chemical analysis. The EPA requires it, but it's a boring job. I'd rather investigate the fauna of an island like Clipperton the old fashioned way, digging my hands into the ground."

"Glad to help you. You mean it when you say you'd fly with me?"

"Of course."

"Seaplane and all that? I have accumulated three hundred hours of flying time; it doesn't take much for me to get the seaplane license."

"I'll start working on the details."

After he hung up, Frank thought back to what Jim had said at the airport. In the past he would have been intimidated by Jim's disapproval, but now the secret delight kicking up in his heart pushed any thought of Jim or his disapproval out of his mind.

7

ON HER DRIVE TO THE SCRIPPS INSTITUTE, Leila got stuck in traffic. Oppressive smog hung over the city and the car radio kept blaring, "You are the wind beneath my wings." She was irritated even though the morning had started well and she'd enjoyed talking to Frank. She felt that he was of kindred spirit. Their conversation made her feel homesick for Europe and family; she realized that he was her closest remaining connection to her departed sister.

Leila had lived most of her childhood with her mother and her sister in a small apartment in Montpellier in the south of France. She often thought back to those dreamy hours spent sitting on the windowsill watching the tangle of clotheslines strung above the narrow street, traffic below swishing like a river, kids darting about in their underwear. It was a smelly, gritty neighborhood flush with life.

On Fridays after school and on Saturdays, Leila would slip into her tightest underwear, something black and lacy, put on jeans, drop a bag across her shoulder and walk *l'esplanade de Charles de Gaulle* to the café Pastiche where she had a job washing dishes.

During breaks Leila would read Camus, feeling a kindred spirit with the writer. She appreciated his connection to Algeria; she loved his reflection that in Africa, at certain hours of the day the countryside is black with sunlight. Like her, Camus had never known his father, who had been killed in the waterlogged war trenches of northern France.

Leila's boyfriend, Jacques, liked to quote Camus. He imitated the way Camus smoked Gaulois cigarettes, dangling them from his lip. Whenever she was with Jacques, the café changed into a romantic harbor dotted with lights—highlighted by metal-hard red of the wines, the milky glow of pastis. Years later the illuminated swimming pools of San Diego would remind her of its opaque light.

In the spring of 1978, Leila's friend Fanny had a job that required her to survey the local oyster beds. Every day Leila would slump into Fanny's Citroen and then, flooring the pedal, would apply the raw force of its twenty-six horsepower to accelerate into the flat stretch of road that leads from Montpellier to the *étang de Thau* with its beds of oysters.

The landscape stretched horizontally in the quivering heat, mountains in a blue haze. Boiling. They drove into Sète and from there to the Quonset hut at the lake where the maritime research was conducted.

In the evenings, Jacques drove in from Montpellier and sat with Leila to watch the purple haze of night weigh down the final vestiges of daylight. A strange, aimless yearning wedged into Leila's heart. Sometimes when alone, she would stand at the beach at sunset, rub wet sand into her palms and inhale the smell of burnt flint, awed at the lure of secret grounds.

Fanny was more practical in these matters. "He's taken out the backseat of his Citroen and I can guess what he's up to," she would say, pulling up the wrinkles on her forehead.

After that summer, Leila's family moved into a farmhouse at the outskirts of Montpellier, where Leila had a tiny attic room with a view of the ocean. On rainy days, it was a distant wash of gray, on sunny days a shield of hammered tin. She often walked a nearby willow-lined creek looking for centipedes, cockroaches and spiders that burrowed in the shallow eddies.

Sundays were difficult: a slow, heavy meal, Mother sitting stiffly with her back to the wall on which hung her departed husband's saber. His books—French poetry, Mallarmé, two issues of Proust—were still displayed behind sliding glass. The bunch of paper flowers his commanding officer had thrown on his coffin sat next to the books collecting dust and paling with every passing day so that they appeared to be made of cheap plaster.

"This is how we were always seated when your father was still alive," Celine would say, first looking at Lucienne then, fixing her gaze on Leila, she would add, "but you weren't born yet."

Quite often during these solemn meals, Leila remembered playing with her knife, holding it horizontally so her sister's face was reflected on the blade then, by slowly twisting it, making the reflection of Lucienne's face slide off the blade.

But these times seemed far away, and now this strong woman who held together a family during the turmoil of the Algerian revolution was a mere shadow of her old self.

Pierre had written that for days after Leila had left Biddeford to search for her sister, Celine would mumble, "Where are they? Where are they?" She kept rocking in her wicker chair. They decided against telling her of Lucienne's death; there was blessing in dementia.

Now, driving toward the Scripps Institute, Leila thought of the fateful weekend in Biddeford, and the night when Lucienne was waiting alone in her bedroom while she was in Frank's arms lying under the bed. She conjured up the image of Lucienne's waterlogged body and a sudden anger pierced her heart so sharp she had to take a deep breath.

It was Jim's fault. He had been keeping her at arm's length, using her. And all his excuses, "This might be my last trip, my dear; we'll see what comes next."

And, for a while, she gave herself up to the resentment that had long been smoldering inside her like a banked fire. It wasn't that she hadn't tried to change their lives.

June of 1985: A bed and breakfast north of Minneapolis overlooking one of the few remaining stretches of tall grass prairie. They were drinking iced tea on the porch. A glazing heat was gathering on the horizon while the morning dew still pearled on the rocking chairs. Her white cotton dress was long and wide and deliciously wrinkled.

She took Jim's hand and they walked toward the wildflowers. They entered between gray-headed coneflowers so tall and dense their yellow rays bent across her shoulders, seeding tassels and prickly awns onto her dress. Where the Maximilian's sunflowers and the blazing stars thinned out, a smell of wet grain and honey wafted in. She stopped, ruffled her skirt and knelt down to touch the swirls of grass that looked like sleepers' hair, wondering if she would have a daughter whose hair will have the scent of grass. But she hadn't told him yet.

Jim kept standing, skimming the horizon through streams of grasses. She moved around on her knees, picked up a sun-scorched piece of deer pelt, threaded her hands between big bluestems, sages, snakeweed, ground celery, purple cornflowers and asters, then touched the ground in a depression where grass flowed in waves of green.

They walked on across a wet swale of swamp thistles and blazing stars then up a slope into bluestem grasses so tall one could walk between the stalks, look upward and see the sky through a quavering sea of blades.

Afterwards, sitting on the porch, Jim talked about his flying adventures in Kenya. How he chanced to fly above the site of a plane crash that had happened in the 1930s, a place the tribes called Naabi Hill. He described the grass that since then had grown around the wrecked airplane, so tall that from the air you only could see a depression forming a cross, and how it felt sitting at dusk at Seronera looking over a sea of grasses sloping down into the valley. "Walk in the grass after dusk and you are a man," the Masai would say. He kept talking about the fields of maize through which a man could run upright and still be hidden. All this gave her courage.

"I'm pregnant," she said.

He took her hand in silence. Barely a pause. "You have to handle the situation. You have the job in Woods Hole, and, of course, I'll go back to Africa."

Not a word more.

Leila shook off her thoughts of the past. This was California, 1990—cars to her left and right crawling toward the ocean like lemmings.

Adventure was before her, a chance to get out of the humdrum of the Valdez cleanup. What a lucky coincidence to have finally looked at that wall map and actually studied its fine print. And the major hurdle for the trip was overcome. Frank could fly her to the island with a seaplane, avoiding the hazardous crossing of dangerous reefs. Of course, she wouldn't tell her section chief that Frank had to renew his license and retrain for a different type of aircraft. Those were minor concerns. She just had to grab this chance to escape from that smelly basement where she had been analyzing contaminated mussels for months.

Returning home that day, Leila felt exhilaration she hadn't experienced since she had studied coral reefs in Chile. Suddenly she felt like lighting a cigarette, drifting on wisps of curling smoke again. She thought of the Gaulois cigarettes she would light up in the café Pastiche, their dark French tobacco.

When she turned into the alley leading to her house, everything seemed fresh and strangely weightless. The wrought-iron gate fringed by climbing bougainvillea, the whitewashed stucco walls and, above them, the tiles seaming the roof like a pizza crust—all this suddenly seemed perfect. She stopped the car in the driveway. Sitting motionless, she held a feeling of utter completeness.

"I don't want to share this," she mumbled.

Upon entering the living room, Leila saw Jim leaning against the doorframe. Wet from the pool and holding a bottle of beer in his hand, he looked like a cheap movie hero wedged into the entrance to some bodega, vaguely threatening, arrogant. But it gave her a kick to see his lean body, his wet, curling hair.

In the living room the TV was on. The news anchorman's voice announced, "And now in March 1990, a historic moment. The first free elections in East Germany since 1933." Leila picked up the remote to turn the volume louder. *I have to make sure to mention this to Frank*, she thought.

She felt Jim's arms sliding around her from behind. "This news is important," she said, feeling herself go limp.

"Sure," he said.

"I didn't have a good day."

He was touching her breasts; his lips were on the nape of her neck. She felt his erection against her spine. Why didn't she pull away? She didn't want it that way. All she wanted was to regain the moment of perfect balance she had experienced in the car, but a white onslaught of raw primal force stopped her breath. She turned around and put her hand into his pants, circling her fingers around his penis. For a moment he seemed startled, then he lifted her and carried her to the bed, pulling off her jeans, his fingers probing her wetness. She felt him inside her and for a second, as if she needed to blunt his power she thought to ask him if he closed the entrance door. But at that moment, he groaned and she felt a rush throughout her body. She arched in response and rocked onto him with such force that everything inside her rose into white bursts and tumbled and rose and tumbled.

Later she went back to the living room and joined Jim. He pulled her down on the sofa and, kneeling in front of her, slid his hands under her bathrobe and squeezed her buttocks. "Tight little ball bearings," he mumbled. He kept rocking his knee into her groin.

"Don't!" She knuckled his chin.

"I can't get enough of you."

Eventually he let go, walked to the refrigerator and removed a tray of sushi. "I bought it on the way here. There are California rolls, albacore, tuna, cucumber—your favorites."

He poured rice wine and they settled on the couch, taking turns with the sushi rolls.

"Did you see the news about Germany?" she asked.

"Frank mentioned it." He kept dipping his California roll into the soy sauce.

"Frank is willing to fly me to Clipperton."

Jim dropped the roll, sucked his fingers. "You always had a

death wish," he said.

"Here we go again!"

"Frank doesn't know how to fly seaplanes, and he hasn't ever crossed ocean water. I'll bet he's going to change his mind. He's gotten wet feet before." Jim was sitting stiffly now.

Leila bristled. "Jim, stop."

But Jim kept going. "It was you who put this stupid idea in his mind. How can you be so damn sure these Egg Islands are really the ones on the back of the photo? And even if they are, what does he expect to find?"

The term "death wish" had unsettled her, but she tried not to show her consternation.

"Frank has time to get training."

"Play it safe! Delay the whole trip."

"We have to get to Clipperton before June."

"Why?"

"That's when hurricane season starts," she said.

"I bet my father will talk him out of that trip."

"Frank hasn't visited him yet."

"Oh, how considerate! First my father adopts him as the chosen son who can do no wrong, then pays his college. And now that my father's living in the middle of this park of tree houses, which Frank gave him the idea for, what happens? The ungrateful adopted son doesn't even show up."

"You'll see," he said after a while, this time in a casual tone. "It will turn out to be just another one of Frank's ideas."

"He's not afraid to stir up the past," she said.

"Some muck in his father's past, is there?"

Leila threw up her hands. "Whatever! I know these photos have shaken Frank up. It's not for us to pry into his past."

"Stay clear of his projects, I warn you."

"That's up to me."

Leila tightened her bathrobe around her hips, unsettled by a mixture of tension and lingering orgasm. She knew her power; all she had to do was drop her bathrobe.

"You know that my upcoming trip to South America will be a

long one, but if you delay your visit I can fly you to Clipperton."
He grinned, and lifted his hands to the side of his face, folding
them like rabbit ears.

"I'm getting my swimsuit on," she said, turning to leave for
the bedroom.

"Put on the red thong! I love watching your ball bearings,"
he yelled after her.

That evening Leila slid into the lit pool and dove down to
the emerald light, trying to shed a sense of foreboding. Jim's
words lingered in her mind. She was unsettled and chilled by
his remark that a flight with Frank was a "death wish," that there
was "some muck in Frank's father's past." And, remembering
her sense of freedom when she drove up to the house, she was
angry with herself for giving in to Jim once again.

So why did she care if he was still pouting about their
argument? She knew they would make up later in bed and
regretted it already.

CLIPPERTON

Nueva Germania

There was a river that ran dark through Hans Herrmann's life. Its headwaters were back in the Second World War, back in the planes of Russia and Poland. At times it would weaken to a trickle and seep underground and no soul would know about it. Eventually, however, it would have to well up, cleft the soil and carve its course.

In 1959, Hans had written Rick several letters begging him to travel to Paraguay to attend to business he preferred to delegate. He gave no reason why he didn't want to take care of it himself. The task seemed straightforward: Carry cash to a German farming community to purchase some private diaries. He was to send the diaries to Germany where they would be authenticated; if they turned out to be genuine, Rick would receive a cut. It was strictly business, the letter said. And Rick's help had been appreciated in the past. When Rick had visited his sister in Germany, Hans' friend who had been in the Waffen SS asked Rick to search out American business collectors interested in Nazi regalia. At that time, Rick found several collectors in Pittsburgh who were willing to put down a good amount of dollars for authenticated Nazi flags, paintings by Nazi authorities, and Special Service daggers, belts, and buckles.

Rick had almost forgotten about this small transaction, and he was hesitant to travel to South America. But his marriage had failed, and he needed money, as some of his patent claims had recently been in litigation. When the tone of the letters became more pleading and Herrmann sent money even before receiving Rick's decision, Rick finally agreed to help.

He flew to Asunción, where he spent the first night in a spacious old hotel with broken stuccos, their color soiled into a flecked brown. The hotel was almost empty. The Swiss waiter kept serving him warm beer from Bremen and talking in German.

Hans had sent enough money for Rick to hire a pilot and fly up to Nueva Germania, about 125 miles to the north; but when the pilot refused to land the seaplane on the shallow Aguaray river, Rick had to take a rickety forty-foot packet boat to get from Antequera to Nueva Germania. The Aguaray was loamy, a channel of slime pinged by lush jungle. And Nueva Germania was but a row of dirty huts.

Nueva Germania had started as the idea of Elizabeth Nietzsche and her husband, Bernhard Förster, a well-known anti-Semite. It was founded in 1886 as an outpost of Arian culture, the crystal point for a pure breed, blue-eyed and blond, which would take over the world. No sooner had Bernhard Förster built a large colonial mansion than he fell into deep depression; he poisoned himself in 1889.

Elizabeth took over the administration and, benefiting from the notoriety of her brother, Wilhelm Friedrich Nietzsche, she lured hundreds of German colonialists to this mosquito-infested parcel of jungle. The earth was acidic and thin; whatever grew barely covered the colonists' needs.

But in the 1930s, fueled by the fires of anti-Semitism, a trickle of dreamers came over from Germany and sustained the colony for a while so that eventually Bernhard Förster's Arian dreams found new life in the Nazi regime. When Elizabeth died, Adolf Hitler ordered a package of German soil to be sent to Nueva Germania in her honor. After the defeat of the Nazis, Nueva Germania was like a sponge sucking in the detritus of the Reich, SS thugs who had escaped with falsified passports, slack-eyed concentration camp guards and doctors, like Josef Mengele, who had blood on their hands.

Rick had to stay several days, as the package boat wouldn't return any earlier. They were strange people, these descendants of an Arian experiment, old and shrunken now, glancing at him with downcast eyes. They sat, sipping yerba mate tea, to which they were addicted, on the porches of their tiny, red huts. They called him inside, dusted off faint prints on walls that were warped by moisture, and pointed to photos of old German landscapes, mumbling German words the entire time, air whistling through gaps in their teeth. On some occasions, they took out their squeezeboxes and played the Mennonite Waltz.

Several days later, Rick was waiting for the package boat. Mosquitoes had bitten him raw and there were sheets of tiny yellow eggs under his skin, laid by bugs at night. The diary turned out to be a fake; even the few details Hans had informed him about were sufficient enough to prove it as such.

He wrote to Hans that Nueva Germania was a dump, that no spirit but that of decay and betrayal could be found there, and that whatever was left of the ideas of an Arian Nation had long ago sunk into its soil.

8

AFTER FRANK RENEWED his flying license in February of 1990, he quit his job and spent time in Florida learning to fly seaplanes. In the evenings he would swim in the ocean for hours, conjuring up the bliss of the Atlantic of the Maine coast. One night, swimming far off the beach, he entered a bank of fog and his thoughts went back to the desperate hour in Long Island Sound. Even treading in dark, murky waters, he still could feel the ocean yielding abandon and enchantment.

At the end of March he was called to L.A. to interview for the position of architectural editor at the *L.A. Times.* When he phoned Leila from L.A., she was too busy at work to see him and reported that Jim would return from Peru before May. Things hadn't worked out for him in South America, she told Frank, and Jim was now planning to charter a trawler and take her to Clipperton.

"Of course you'd still fly the plane," she said, "the reefs around Clipperton are razor sharp and we do need you to ferry our equipment by plane from the boat to the island."

"I hoped that this would be our trip," Frank said. Every word felt like a pebble in his mouth.

"Please understand," she started out, "this gives me a chance to carry out investigations on the island that need heavier equipment." And when she realized the dead silence in the line she hastily asked, "You aren't put off?"

He caught himself before blurting out that he'd hoped for times like the ones in Biddeford. But it was better to sheet in his sails now, and he started to mumble something along the line that Jim's experience would be helpful. But even as he was talking, he knew that he wouldn't forgive himself for not speaking his mind.

During the next few days, he phoned Leila often, but he sensed that the thread between them was slipping away. Their conversations fizzled. She hadn't heard from Jim again and had no more information for him.

"I'm in a holding pattern here," Leila said.

"That's Jim's fault," he complained. "And if we wait for Jim too long, we might get into the hurricane season."

But Leila didn't respond and simply changed the subject.

Mid-April, Frank returned from Florida to put the house on the market. Despite being preoccupied with packing his belongings and storing furniture, Frank found time to visit Uncle Rick. Frank always had loved driving through the Appalachians, which reminded him of the glacier-scraped ridges north of the Alps, and he looked forward to again following the familiar highway alongside the blue band of mountains until it turned and tunneled through and broke out into a high landscape dotted with knolls, a landscape that muted the harshness of light. At sunset a last fractured light would fan into the valleys and across the fields. He knew he would miss it.

Frank thought back to April 1961—his last spring in the old country—the night drive toward the Bavarian Alps, his Uncle Rick following the limousine that carried his dead father. He was only ten years old at the time, but when the chips were down, Uncle Rick was always there. He took him in when Frank's mother was busy starting a new life in the States, and he paid for Frank's education as an architect at a time when his mother was scraping every penny to help build Joel's paper business, which eventually would bring them prosperity.

Rick, too, had made himself a small fortune. He started as a miner during the late 1940s then specialized in underground and underwater blasting. Soon corporations in Pennsylvania, West Virginia, and Kentucky were consulting him. His marriage, however, didn't fare well; after Jim's birth in 1950, the couple separated.

Jim stayed with his mother in their small house along the Stonycreek River in Johnstown. Some people in town would say the separation drove Rick to drink. But good fortune was not absent from Rick's life; it just came to him in different ways. Shortly after his divorce, Rick patented an underground shaft support system, which was quickly adopted as the standard in mines across the country. Suddenly Rick was independently wealthy. He bought a large farm overlooking the Juniata River and petitioned the court for Jim to visit him more frequently.

But Jim wanted to visit his father infrequently, only during the weekends and then only, so his father would say, because he loved the rough life in the woods along the Juniata.

Rick began to withdraw and devote more of his time to his interests in architecture and the cultivation of rare species of trees and plants. He became reclusive, and folks from nearby Johnstown began to gossip about his peculiar tree houses, his night walks and his spelunking in a cave in the limestone cliffs overlooking the river. During the summers, Rick would invite Jim and his friends to outings or gatherings around a bonfire, and Rick would always end up drunk and carry on about his various projects. Everybody knew about his problem and his visits to one rehabilitation center after another where he would dry out temporarily, only to fall back into drunkenness soon after returning to the woods.

It was early afternoon when Frank drove up the rutted dirt road toward the farmhouse now almost hidden behind wickerwork of shrubs and trees. Frank didn't see Rick or his old, battered Mercedes, so he sat down on the porch steps and took in the familiar sight. Behind the stand of gnarled apple trees, the land sloped down to the cliffs of the Juniata then hooked away from the river and dropped off into underbrush.

Gradually he became reacquainted with this landscape, its uneven tufts of grass separated by rills of clay, stands of maple along the river and humps of vegetation covering what was left of Rick's disheveled tree houses. The smoke of a distant wood fire sharpened the air with a sense of autumn. He felt the comfort of things familiar but also the tug of shame reaching him from summers past when Jim, master of the dark woods, would jump on Frank, throw him to the ground then roll his knees across Frank's biceps.

Frank tried to shake off his memories of Jim and began to thumb through a pile of old architectural magazines stacked into the corner of the porch. How much of Rick's enthusiasm for architecture was still there, Frank wondered. Not that many years ago, he had been sitting on this very porch with Rick, who had been eager to spend the night talking about his belief in the deep quality of life that could emanate from building a structure.

Frank stepped off the porch to walk around the house, but circling this building was sobering; nature was reclaiming it unceremoniously. There was no drama to this decay. Eventually Rick's old Mercedes came up the access road, his car heaving in the ruts. They embraced each other warmly, the motor dieseling behind them.

Rick's face appeared rough, as if cut from a hide. His skin was so sensitive that shaving his beard had left a field of tiny red bumps, and his small, intense eyes looked like chestnuts sunk into creased faults. Despite his age, gray had not taken over the reddish tint of his hair. While Frank helped carry grocery bags into the kitchen, he noted the two beepers stuck into Rick's belt. On the kitchen table two radio phones recharged in their cradles.

"I could open an electronics store with all that stuff," Rick commented while preparing his special diet, a bland meatless mush. He kept talking endlessly about the transplant unit, the lack of liver donors and the painful wait for the decisive call announcing that they had found a donor.

They took their plates and sat down in the living room. It was almost dark, but the light coming from above drew Frank's attention. Rick had angled the ceiling windows to flood the sunken center of the room with the last light of day, making the walls recede into darkness while the middle of the room still captured the remnants of day. It was a magic balance of openness and withdrawal.

"Without your help and enthusiasm, I would not have become an architect," Frank said.

"Jim wasn't interested." Rick wiped his mouth. "When that boy was five, he drew a picture of the farm, rolled the drawing up, stuck it into a bottle, then corked it and sent it down the Juniata. All that boy wanted to know was where it was going, to what foreign lands and distant shores. Always driven, that boy. One Christmas I gave him an erector set and sat down with him to construct some buildings, huts, windmills and whatnot, stuff like that, but he refused, only wanted to build objects on wheels. They had to move!"

"It makes for an interesting life," Frank said.

"Maybe he'll settle down eventually," Rick said. He paused then looked up. "Did he say anything to you about getting engaged?"

"Engaged?" Frank said.

"I guess he's too busy. Wouldn't find time to tell his father anyway."

"I haven't heard anything about engagement. But Jim might join us on our trip to Clipperton," Frank said. "Our trip," it sounded so hollow.

Rick pulled on his lip then suddenly pushed back his seat as if to flee from the light toward the dark walls. "You want to find out what I know, don't you?" After a long pause, he continued. "It is possible that your father had been sent on a U-boat mission to Clipperton Island. Think of it! He knew enough details of the Messerschmidt Me 262's jet engines, and it would have made sense to give that knowledge to the Japanese. I know for sure that in 1945 the American occupation forces found a working Japanese jet fighter."

"A copy of the Messerschmidt in Japan?"

"Every inch of it."

Frank set down his plate and stood up. "The Nazis wouldn't have sent anybody whom they couldn't trust."

Rick nodded in agreement.

"I didn't know," Frank continued. He was pacing in and out of the light. "Talk to me for God's sake! How much was my father into it? "

"Your father had an eight-millimeter movie projector in his glass house," Rick said. "Don't you remember the old news reels he would watch? Hitler and Mussolini striding into the darkened Nürnberg stadium, haloed by two searchlights. They stepped up to the podium as if they were to be taken up to heaven. The moment they reached the top, lights flooded the stadium and there rose a hundred-thousand hands. Another reel he liked to watch showed Hitler waving from the Reichstag window, the crowds going wild."

"How did he kill himself?" Frank asked, standing beside Rick's chair now.

Rick sidled away. "Your father took cyanide seconds before he drove the car into the lake."

Himmler and Göring took cyanide, Frank thought.

"Why didn't you tell me that detail?" Frank's voice was as sharp as glass. Rick rose from his chair and started to edge away, but then he slowly put his arms around Frank and laid his face on his chest. Frank stood motionless until Rick let go, sat back down in his chair and buried his face in his hands.

"Don't you ever forget that I broke my promise to your mother not to tell you about his suicide! It was I who told you the truth years ago." Rick's chest kept heaving.

"Why did he do it?" Frank asked.

Rick thinned and tightened his lips; he had said too much already.

"You were his friend," Frank said.

"I didn't help him. I failed." Rick stood up and wiped his eyes. He was close to crying. "There's not much between me and death now, and all I can hope for is an icy road at night, a car slamming into a tree, somebody ripped from a life and pulled under the lights of the treatment table. The call . . . the call." Rick was shaking. He started pacing the room but then changed his mind and pulled his coat off the rack, motioning to Frank. "I need fresh air."

When they stepped onto the porch, neither the cold air nor the slanting light of the low sun could pierce the thick mat of thoughts that lay upon Frank's mind; he was the one who had been stifling his own suspicions.

Walking toward the cliffs of the Juniata, they crossed a wide-open field where Frank stopped in a swale of broom sage reaching up to his knees.

"Why did he kill himself? Why?"

"Your father never was able to open up," Rick explained. "And it was a different time, a different generation."

"Was he involved in war crimes?" Frank asked.

"You see, in the spring of 1945 when I arrived as a G.I. the war was almost over, and the only action I saw was mopping up sharpshooters, and cleaning up the rubble, of course. I was young; I could even visit my sister who was serving in the Army as a translator. At that time I didn't give politics much thought. The cities lay in ruins, but the Bavarian countryside was bursting with flowers, and I had no reason to hate the Germans. I sought out their plants and trees and lakes and castles."

"What did my father tell you about the war?" Frank asked. They had reached the bluffs above the river. Frank yearned to return to that time before history claimed his father's life, before things went wrong in that muddy, opaque past.

"Your father kept to himself," Rick said. "I was the American, the enemy. He never totally lost that feeling." He kept staring at the cliffs across the Juniata, and for a moment Frank wondered if Rick was conjuring up that cold morning when two sled-riding boys were hurled into the crowns of icy tall trees and had hung on for life. Rick kept staring in silence then briefly took Frank's hand. It felt awkward wearing gloves.

"I looked forward to talking about architecture with you," he said. "And I would like you to see my new tree house."

Frank looked at his uncle. Even through the winter coat, he could make out Rick's gut swollen grotesquely by retained fluid. Rick was a dying man.

"I often think of the quality without a name," Frank said after a pause.

Rick's face lit up then turned pensive. "I still remember the first lines," he said. "A building or a town will only be alive to the extent that it is governed by the timeless way, but to seek the timeless way we first must know the quality without a name." He was quoting from *The Timeless Way of Building*, a Christopher Alexander book they both had come to appreciate.

The exercise and the conversation put a bounce in his steps. He started slapping together his gloves, and his voice turned forceful, his breath sending small flags into the frigid air. This was the Rick Frank had known decades ago, the Rick who had instilled in him a love for architecture when he was still in Catholic high school in Pittsburgh; this was the Rick who made him study how the light was streaming from the sky and how the shadows of the evenings were fingering toward the walls, who taught him how to plan the layout of a room so that one could watch the street from a window seat and still retreat into the soft light of a cozy reading corner, who taught him how to mold a house into the hill such that the midday sun would be hidden yet the evening rays would reach over the crest.

"Architecture still is the most powerful of all arts," Rick said.

"It studies what surrounds us all day. It faces the ordinary," Frank agreed.

It had been with Rick's help that Frank studied architecture in Berkeley, California. He remembered sitting late into the nights, filling yellow pads with arrows and circles. It was not the individual object that was important—it was the pattern, the web of relationships that evolved; it was structure that counted. Concrete guidelines were applied—a room should have two sources of light; a window should be a place with a soul, a place to sit and reflect. He learned to appreciate organic patterns so that the architectural communities would resemble living plants that could repair damage and redirect growth. And, always, there was Christopher Alexander's *The Timeless Way of Building.*

The two men continued walking silently between tufts of grass. Frank's thoughts drifted. Maybe there had been good will in Rick's long silence, a benevolent clamming up and an attempt to protect him. But things can't be worked out by looking away. A fog, a sticky miasma, always had clung to Frank's memories of a father who drank night after night in his greenhouse in the company of orchids and movie reels of Nazi glory. These were the memories he'd chosen not to face.

"I'll show you a secret," Rick said. They crossed a narrow swale then walked up toward the limestone cliff. Hidden among tall grasses there lay a huge, rusted contraption; it appeared to be a press of some kind. "What is it?" Frank asked.

"Look at the blocks of concrete lying around."

"Something to do with making building material?"

"One last hint. It has an Italian name!"

"*La Rosacometa! La Rosacometa!*" Frank said. "How did it get here?"

"I had it trucked in from Mexico," Rick explained.

Frank's memory reeled back to the hot summer of 1976 when he participated in the University of Berkeley's workshop at Mexicali, Baja Mexico. Christopher Alexander had shipped the block-making machine—*La Rosacometa*—from Italy to pour concrete blocks right on the site in such a way that the blocks did not have to be joined by mortar but could be stacked. They had experimented with variations of the cement-soil ratio, and always mindful of cost, they had woven the roofs like baskets, which they covered with burlap then sprayed with light concrete; when laying the cement slab, they had used palm fronds instead of steel rods. Building houses with soul at half the price! Eventually five families were to live in the small village. From the start, they had worked with their own hands, pouring one concrete building block at a time.

"I haven't seen that spirit for a long time," Frank said. "It carried me like a river."

"I could sense it from the letters you sent from Mexico,"

Rick said.

"And then the river went underground," Frank said, and Rick continued, "from where it will rise again."

"This is a heartfelt reminder of exciting times," Frank said. He smiled at Rick and laid his hand on his shoulder, and the two men returned to the house where Rick served two bowls of vegetarian stew.

Near the end of the meal Frank broke the silence. "I need to know what had such a hold on my father." Frank sensed Rick's hesitation, his struggle to find words.

"There is a fanatic bent in all of us. Something inside calls us to aim for the most intense feeling of being alive, to deliver our senses and our minds to the highest pitch, to abandon ourselves to any idea that quickens our pulse."

"Are you saying the Nazis gave him that pitch?"

"Yes! Many of Hitler's followers immersed themselves into this strange transcendental fog; they were continuously walking at the edge of rapture—whatever you want to call it—but it made them feel that an inalienable meaning had been bestowed to their lives."

"This rapture was evil," Frank said.

"It was religion," Rick stated.

Rick had detested anything religious and—as he would put it—had saved Frank from the clutches of priesthood. He hadn't ever seen eye-to-eye with his wife on this topic, and Frank's mother had blamed the quarrel over religion for the breakup of Rick's marriage. It was better to shun this topic.

"I don't know how to thank you for making me an architect," Frank said. "It was the most generous thing anybody ever did for me."

Rick took his spoon and waved it across his plate. "Jim wasn't ever interested in architecture," he said. "Once he had his flying license and became a member of the Pittsburgh Adventure Club, he was as good as gone."

He spooned some stew again. Startled, Frank noted that a number of Rick's teeth were missing; then he remembered

Rick telling him that eradication of herd infection was one of the preparations for liver transplant. They finished their stew quietly, as if waiting for the moment Rick was living for, the moment when the call would come and Rick would jump up and race down the driveway for his transplant.

After the meal, Rick asked for the photographs that Frank had brought, and they went to Rick's upstairs study to inspect the prints. Rick kept moving the lens of a strong magnifying glass across the print like a magic wand, scanning every detail of the U-boat's hull.

"It seems possible he might have gone on a mission like that. I do know that he did long-range supply flights, linking up with the Japanese forces in Mongolia as long as the Luftwaffe had airports close to the Volga."

"They used diesel planes," Frank interjected. He told the story as best as he could remember it. Rick listened attentively then slid the prints back into the folder.

"Wouldn't mind going to that island myself if I wouldn't be so sick," he said. "Jim hasn't been here for a year; I might actually get to see my son."

Jim's infrequent visits always had been a sore point, and Rick began to suspect that Jim would visit his mother, who was still living in Johnstown, without making his way up to the farm.

"You wanted to show me the tree house," Frank reminded Rick.

"That's where you're going to spend the night," Rick said and, recognizing Frank's bewilderment, he added, "It's quite comfortable; there's even electricity."

Frank expected that the tree houses he'd seen decades ago would have crumbled by now and would be nothing more than vine-covered mounds of rotting material. But Rick explained that he had rebuilt the helix house. To live in a tree house would befit Rick's bizarre taste. He always had nursed this love for odd architecture, a trait he had inherited from his father, whose own unconventional sensibilities brought him to western

Pennsylvania from Italy with a mission to start a contractor's business.

Rick always had been an eccentric but didn't seem to care. "When the town folks began talking, I just turned my ass toward town," he'd say, and so he'd decided to move into the woods and nestle houses into trees.

The wheel house was wrapped around a burly oak, its ceiling peaking into branches such that leaves would sprout inside the house. And the helix house, which had the appearance of a pack of riffled cards twisted around a tree trunk, was by far the most awkward and most interesting of the houses.

As they were walking up to the edge of the woods, the sun setting as a sharp disk of white between the trees. The wind had shifted to the southeast, a harbinger of snow and sleet.

The rebuilt helix house was one long room framed intricately with many angles and corners. It had three distinct levels, which had to be set on corners to bend them around the large oak tree trunk. The middle room served as the kitchen; the upper and lower parts were living units with a table and a pullout couch. Rick had even managed to wedge a toilet and a shower between the kitchen and lower unit.

"I first had the privy bolted right onto the tree," Rick commented. It didn't take Frank much to imagine the jokes that this might have inspired. The folks in western Pennsylvania had the habit of cutting everything down to size anyway.

Rick flicked on the overhead light in the upper room then drew out Frank's couch and set down the pillows and blankets. The oak-paneled walls, two large windows, and a table with three chairs gave a sparse, but tasteful, impression. Frank noted two photographs hung on the wall. One showed Leila in a water park feeding fish simultaneously to two dolphins jumping up on either side. The shot was playing to the common taste, but it made Frank jealous that Leila had been willing to work with Jim to make this perfectly timed shot possible.

"This one he took in Tanzania from a plane." Rick was pointing to the other large print, which had been taken in low sun slanting in from the side. On first glimpse all Frank saw was a sea of grass, but the print was exquisitely sharp, and every single blade stood out bathed in silvery light. With a closer look there seemed to emerge a pattern from the tapestry of blades.

"Can you see it?" Rick asked.

"It looks like a cross. But how?"

"Jim told me that years ago a plane crashed there. The pilot survived, but the plane was so badly damaged that they left the hull and wings and, now with grasses growing over it, all that remains visible is the pattern of a cross."

Frank nodded silently. The picture affected him strangely. He believed that he had the higher ground, that he was the one who had the refined feelings, the multi-layered sensibilities. And here was Jim's picture showing so much beauty! This room was Jim's, and in more than one way it should have been Jim who was here.

Rick started a fire. It flared up quickly, and as the fireplace was almost entirely glass they could watch the light whip into the branches, pour a yellow sheen onto the mossy ground and send a faint glow as far as the stand of dense laurel crowding alongside a creek. Some snowflakes had drifted down—not unusual in these highlands in April. The flakes tumbled playfully between the branches lit orange by the fire.

Frank thought back to Easter night a year after his father's death; he had just come to the States. In church they gave him the honor of holding the candle that night, he remembered. It was he who carried the flame through the darkness to the altar. He raised the candle. Light flooded the church in resurrection. Lumen Christi.

"Light is everything." Rick stood up to leave. "Good night, Frank."

Frank lay down on the couch and kept watching the flames. As they dwindled, he anticipated the faint chills that would soon rub him and how he would pull deeper under his blankets in a delicious retreat to find shelter in his own warmth.

Sometime in the night he woke up confused until he

remembered he was at Rick's farm. Even in the dark, the fireplace panels had a metal glaze to them. Glass glistening in the dark. He thought back to an evening in the winter of 1961, just weeks before his father's death. His father and he had driven out into the snowy landscape south of Munich following a narrow road between fallow fields. It was dusk. His father stopped at an abandoned farm, left the car and walked to a ruined green house. Some of the glass panes still hung in their rusting frames, but most were broken. It was odd, but he could still remember the small, triangular snow piles the wind had blown in beneath the fragments.

His father picked up a stone from a small pile and threw it through a glass pane, and shards of glass came raining down. And then he took another stone and threw it, then another. He went on this way for several minutes, working himself into a frenzy. Frightened, Frank stood close to his father, thousands of broken crystals silently spiking the snow around him.

"Ten Deutschmarks if you throw a stone. Once in your life, act like a real boy!"

He didn't.

Maybe it was in the far reach of a high beam from some distant car—for a moment he could see his father's eyes, wide and bulging by strange forces.

In the wee hours of the morning, a wind came up, leaned into the tree house and shook it like a boat on an angry sea.

Rick woke early and made breakfast. He threw some eggs and Canadian ham into a skillet and forked his egg whites over to Frank's plate. "My liver can't handle proteins," he said. "Everything inside me turns into toxins."

"There will be a donor," Frank said.

Rick didn't answer.

Outside the wind drove in the last of a southerly flow. Walking out to his car after he had packed his belongings, Frank felt the push of acid air into the nostrils, the tart smell of decaying grass. While Frank felt sad leaving his uncle, he was grateful to be alone with his thoughts.

The road back to the turnpike led through Johnstown where Rick's ex-wife worked in a convenience store. She recognized Frank immediately and paused from making one of the store's specialty sandwiches to lift her gloved hand. She spread two fingers, signaling she would take a break, then mumbled something into the ear of her supervisor and left from behind the counter.

"You wouldn't expect me to give you a hug," she said, laughing.

"I just hugged your ex," he teased.

"Oh. Lord. You had to camp out in his vodka cabin."

They sat down on two rusted folding chairs behind the store. She shook a cigarette out of the package, lit it and inhaled.

"Sorry I couldn't come to your mother's funeral," she said. She laid her hand on his elbow as lightly as a feather. It was only now that he saw the red patches on her hand, evidence of the abuse her hands had taken. She always had been a proud woman, bitter maybe, but with good cause. Though Frank loved his uncle, he realized Rick had not been kind to her and, in the end, had cheated her out of her share of his royalties. She still had her round face with the high cheekbones and those alert eyes, which now were crowded in by wrinkled skin that looked like the dark bellows on old cameras.

"Jim wrote me about this island . . . Clipperton? Is he coming with you and Leila?"

"It looks like it," Frank said.

She lit the second cigarette. "How is my ex?"

"Countdown to a liver," Frank said.

"I wish him luck."

"I told him the way folks here keep driving on those icy roads, he has a good chance for a donor."

"I surely hope so," she said. Suddenly she was quiet. She looked up toward the railroad tracks, which crossed on an elevated bed several blocks behind the store.

"We had a good life," she said. "His drinking destroyed it." She pointed at her house, which was so close they could see it from the store. "He'd leave at dawn," she started, "cross the trolley lines then trudge up the cinder-covered mound to walk along the abandoned railroad line. Maybe it was stepping on the wide-spaced sleepers that made his walk seem mechanical, as if he were jerked around by invisible strings, a jumping jack. And the tin drum he used for a lunchbox bounced beside him—that was the last thing we would see as he disappeared between the tufts of tall grass that sprouted between the ties, Rick sinking into a sea of grass. I always wondered about that, how there was so much grass in this steel town."

Somebody knocked on the door.

"I'm coming," she yelled. She turned her gaze back to Frank. "There's always something that destroys our men," she said.

"And our fathers," Frank added.

She opened the door. "Walk with me through the store," she said. "It looks strange you slinking around the back."

She hugged him and disappeared behind the counter. He took one of the order forms and one of the stubby pencils the store provided. On the backside he wrote," You are a wonderful person. I learned a lot in the time of two cigarettes."

He placed the order in the plastic slot and left.

9

JIM LEFT SAN DIEGO on a flight to Lima and from there took a small turboprop plane to Cuzco where he met O'Reilly, a free-lance writer. Jim smelled whiskey on O'Reilly's breath. Later, at the hotel bar, O'Reilly had no qualms admitting his love of the bottle.

"You have to know that I do my best work with a flask at my hip."

Jim looked at the Irishman's face, burnt and seamed by the sun, and saw two quick eyes and a smile that impressed him as just a bit too obsequious.

He shook his hand and said, "I've worked with worse; I can live with it as long as you don't touch the steering wheel when you are drunk."

Then there was this other side of O'Reilly. He spoke Spanish fluently, and he had quite a way with people. But most importantly, he had done his homework lining up the itinerary. They were to start at the Apurimac River and work north from there. Jim's and O'Reilly's contracts asked for an illustrated article of original rope bridges."

"How many are still there?" Jim asked.

"Originally, there were two hundred rope bridges in the Tahuantinsuyu," O'Reilly explained, "but many are tattered or worn down now—most tribes quit growing ichu grass, and they can't repair them anymore. I'd say we might find about a dozen bridges.

The next several weeks they drove their Land Rover up east of the Andes checking out river gorges in search of Inca rope bridges—the Rio Apurimac, the Rio Pampas, then Rio Mantaro and further north Rio Huallaga—but the only well-maintained bridge was to be the one spanning the Rio Apurimac. When they arrived at the small village, the locals were repairing the bridge, and women were carrying bundles of straw-colored ichu grass toward the gorge. Jim took photographs of women carrying bundles of grass on their backs as the setting sun came bursting through thousands of strands. In the middle of the bridge, the roar of the river in his ears, Jim swayed between light and shadow.

During their three days at Rio Apurimac, Jim documented the tribe's work on the bridge, and when he was done, he knew he had taken some great shots. The rest of their trip was less successful. As O'Reilly suspected, most rope bridges had long ago frayed, and many had lost one or two of their four strands, making them passable only to those thrill-seekers crazy or drunk enough to attempt a crossing.

They stayed in Huánuco for a week and hung out at the hotel bar. Jim got to know Carlos, a local farmer who owned several wooden planes, among them two East European models. Nearly done with the assignment, Jim could not resist Carlos offer to take one up for a spin. On the first flight, Carlos and Jim took off from the short dirt strip on Carlos' hacienda, and Jim had a chance to show his stuff. Carlos was impressed and allowed Jim to use the plane to survey the area. After four days of flying and practicing his landing on high mesas, Jim told O'Reilly that none of the rope bridges he'd spotted was worth a visit. When Carlos asked Jim to ferry one of the wooden planes to friends in Uchiza, O'Reilly took the opportunity to ride along. After several weeks of driving over barren passes with the sun bursting open his Irish face, O'Reilly had had enough and wanted to reach Uchiza, where he could catch a commercial flight back to Lima.

Jim and O'Reilly ferried the plane onto a dirt strip on a farm close to Uchiza. It was already evening when he landed, and a room in the farmhouse had been prepared for their stay. To thank them, their host roasted a pig over an open fire and opened his best tequila. A group of young women that were staying on the hacienda joined the workers, and the festivities went on long into the night.

A tall blonde from San Diego kept dancing the tango with Jim; rushed on by the clapping of the bystanders, she made Jim lick tequila salt from her lips then whispered into his ear, "I have softer lips to try, stranger." But she didn't divulge why she was there, rather shook his question off with a flick of her neck. "You didn't come to talk."

O'Reilly left the next day, taking with him undeveloped film and most of Jim's photography equipment. Manuelo, the owner of the farm, asked Jim to stay on and help train another pilot to fly the wooden plane. Only after several days of flight training did the real intent behind what initially had appeared to be a few favors become clear. It happened when Jim joined Manuelo for breakfast and found him sitting at the table with bundles of dollars as thick as bricks before him.

"We need pilot who knows fly wood planes. Federales have radar now. You fly from Jeberos to San Cristobal in Colombia. Each time return, you take bundle of eight thousand."

"For how long?" That was the only question Jim asked.

"As long you like," Manuelo said.

At Jeberos, the cocaleros had marked an airstrip with drums of burning kerosene. Jim decided to fly at night because the plane handled better in cooler air. He followed the glistening band of the Marañón River but stayed far to the north of Iquitos, from where the Federales planes were operating. He knew he had to arrive in San Cristóbal before one in the morning when the local radio station, the only navigation aid, was still on the air. To Jim, this was flying at its best—the raw sound of the propeller and, beneath him as wide as he could see, the canopy of the Amazon. At least this adventure would pay out, Jim told himself. One night, he bribed the mail clerk to open the San Cristóbal post office and called Leila.

"Frank and I were able to arrange for a seaplane," she told him.

"I never thought he would be foolish enough to go through with the trip to Clipperton.. How about supplies?" The line stuttered.

"The Navy will air drop them."

"Hell! No! . . . Anyway. What's the model he's trying to fly over?"

"Cessna Turbo-something."

"Leila, listen! He doesn't have the experience."

"He's leaving New York tomorrow," Leila said. The line suddenly filled with the sound of crackling cellophane and then went dead.

Mulling over the situation, Jim decided to return to San Diego. He was not about to let his cousin take off on a private vacation with his woman.

But the next day, Jim landed during a gust of wind, ground looped the plane and hit a tree. The wing's mid-spar was broken, and it would take weeks to open the wing and replace the spar. *One reason more to extricate himself from this adventure gone sour,* Jim thought.

The owner of the hacienda, however, didn't want to hear about it. "We give you other plane," he said, jerking his hands. "Friends not walk."

"I wouldn't push the point," one of Manuelo's men whispered into Jim's ear. And the cocaleros meant business: in less than a day Carlos had the other plane ferried onto the hacienda's dirt strip. Several days later, one of the ground crew gave Jim the sign of the slit throat. "Carlos no problem any more," he said. Jim's blood suddenly ran cold; he knew he was in too deep. But could he quit without the danger of retribution?

At San Cristobal, Jim eventually came up with a plan. He claimed he had trouble with the plane's engine and had to keep the plane light, even refusing to load the usual stack of cash on the return flight. Flying low over the jungle at night, he turned to the north, then followed the Putumayo River, which marked the Colombian border, and eventually landed at Puerto Leguizamo. He left the plane at the airport and took a flight with a group of loggers in an old, rickety DC-3 to Bogota. From there he sent telegrams to Jeberos and San Cristobal: "Plane is at Puerto Leguizamo. Our contract has ended. *Gracias.*" Then he called Leila and announced his return to San Diego.

10

THE END OF APRIL 1990 MARKED seven months since Lucienne's death. Earlier, Frank had packed the last of his belongings, and now he watched the moving van careen slowly down the alley. It left behind a rustle of flapping branches showering white lilac blossoms onto the driveway. He walked back to the house and, for a moment, he felt as if Lucienne were still alive, as if he could kneel down beside the rocking chair, look over her shoulder while she was reading a manuscript, touch her slightly tilted neck and kiss her gently behind the ear.

The living room was empty except for the sleeping bag in which he would spend the night. An oppressive quietness overtook the house, and he slept fitfully. When the morning light invaded the room, he gave up and walked out to the garden, taking in the smell of wet soil and sweet lilac. He stood still, suddenly aware of the burden of time. He walked across the lawn to the swale of grass Lucienne had planted. The full juices hadn't entered the blades yet; the stems were still bent, the spikelets still tousled. Frank knelt down and began pulling weeds; it was the way Lucienne would have said good-bye to the house.

He drove west. The relentless plains of Indiana dragged by, the soil heavy with freshly plowed clods. Flocks of black birds in tight formations whipped across the sky. Then came Missouri, the rolling hills of Oklahoma, flatlands and fields peeling away on a highway that ran into the horizon far and thin as a needle. A clear light began pouring on him in New Mexico, and his raw soul yearned for the cry of sea gulls. He was drunk with the sky, with the lightness.

During nights in roadside motels, he lay on the bed and stared at the ceiling, a bottle of scotch on his night stand. The immensity of the continent wore him out. But as Frank floated between the confines of two coasts, the denseness of existence seemed pleasantly lifted. He had been driving for days without calling Leila or glancing at Jimmy Skagg's Clipperton book. He found himself indifferent to the future, his mood suspended, weightlessly numbing the hurt that his father's past had stirred. His soul was appeased by this state of indifference.

After several days, he called Leila from a motel in Albuquerque.

"Finally!" she said. "I wanted to tell you that I did a job on my section chief. Believe it or not, this sucker is going to pay for Jim's trawler and everything!" Her voice sounded shrill. So that was it now: Jim's trawler.

"So he's no more . . ." Frank started to say.

"Where have you been? Jim's back in San Diego," she interrupted. "In two days he sewed up everything; trawler and plane and whatnot."

"Well . . ." He paused to keep from stuttering.

"Where are you calling from?"

"St. Louis." Frank lied.

Talking to Leila, he came to grips with his need to take pause, to give one last moment to his melancholy, to seek refuge, and he felt driven to deliberate over the seriousness of life. And more than once he sensed that Clipperton might bring them all to ruin.

"Get over here!" Leila's voice came through the phone. He didn't respond, and his silence must have given her pause. "I know you wanted to hear something else," she added. Now her voice was mellow and soothing.

Frank stayed two more days, occasionally reading Skagg's book, still hoping to hold onto some romantic notion about the island, however faint it might be. It was a lost cause: Clipperton had never been much of a territory; mankind should have left it alone; ships should have turned away.

CLIPPERTON

Why the French, chancing upon the island on April 3, 1711, had laid claim on this burnt out volcano was beyond him. Predictably, they soon lost interest. Then, in 1908, the Mexican Army claimed dominion by establishing a garrison under the command of a Captain Arnaud. The garrison never amounted to more than some ramshackle huts bordered by pigpens with a few skinny hogs chewing the few spare greens and a helter-skelter of rusting winches and shovels strewn across the pitted soil where soldiers had scraped the phosphate deposits.

Yet every day, Captain Arnaud would show up in a spotless Prussian uniform to hoist the Mexican flag. The bare-chested soldiers who had to stand in attention could not have cared less about the ceremony; the phosphates were raw material for gunpowder, and it was all about power and money for them. Day after day, they toiled, heaving lumps of phosphates into lorries and then dumping and stacking them, eventually loading the piles into a gasoline-powered haul and onto a steamer scheduled to arrive from the mainland every six months.

There was a man who walked between the soldiers talking about exploitation and the coming rule of the proletariat. Rumors were budding like yeast. One soldier of German origin would sit for hours on the beach waving Nietzsche's *Also Sprach Zarathustra* and yelling into the roaring breakers, "God is dead."

The soldiers began to fight. There were stabbings. Captain Arnaud knew the isolation and the cacophony of shrieking boobies, the constant roar of the surf and the blistering rays of the sun all could turn people mad. So he decided to bring the soldiers' families to the island to give the men a measure of private life. At first the fighting eased, but a mulatto, a certain Miguel Alvarez, continually harassed the men and their women and children. One day, a soldier walked toward him with a raised Bible and called him the Antichrist. Alvarez pinned the man, broke his arm and, ignoring his cries of pain, wrenched him mercilessly.

After the incident, Captain Arnaud decided to keep Alvarez

away from the rest. He ordered him to construct a lighthouse on top of Clipperton Rock, supplying him with cement, iron rods and bricks; once it was finished, he made him the warden. From then on, this new light would guide the supply boats. Events on the Mexican mainland, however, were set to change everything.

In August 1914, Venustiano Carranza overthrew the Huerta regime. A civil war broke out, chaos reigned and the supply missions to Clipperton were forgotten.

Fruits and vegetables ran out first. Arnaud ordered rationing of whatever was left. The available supply of coconut and coconut milk would first be given to breast-feeding mothers; next in line were the children, then women, then soldiers.

Discipline broke down fast. Groups of soldiers roamed the island in search of food, clubbing crabs and shooting birds. The few fish they caught tasted foul, and the watery meat wrenched their stomachs. One mother gave birth to her child but was so wrought with fever she never recognized her newborn; as she died, the women at her side fought for her ration of coconut meat.

As food supplies dwindled, Captain Arnaud made the fateful decision to ration the coconuts to women and children only; the men began to develop scurvy. Their eyes became bloodshot, their muscles bruised, and blood oozing from their lips. Most of them were already too weak to walk, and those who were able slouched toward the beach and stared into the surf as if sintered in place by the burning sun. Some lay in their huts, faces swollen like gargoyles. They woke up with teeth rattling like loose gravel in their mouths.

The two smaller rowboats, each less than twelve feet long, would not make it through the surf safely, and the only seaworthy vessel, a fifty-foot gasoline-powered launch, had run out of fuel transporting guano to the larger ships that once had been waiting offshore. Out of desperation, they tried propelling it by oars through the surf, but exhausted as they were they gave up. Besides, there was no way to pull at oars all the six hundred seventy miles to Acapulco. Escape proved impossible.

Like a bird of prey, Alvarez would come down from his lighthouse to walk among the soldiers, trading cigarettes here and there, but mostly remaining silent and aloof. Rumor had it that Alvarez had magical powers. Some claimed he had stolen supplies and stacked them away in his fortress hideout. Others looked upon him as the devil and tried to plead with him— praying for him to spare their lives. But Alvarez would just laugh and say there was no devil and no evil but the one created by man. With a wave of his hand, he would command them to kneel down and then would call them fools, turn around and trudge over sun-scorched spits of sand toward the lighthouse on the rock, which had become his fortress.

There were others who gathered at night on the beach and huddled at low fires to read from Revelations, where it was written that a time would come when man would worship the beast.

When it didn't rain for weeks, they had to drink brackish bay water that reeked of fish. Every week somebody died from malnutrition or scurvy. In the beginning, the survivors erected a primitive cross at each burial, and some friend or family member would read from the Bible; eventually they merely tossed the bloodied bodies into the surf.

A peculiar state of mind overcame those who still lived— the *maladie de mer*—brought on by shrieking boobies, pounding waves and the relentless sky of molten pewter. At night, a distant glimmer of a thousand red eyes smoldered when the crabs gathered in their rusty armor to shred to pieces anything living or dead.

Ramon Arnaud was close to insanity. One day he took his revolver ran to the beach and yelled, "Ship! Ship!" As women, children and soldiers gathered around him, he forced the remaining six men to launch the boat, and when he boarded it, ordered them to row through the surf to the open sea. Then a fight broke out and shots were fired —so it was reported by Senora Arnaud, who observed the boat through her binoculars—and the boat overturned. All of the men drowned in the shark-infested sea.

The only man still alive, Alvarez, came down from the rock and walked from hut to hut gathering all the rifles, most of which he threw into the bay. One day, when twenty-five-year old Randon crossed him, he pointed his gun at her. She fell to the ground and kissed Alvarez's feet; she promised him a meal of fish and crabs every day, crying out that she would mend his clothes and do any chores for him. Laughing and ignoring the shrieks of the others, Alvarez grabbed her hair and dragged her to his hideout. Two days later, he brought her back, and threw her at the feet of the terrified women. Randon's body was bloody, her face bruised. Terror settled over the small camp of women. They cut their hair to appear ugly, but each time Alvarez descended to the camp, he took one of them up to the lighthouse.

When Alvarez demanded food they would climb to the lighthouse and place the best of their meager catch in front of the iron door. Some of the women accepted that there was no way of escaping and collaborated with the half-breed to keep him in a good mood. Some tried to get favors by offering fish, but Alvarez just tossed the smaller of the catch into their faces. Others thought of killing him at night but could not think of a way to break into his fortress.

Alicia, the wife of Captain Arnaud and mother of his three children, kept her hatred boiling. Perhaps out of some strange respect for the captain, or perhaps by chance, Alvarez had not yet molested Alicia, but eventually he took her. Down in their huts, the women heard her scream all night, and when she crawled back to camp the next morning, she was battered almost beyond recognition. The morale of the women was broken.

It had been three years since the last supply boat had arrived and twenty-two months since the men had so foolishly launched the boat. Malnutrition had killed several of the women, and the survivors prayed that their pale gray faces and their flaccid skin coming off their bones in wrinkles might keep them from being raped so often.

CLIPPERTON

On July 18, 1917, Tirza Randon was heading toward the lighthouse with a basket of food to be placed at the door; she had Alicia's little boy Ramond in tow. Alvarez had been holding Alicia for several days, and Tirza hoped that Ramond's tears might urge Alvarez to release her.

Alvarez opened the iron door, sneered at the basket and tossed Alicia Arnaud onto the concrete slab at Tirza's feet. "She's no good," he yelled.

Tirza, choking with hate and despair, asked for an ax, explaining that the women needed to cut a coconut tree. At first, Alvarez did not answer and continued to kick Alicia. After a few minutes his anger seemed to subside and he turned around and came back with an ax in his hand. He threw it onto the floor beside Tirza. "You report to me every day!" he commanded. "Take that dirty whore with you!"

Tirza bent down to help up Alicia, who lay crying on the floor. Disoriented, Alicia started to crawl back through the door. Alvarez stared at Alicia as she was crawling by him. He turned back and kicked her buttocks. "Get out of here, you bitch!" he yelled. Alicia did not react. Alvarez bent down to pull her out of the room, turning his back to Tirza. That moment, Tirza clutched the ax and swung the blade into Alvarez's back. Alvarez slumped over but managed to push up on his elbows and turn around. Suddenly alert, Alicia pulled him down and Tirza swung the ax for the second time. Alvarez collapsed and rolled sideways. Tirza grabbed the handle, jerked the ax out of his back and landed the blade between Alvarez's eyes. Alicia grabbed Alvarez's knife and in pure rage cut his face into a bloody pulp.

Eventually Tirza and Alicia staggered out through the door and slumped down outside at the wall where the boy was hiding; he was trembling with fear.

What was to happen now would turn out to be one of the most peculiar coincidences in history. Only minutes after the murder, the boy yelled, "A ship! A ship!" Indeed, Ramond had spotted the American cruiser *Yorktown*, which had been sent into the Eastern Pacific to search for German submarines.

On that same day, all the women, and children were aboard and safe. The landing crew had informed Captain Perrill, the commander of the *Yorktown*, as to what they had found, but feeling empathy with the raped women, he wanted to spare them a prolonged investigation and did not enter the facts surrounding Alvarez's death into the ship's logbook.

The story was soon forgotten. The war took the headlines in 1917, and the *New York Times* reported the rescue only in a brief paragraph on the back page. For their part, Captain Perrill and his crew kept the story to themselves until seventeen years later when the captain's widow found her late husband's diary and broke the silence.

The murderous story was still on Frank's mind as he drove into San Diego and turned toward La Jolla.

CLIPPERTON

Strait of Gibraltar
May 6, 1944

The Requin class U-boat was sliding under the thermal layer at crawling speed. The captain's face lit by the green board looked like an olive rubber mask. Everybody else's face appeared purple, as all overhead lamps had been dimmed to a faint red. This would be the most dangerous part of the mission: passing the Strait of Gibraltar.

In May of 1944, German U-boats did not rule the oceans anymore. The few U-boats the Germans still had left in the Mediterranean were in disrepair and bottled up in harbors, and all ambitious plans had been abandoned. At the start of World War II, the Italian Navy had commissioned several U-boats for long- distance missions and some of them had reached Japanese waters, but in 1944 the Italians had already defected to the Allied camp, and the Allies now controlled the Mediterranean water and sky. A few tattered U-boats were still hidden in Genoa harbor, but they hadn't cut their mooring lines for months. Requin class submarines were among them.

Even at the start of the war, Requin class submarines were outdated already. Those submarines were long-range boats built by the French navy after the First World War. After the defeat of France, they were incorporated in the Italian navy. Some were lost to mines, one was sunk by Allied forces in 1941, some survived, and when the Italians joined the Allied Forces, three were captured by the Germans and one at least was moored in Genoa.

There it floated about and for months was merely used to reload batteries. The Germans had given up on it, and the Allied Air Force didn't even bother strafing, as the AA batteries in the hills above Genoa were very accurate. Requin class submarines had been written off as junk.

In the beginning of 1944, the Germans decided to supply the Japanese with jet fighters, but the naval situation was now so desperate it was decided to use Requin class boats in one of these attempts. The order went out to make the mooring site appear as tattered and slovenly as possible. They let chickens run free on the quay where they picked on rotten vegetables. Batteries were scattered all over the pier. No sailor was ever to wear uniform. But in the nights, a small crew began to install snorkel and radar detection equipment. Then, at the end of April 1944, the trucks with the jet engines and crates, some containing dismantled hulls, arrived.

Captain Mintmeier was keeping the U-boat just below the thin layer of warm water. He was an experienced veteran of the Battle of the Atlantic; he was resourceful and it had been his idea to equip the boat with temperature gauges, which now were floating above the U-boat at different depths. He knew that with a speed of seven knots only cunning and good luck would make this outdated U-boat ever pass the Strait. At least for the time being, the thermal layer would deflect the acoustic waves of the propeller and prevent detection.

The four Luftwaffe soldiers in the aft battery spent most of their time playing cards, except the one who for most of the voyage would stay on his cot, which he shared with a tray of gel-filled flasks, tin boxes with flowers pods, tools and chemicals. Often he would place the flasks under fluorescent lights, which— so he'd told his comrades—would help the seedlings grow into lush yellow-tongued orchid flowers once he'd decided to replant them. But as for the fact that everybody had brought something feminine onto the boat—a wife's slip, a stocking or some perfumed trinket—they might on occasion call him orchid freak; but for the most part they left him alone.

On their journey across the Atlantic and the Indian Ocean, one refuel procedure was scheduled mid-Atlantic, another in the Indian Ocean. And there was a Plan B if they could not refuel: reach the east coast of Mexico, scuttle the U-boat and transport just a few selected crates with documents and jet engine parts across Mexico to Acapulco and from there to Clipperton.

The next day, the U-boat reached the open Atlantic.

11

FRANK TOOK OFF from the San Diego seaport several days
after he watched Jim steer the trawler, a pathetic piece of scrap,
toward the open ocean. Dark streaks on its hull looked as if
black piss had run down from the portholes, and its cabin was
banged up worse than the body of a demolition derby car. But
Frank knew Jim would have rowed Leila to Clipperton in a
bathtub if need be.

The route Frank chose took him along the Mexican coast to
Manzanillo where he would spend the night. Only then did he
intend to cross open waters to Clipperton. The distance between
San Diego and Manzanillo was thirteen-hundred miles, which he
intended to fly non-stop in ten hours. It was his way of preparing
for the flight to Clipperton, of building up his endurance, and
becoming familiar with switching the two inflatable tanks on the
back seats. He'd been skittish about flying to so far off an island
and had insisted on installing a Loran navigation system. But
he learned quickly that his trip to Clipperton wasn't anything
special: at the San Diego airport his Cessna 206 seaplane was
just one of several planes waiting to cross the ocean. Two sleek
Moneys were headed for Hawaii, and so was an old Cessna 172,
beside which his Cessna 206 looked like an oversized truck. And
none of the pilots he talked to had shown the faintest interest in
his trip. Hopping six hundred miles across the ocean was no big
deal to them.

When after hours of uneventful flight Frank finally contacted
the tower at Playa De Oro, every remaining shred of thought had
been hammered thin by boredom. That seemed to be a common
affliction as even the customs inspector seemed to be barely

135

awake. After he had the plane refueled, Frank took a smoke-spewing Mercedes cab to the local Holiday Inn. The bar was crowded with young Germans, but even understanding their chatter did not prevent him from feeling like an outsider. And why use his German? Nobody would listen anyway. They had already spun off into discussion groups of gesticulating buck-toothed blonds, eagerly waiting for their turn to blabber about ice biking in Canada or flying ultra-lights in Uganda.

Frank imagined for a moment mustering the courage to join them. Here's my story, he'd say. They even might fall silent and listen, sheepishly watching the tips of their Birkenstocks. But what was his story? His mother abandoned him and left him with a drunken uncle. His German father's mind, bled white by war, could not see hope, anywhere but in death among floating orchids. This cagey man who would bequeath to his son a mind haunted by self-doubts, a mind strangely hollow, weakened by a reckoning that life was shallow, that the floods of passion and rapture merely lap at the soul, and that history, too, would pass him by.

Later, in his hotel room, Frank dreamed that the continent he had driven across had, broken into pieces and the parts kept sliding into dark bodies of water. He saw his father as he appeared on the old sepia print, standing on some knoll in an unknown country, wearing a shiny uniform, and though he appeared misplaced and remote, he seemed to have a strangely comforting power.

Frank rose very early the next morning to open his flight plan. He expected some inquiry as to the unusual destination, but the controller cleared him for take-off without delay. Climbing out over the ocean, the Cessna followed the radial off the VOR until Frank was sure the Loran was working properly and could be coupled to the autopilot. From that point, it was a straight line of about six hundred miles to Clipperton.

I'll be there for *lunch*, he told himself.

He signed off with the tower and took his headphones off. He saw several fishing boats, here and there specks of birds cutting through the glare, then nothing.

Not even an hour into the flight, the engine noise began to numb his mind. He fingered some dried apricots, somehow managing to smear the gooey sugar coating all over the yoke. He didn't do better with the M&M's, which had melted into sticky protoplasm. How could he be so stupid? He pulled off his T-shirt and wiped his fingers. Mid-morning and he already was annoyed! His armpits were turning swampy hot. He downed half of a six-pack of diet cola and waited for the caffeine rush, but all it did was drown his bladder. The worse part was that he'd forgotten to unpack the urinal from Sporty's Pilot Shop.

The best he could do was to widen the triangular opening on one of the cola cans, bend away the aluminum, make room to dangle his penis in there and let loose. Nice and steady it went, until the devil twisted his mind, tempting him with visions of Leila doing morning stretches in her thong, making his imagination reel off into the wonderland of unfulfilled dreams. But now his penis was wedged into the slot so tightly, he felt the icy sludge of panic in his stomach. Eventually it did curl and slip back out of the can. Hell! This was a ridiculous start if there ever was one!

But eventually boredom would win out. The flat green of the ocean reminded him of the blind green of telephone insulators his uncle had collected a long time ago. Nothing but empty, dead space. With the autopilot working smoothly, he stretched out across both seats and, for a brief time, closed his eyes and drifted off, imagining how he was tracing the arc toward a distant island. Maybe if he dozed off and let go, he might enter the realm of levitation, find that crack in reality he yearned for, that rift out of which would burst a leavening force.

Sailing through space, Frank felt lost and disconnected, yet content in a strange way. He yearned for a sense of abandon to snap him out of the denseness of being. Or was it the other way? For the moment at least he didn't really care.

Eventually reality would pinch him awake. The altimeter had to be checked, the gyro realigned. When the Loran receiver indicated twenty miles to Clipperton, Frank sat back up and started to gaze out alongside the propeller's flutter. The glare of noon scraped his eyes and swirled his senses. The sky above appeared like quicksilver spread on a cloth that tilted and warped before it dipped into the bleached green of the sea.

Out of this wash, Clipperton would rise first as something crystalloid, like a frozen smudge on the windshield. Then it expanded into a smoke ring, boiling up from the ocean, a sintered circle of sand and brittle rock broken and smashed and ground down through thousands of years of pounding waves.

He throttled the engine, circling toward the trawler anchored outside the surf line. He descended through a thin, yellow cloud that, like a wind-blown finger, seemed to emanate from the center of the bay. It left a brownish slime on the windshield. Skimming close to sea level, he caught a glance of the trawler and of Jim standing upright at the ship's bow, naked so it seemed, his body covered with black slick. He appeared like a galleon's dark figurehead, not giving any signal of recognition even as Frank tipped the wings. At stern, he spotted Leila frozen stiff on her knees, bent across the taffrail as if somebody had stabbed her. Frigates and boobies and albatrosses flew madly around the trawler, squawking at the intruders. Frank suddenly sensed a crack in reality open, and, instead of excitement, he felt immense dread. This trawler looked like a ghost ship. It was as if all the rules had changed and nothing could be counted on, and that anything—anything—could happen now. Frank rubbed his eyes. Was that an albatross with its wings nailed onto the mast, its belly sliced open and bursting forth a loop of guts? This couldn't be. A brimstone illusion — it had to be the damn slime on the windshield!

He pulled the plane up in a panic. Only the sky seemed safe now. He felt the urge to head back to Mexico, though there was not enough fuel. But once he'd reached altitude, it suddenly seemed laughable—maybe it was all a practical joke.

After circling for a few minutes, he turned the plane into the wind and touched down only yards away from the trawler. It was a rough landing, and the plane rolled and yawed: Frank had to rev the engine to keep from drifting in the low swell.

While steering with rudder and aileron, Frank kept looking for Jim to row the rubber dinghy across to the plane as planned. Jim donned a swim vest and took his time coming down the rope ladder. He finally slid into the dinghy and rowed over.

Lifting himself out by hooking one arm across the wing strut, Jim eventually wiggled out of the vest and brought his face up to the cockpit window, yelling above the propeller noise, "I'll take it!"

Frank grasped the top of the doorframe and slid backward out of the cabin, coming to a stand beside Jim. "What's that mess on your skin?"

"Damn engine repairs!" Jim started to pull himself up into the pilot seat.

"Don't mess up the seats!" Frank was ready to pull Jim back out, but right then the plane started to tilt and turn so that, for a few seconds, Jim had his hands full stabilizing it.

"The plane's anchor is still in the dinghy!" Jim yelled through the side window to Frank who was outside holding on to the struts.

"How is Leila?"

"She's seasick. See for yourself."

Frank loaded the anchor through the rear cargo door then rowed the dinghy across to the trawler and climbed the drop ladder to where Leila was kneeling bent over the gunwale. She seemed to have been retching for some time. Her cheeks were white as flaked gypsum.

"Get me over to the island," she stammered. "Now!" Then, looking up briefly, she insisted, "I don't give a damn what he told you."

"Doesn't he want you to go?"

She just dropped her head.

"The plane ride doesn't help," Frank said.

"Now! I said." For this moment, she mustered a determined look, her green eyes stuck like bullets into her doughy white face.

One arm slung around her waist, Frank half-carried her down the rope ladder. She plopped into the dingy, retching all the way to the plane, but eventually managed to clamber through the drowning sluice of prop wash into the copilot seat. Jim, who was still sitting in the pilot's seat, helped pull her into the cockpit. Irritated that nothing had gone according to plan, he yelled, "You can't be that sick!"

"Shut up!" She pushed her fist into her stomach, waving her other hand in front of her mouth.

"Don't throw up on me!" Jim grunted. "I'm out of here." Frank dove beneath the floats to the other side where he pulled himself up as Jim was sliding out of the pilot seat and was putting on the swim vest.

"Couldn't you be nice for a change?" Frank hissed.

"Why don't *you* repair the diesel engine?"

Anxious for Jim to leave, Frank ignored him and tended to Leila. He revved the engine even before Jim had rowed the dinghy to a safe distance, showering him with water.

It was a skittish takeoff. Leila kept her head down at first, but soon she was able to help Frank locate the stretch of water inside the bay that, on aerial photography, had appeared to be free of reefs.

"You must stay inside that rectangle," she said.

"I have the photo right here on the clipboard," he reassured her. He managed to touch down very gently inside the outlined area and let the plane drift onto a shallow beach at the island's western rim. After helping her ashore, he made her sit down on a low dune covered with spiny gray grasses.

"Is Jim nasty or what?" she said.

"Take some whiskey. " He handed her a small flask and she took a mouthful or two.

"That's what pilots use for hydration?"

"At least your humor is back," he said.

"It's a wonder after these three days." She looked up and tried to grin. "Don't ask."

Frank noted that he had beached at the site of the former Mexican camp as planned, half a mile south of the Egg Islands, although with the island presenting nothing but a featureless rim, it was difficult to be sure. He remembered Jimmy Skaggs' book pointing out that the rim formed the outline of a skull laid on its side: Forehead to the east—the site of Clipperton Rock—chin to the west. Picturing the island this way, he was standing at the campsite halfway down the skull's left cheekbone. He looked around for some elevation, a ridge or a firm slate of soil, but nothing snagged his gaze. Leila's face had now regained some color and her puckish cheek dimples had come back. She kept scooping up grains of sand and tossing them into the breeze— like she did that summer day in Biddeford, Frank thought.

"Jim is pissed," Leila said. "First, the engine repair— something with the sump pump—and now he has to stay on the trawler to repair a broken anchor chain. He had it coming, of course! You should have been on that trawler; it rolled, it squeaked, it leaked. What a wreck!"

"Who rented him that piece of junk?" Frank asked.

"He didn't say."

Jim's secrecy made Frank angry. "He finagled to shorten his South America trip so he could join us!"

Leila looked at Frank with a sudden alert in her face. "It makes me feel uncomfortable when you say that."

She took several long breaths and stood up. Her curly reddish hair had left a spatter of tiny scratches in the sand that looked like ant tracks.

"What did Jim really do in South America?" Frank asked.

"Why do you ask me? Are you trying to spoil everything from the start?"

"But you must have asked yourself that question," he blurted out, but then he bit his tongue. Leila was right; it was better to avoid the topic. "I'm sorry I upset you," he said.

There was no time to quarrel. The supplies had to be flown onto the island. When Frank landed back at the trawler, he threw the plane's anchor, then waited until the plane had drifted leeward and the anchor snared. Frank swam across to the trawler where he found Jim kneeling in the stern crawl space. Jim's body was slicked with black oil like a devil's out of Dante's hell. His white, rabid eyes made him look like an apparition from a nether world of dark space and fierce deviance.

"Took me an hour to even spot that fucking leak," he yelled. A stream of curses. But it seemed as if he were talking without moving his mouth, as if his voice escaped from some indeterminate region where all human sounds were as dead and machine-like as the hum of the bilge pump and the low stump of the ship's diesel.

Back up on deck Jim lobbed a blob of sludge onto Frank's head. "Have a sample."

"Don't be mean." He had to say something.

"Just for the record: I feel mean right now."

Jim started to wash off the oil slick on his body with bucket loads of soapy water. He was almost naked, wearing only bikini trunks, his abdominal muscles twisted like ropes. Pushing back his hair, he appeared tall and lanky, sure of himself. This was Jim the wrestler, intimidating Frank with a stare that said, "I know you are afraid of me." The awkward silence felt like a stumble in the flow of time.

For the next several hours, Frank shuttled between the island and the trawler. He would taxi the plane as close to the trawler as was safe; Jim would appear from his underworld, don the swim vest, let down duffel bags, containers or metal boxes into the dinghy, and, after having rowed the short distance, stuff them through the plane's rear cargo door. A clumsy and hesitant swimmer, every time Jim touched water, his lankiness would disappear. But eventually the two men had a routine, so that by mid-afternoon, the supplies were piled up high near the dune. Leila, recovering quickly, had already opened a few of the duffel bags and pitched a small tent.

On his return, Frank signaled Jim to stop. Jim acknowledged, but to Frank's surprise, he started to swim across to the plane with awkward paddle strokes. Frank knew that, despite the swim vest, it would take all of Jim's courage to swim in the open ocean, and he felt vaguely threatened by this display of pluck. Eventually, Jim pulled himself onto the plane's float. He moved his face close as they talked through the half-open door.

"I guess you quit flying for today."

"Leila needs me."

Jim ignored the remark. He told Frank that he had stopped the oil leak in the sump pump but had not yet welded the broken anchor.

"I have to stay on board," he said. "How's Leila?"

But he didn't wait for an answer.

"Fly her back over."

"She's still seasick."

"You told me she's feeling better."

"Don't you get it? She needs to be on land—not in a rocking bunk bed," Frank yelled. Jim tried to argue, but the propeller kept spraying in his face, and all he could do was spit.

"Hold it! I've something for her," Jim finally shouted. He pulled a tiny square box from a vest pocket.

"What's that?"

"Give it to her!" He slapped it into Frank's hand.

"Can't you do it yourself?"

"Don't ask questions."

The way Jim hissed the words at him angered Frank to no end. "Why do you always have it your way?" he yelled.

He revved the prop, whipping water onto Jim with a force that made him let go of the struts. He'd been cowed by Jim far too often! He looked pathetic, a clumsy sailor, paddling his way back to the trawler. And that stupid box. Looked darn well like a jewelry box. Frank couldn't imagine that Jim would propose marriage to Leila like this, letting him make the presentation. No way! It was just another twisted way to humiliate him. Better to make a joke out of it, he told himself. Frank felt better after kicking up some defiance. Man, it was time! Jim deserved it. And damn the box, whatever was in it! But despite his indignation, he felt doubt and insecurity clawing his heart.

On this last flight back to Clipperton, he circled low above the Egg Islands, shallow piles of coral and pebbles studded with boobies that immediately flew off, spreading a flickering white net above the bay. He spent some time circling—mostly to put distance between himself and Jim and to forget about the little gift box. Then, anxious for time alone with Leila, he landed and let the plane drift onto the beach. Leila waded out and stepped on the float, holding on to the struts. She lifted her face so close to Frank's that, against the low sun, he could see the downy hair on her cheeks.

"How did it go?" she asked.

"He'll stay on the trawler."

"I thought so."

"He's pissed like hell."

"He probably made it sound as if you abducted me," she said. She threw her head to the side, smiled at Frank, then let go.

The plane was easily secured by pulling it onto the flat sand beach. They sat down on the dune and watched the low sun. Already, the reef's shadows threw purple fingers across the white foam inside the backwaters. Salt spray and whiffs of moldy kelp blew in from the ocean, and boobies kept tumbling, graceless and clumsy. Frank suddenly felt as if he were sitting on a beach on which all the umbrellas had been put down. A sense of joylessness and void came over him. He squinted his eyes and looked at this sliver of land, and what he saw was a rim of sand drowning in the ocean, weighed down by a sky that lay on it like a millstone.

"What's wrong?" Leila asked.

"I need to get used to this," Frank said. He felt a sudden urge to return to the East Coast, to see woods and moss, and walk barefoot on dewy meadows. All day, the light had been harsh and relentless, so different from the fractured light back east. If she guessed his thoughts, she didn't say so.

"I found a beach already," she announced, dispelling for the moment his somber thoughts. They walked the short distance to a shallow eddy just west of the campsite, and Leila sat down crossing her arms in front of her knees. Frank squinted into the low sunrays that burst through her hair and then, very gently, laid his hand on her arm. She didn't pull back.

"It isn't like our beach at Biddeford," he said.

"Well? So?"

"I would do everything different," he said.

"Why didn't you try to win me over then, Frank?" she asked. How could he explain? He'd been afraid to compete with Jim—she had to know that—and what sense would it make now to admit that he was timid and cowardly.

Leila did not press for an answer; she kept scooping handfuls of sand, making them trickle through her fingers, and somehow this seemed to settle her mind.

"I'll tell you a story," she finally said. "Sometime after your wedding—maybe it was your first anniversary—you planted a larch in Pierre's yard. But the sapling didn't grow well, so I replanted it in Maine and kept nursing it. But you never, even once, asked me what became of it."

"Believe me, I kept thinking of you."

"But you kept it to yourself." She stood up and wiped her hands. "It is what you didn't say that day on the beach in Biddeford, for whatever reason. But I can't live with nothing to hold on to." She slapped the sand off her hands, a gesture of closures that made Frank wince.

But then came one of Leila's mood changes, an emotional flip-flop that would overtake her. It had been that way as long as he'd known her.

Leila, wearing a miniscule thong, waved Frank to follow her to the swimming hole where she kept sliding through the lacework of snaking reflections as lissome as an eel. When she returned, her body dripping wet, Frank couldn't take his eyes off her tanned breasts, her tits bent upward like the tips of soft ice cream cones. Back at the camping site, Frank handed her a glass of red wine. "Côte de Rhone," he said, biting his lips.

"My corner of the world." She took a sip.

"Are we done with the past?"

"Not really." She laid her hand on his shoulder. "But the situation is quite different now."

"All right then . . . the day after you left San Diego I received a phone call."

"What could that be? Oh God! You got the job!"

"Yes! Yes! I am the new architectural editor of the *Los Angeles Times*."

Leila started jumping up and down. She threw her wet arms around Frank, hugged him and smooched his cheeks. He steadied her neck and kissed her, and she allowed his gentle probing. Getting his nerve up, Frank started fondling her breasts, but she pulled back.

"I have prepared everything for tonight, so that we have time to look around before sunset," she said.

They took off their sneakers and started walking alongside the bay in the opposite direction from the tangle of coconut trees that bordered the tent site to the east. The land at the tent site was sandy and folded into small dunes, but there had to be some clay deposits as recent downpours had filled some of the small pits with rainwater. Always the observant scientist, Leila pointed out the puddles, explaining that fresh water would be available after rainfalls.

They walked to the northwest where the land flattened into deeply rilled washes. Soon they were sloshing about in the island's mud flats, muck squishing between their toes in a delicious tickle.

"Build me a house of your imagination. What would it look like?" Leila requested.

"I'd start with a tree," Frank said, pointing into the darkening sky. "It will serve as the anchor. Part of the earth — nothing less will do. And let's build the kitchen around it. Some of the branches will spread out inside, just below the ceiling, and at night you will hear boughs rustle against cedar shingles."

Leila was leading him on further into the soft muck as he continued to stitch his dream circles into the evening sky.

"Beautiful. Go on!"

"And a brook will rumble right under the bedroom," he continued, "and I'd build a window into the floor so you could watch leaves and twigs drift by below you. You'll have benches tucked below the windows and wide sills for cats to perch on gazing outside with dreamy expressions on snowy days."

"And the light?"

"It will dance," Frank said.

That very moment, Frank realized he had sunk into the muck up to his knees. But Leila wasn't stuck yet, and she kept moving in a circle with her hands high up in the air, acting giddy when her cloddy feet pulled out of the mud with a sucking sound. She turned toward Frank, taunting, "Catch me!" He reached toward her, but with his legs stuck in the mud, his arms merely flung about like windmills. "You're just too heavy and clumsy," she laughed, hands on her hips.

Leila came closer again, her almost-naked body set white against the flats' blackness. Deep inside the mud, Frank felt her feet slide above his, weighing him down, sinking him deeper. What was she doing? He tried to put his arms around her hips but she wiggled backward and he lurched and fell belly-down into the mud. Before he knew what was happening she kneeled behind him loading huge clumps of wet muck onto his skin, and then straddled him and splashed his back with a thick paste that oozed around his neck. A warm brine ran dark in the receding light. He felt her thighs hard against his hips, pushing his lower body deeper and deeper. But it did not frighten him, nor did he fear drowning. The mud was warm and soft, providing a strangely inviting lift.

For the moment they had stopped struggling forward, breathing heavy from the exertion. Frank could feel her hands reaching between his legs. More than anything he wanted to get on top of her, lay her down on a spit of sand, fuck her for good. Scooting forward again, he dug his elbows into the mud and kept rowing with his hands. She kept laughing. His swimming trunks were now slung tight around his legs, and Leila kept plastering blobs of mud on his ass and in between his legs.

Eventually she grabbed his legs and half-lifting, half-pulling on his swimming trunks, she dragged him out of the mud hole. He immediately turned and pulled her down into the mud beside him and held her. As she tried to wiggle off, he straddled her back. He scooped mud onto her butt, her back, and her calf and ladled blobs of muck onto her with a slapping sound. Leila slid forward but he snared her legs. She squirmed sidewise; Frank wrapped both arms around her legs and pulled her back and then he reached under her and pulled a solid wave of mud under her breasts, under her stomach, in between her legs. She curled sidewise to move her face away from the mud, panting; he pushed a mound of wet mud against her belly, down to the bikini bottom she somehow still managed to wear, packing it all in.

"Enough!" Leila gasped. "Enough." He grabbed her from behind and pulled her up to her knees, but she wiggled and threw herself forward and now, scooting away on her knees, gained some distance. Though he crawled on all fours after her, he kept sinking in too deep and couldn't reach her. Kicking off his trunks, Frank was still far behind her when they started running on sandy ground. Naked, he dashed after her, flinging mud right and left, but she kept ahead of him until she dove into the waterhole close to the campsite. Her muddied body sliced through the sky's reflections, dappling the water with a pale yellow and leaving behind billows of muddy water that looked like pea soup.

"Peace!" she said. Still panting from the run, Frank plunged into the swimming hole. Leila shook his hand. Then with a quick giggle, she shoved him into the water and ran out on the beach toward the campsite. After he had washed off the mud, Frank headed after her to start the fire.

This is what he looked forward to: watching the curling flames and yielding to the feeling of closeness inside the circle of fire. He nursed the first flames while watching the sun spin into the horizon without drama. Darkness followed swiftly. From somewhere between the piles of duffel bags he heard Leila call that she would join him. In Maine, the setting sun brought a tart bite to the air that instilled a sense of wistfulness. But on Clipperton, the air was mellow. Its gentle caress eased them into the night, and the fire's warmth drew a pleasant prickle before the nip of cooler breezes could sting their salty skin

His thoughts were still going wild from the chase in the mud fields. It had been a long time since Frank had seen Leila so playful, but he'd never seen her as ferocious, nor heard her speak so frankly. Burdened by her sister's death, her actions had appeared hobbled, her demeanor depressed, so that even her enthusiasm for the Clipperton trip seemed to be a form of escape. And now this! Memories of that fateful night in the Long Island Sound tried to creep in, but Frank refused to let them pale the present.

It was almost dark when Leila sat down beside him, tucked her feet under, then unwrapped two sandwiches. She laid them on a cloth beside her. "What are you thinking?" she asked.

"Muddled mud stuff."

"I bet you are."

They both burst into laughter.

Frank stabbed more fire out of a smoldering log. Then he leaned back on his elbows and began lifting the hair on her nape very gently.

"Feels good," she said.

"It was supposed to be *our* trip," he whispered.

She sat up straight and slid her hands on top of her knees; Frank could not miss a hint of exasperation.

"Let me get this straight! Jim and I — we've always been like pool balls — we keep bouncing off each other exchanging energies."

"Stop playing pool!" Frank blurted out. A doltish remark, but it was too late to take it back.

"So I make room for your game, is that it?"

As Leila turned halfway toward him, she scooted closer to the fire, where stacks of coconut branches gave off a dull-brown glow and laid back, propping herself up on her elbows. Frank

149

did not answer, reckoning that his response had dismayed her and silence was the better choice now.

He kept poking the fire, and made more sparks shoot off the fronds. Then, slowly, he bent down and caressed her breasts. Leila was staring into the fire trying to balance her glass of wine on her stomach. In the process, she poured it across her chest. She giggled and stroked Frank's forehead. He started kissing her nipples, flipping them gently with his tongue—circling, sucking, circling, raising them hard. Frank heard her breath quicken then thicken into groans. The wine glass forgotten, she dropped her arms to the side and tilted into the sand.

He kept moving his hand across her endlessly flat stomach, which stretched down to the bikini slip so tiny it revealed the roughness of her shaved pubes—a slip so tight that, in the flickering fire, Frank could see her labia bulge the cloth into small mounds. With one hand, he began kneading her crotch, sliding the other beneath the tiny triangle that covered her ass, slowly pulling it down. Suddenly Leila tensed up and jackknifed into a seated position.

"Damn crab!" She jerked her legs away.

"What?"

"Right there!" She shook off a crab. Frank rolled on his back and bolted up. Several crabs were scurrying across the sand only a few feet away. Then Frank spotted hundreds of crabs dug into the sand toward the bay. They seemed to form an arc around the fire. In the hostile flicker of their eyes and the whipping gyration of their feelers, Frank saw a phalanx of cunning war machines. He threw a couple of burning twigs at them. Lit by the rush of air, the twigs sailed in a bright trajectory, shooting off sparks as they hit the sand. The crabs didn't budge.

"I'm sorry," Leila said. "It bit my leg and scared me." She was standing now.

"Where the hell did they come from?"

"They crawl out of their holes at night."

Frank was sure Leila had spotted the line of crabs, but had decided to make light of it, dropping only a few remarks about not leaving food outside. "They could have gone for the sandwich, not your legs."

Suddenly he felt awkward being naked and pulled on his khaki pants: Adam running for a fig leaf. Paradise closed. Perhaps this was to be the night of the crabs.

"What are they up to?" Frank asked.

"Upon awakening, Gulliver found he was held to the ground by hundreds of crabs."

"I'm so grateful you're well read."

"Don't blow it out of proportion! They'll hunker down and that's it."

"Can we eat now?"

"Keep food in your hand!" Leila ordered.

While eating the sandwich Frank kept his eyes on the perimeter, looking for any stir in the phalanx of crabs. For now it seemed that Leila was right, as none of them seemed to sally forth. Frank poured more wine, hoping to loosen things up now that darkness had fallen and the crabs were less visible, but he couldn't help staring at their green eyes. Worse, he found himself embarrassed and angry about his apprehension, which only made him more tense. He wasn't one to take conflicting feelings lightly.

They stumbled into conversations about ecology and the history of Clipperton. While these were topics he liked, he couldn't draw his attention away from the lurking crabs. To his consternation he found himself becoming irritated listening to Leila talk about Alvarez, the murderous lighthouse warden,

When she made the point that all evil on Clipperton "had come, and would come from humans," Frank interrupted. "How about those crabs? They're ready to eat us alive!"

"Trust me, they won't," she said. An impish smile flickered into her face. "You almost had me in that mud." She slowly pulled him toward her and rolled him with her arm slung around his hips in a forceful movement that left nothing unsaid. He put his hands into her slip and fondled her. When he pulled it down, she spread her legs. He found her so wet and soft, entering her felt like sinking into warm silk. He worked into a rhythm, his face rubbing the sand. When he lifted his head, she had her eyes closed and her lips slightly parted, sweet little moans escaping as she panted. He wanted to fuck her to eternity.

Then Leila leaned forward and started thrusting into his groin. "I'll let you have it," she said, rocking herself into him. "I'll let you have it!" And all wires were sprung. Frank came violently thrusting till there was nothing left. He collapsed beside her, his heaving settling against her fading quivers and shakes.

With Frank's arm cradling Leila's head, they found a private space to drift into satiated indifference, yielding to a delicious ground of neutrality. Slowly the world would filter back. First, it was the pleasant warmth of the fire, then thoughts floating in but not yet penetrating. At one point, Frank tried to say something, but Leila just smiled, holding one finger across her mouth.

When did it end? When Frank looked for the crabs? When he stood up and laid more fronds across the fire? Or was it when Leila rose and poured wine, and the ring of glasses touching was lost in the steady rumble of the waves rolling onto the shore. They kept looking into each other's eyes, searching for reassurance, trying to push away thoughts of Jim who, by now, had probably finished welding the trawler's anchor chain and would arrive in the morning.

Eventually Leila walked off to the tent she had put up between two dunes nearby. After Frank helped her to get settled he kissed her good night and returned to the fire. It still threw off a few sparks, and small pockets of water in the wood exploded with a cracking sound. He should feel exalted, he thought, but a wedge of fear had worked itself into his heart. Why was he letting Jim intrude on this moment? He conjured up the house he had drawn in the sky to Leila's frank delight, their abandon in the mudflats, the image of Leila's lithe body in the tide pool, making love. Already the sexual act seemed to have crystallized into images of her impish smile, the jolt of her rocking into his groin, her taunting, "I'll let you have it!" Her words still sent a tingle into his groin. But in a dark moment, it seemed to him as if he'd spliced together a film of events to be remembered, but never to be repeated.

Frank walked away to a distance where the flicker of the flames washed into the dark, then looked back over his shoulder to what he knew was the only fire for hundreds of miles—a thought that swirled his senses. Then he looked across to the Egg Islands that were floating in black waters, slabs of rocks studded with hundreds of boobies folding their wings in white sleep. He should be sitting back at the fire suspended in some post-coital bliss.

Wasn't what happened the fulfillment of deeply buried desires? Instead he found himself recalling the waters of the Long Island Sound on that fateful night, drawn to it by the recall of dreams he had been fighting to forget but could not shake, dreams in which he'd see his wife's arm reaching from the water, her fingers floating like white flower petals. On awakening, he struggled to return to reality.

Of course he had not talked about it. Yes, he had given hints and received consolations of some kind from friends and colleagues. But a sense of deceit clung to their gestures. They spared him the truth, Frank told himself; he was labeled as the grieving partner who needed to go on with his middling life. But what would they think once it was known that he was sleeping with his late wife's sister, that what emerged from the cover of his guilt was not atonement and redemption, but pretense and lust?

When he returned to the fire, Frank noted the green flashes of a few crabs dug into the sand, their eyes reflecting the fire's remaining flicker. First the crabs did not move, except that their eyes kept sliding out on square cantilevers, and then some of the crabs retreated in bouts of hasty crawls followed by stop-and-go advances. In the low light he could not see the reddish color of their exoskeletons, but it was easy to discern their armored plates, how they were angled into each other to encase the beast and make it impenetrable. They reminded Frank of the WWII tanks his father had told him about.

After having laid down more fronds and having stoked the flames, Frank remembered a winter day the year the greenhouse in Munich had been shattered. His father, with a voice, raspy, drunk and choked by distant emotions, was telling him about the battle of Kursk.

Oddly, Frank still remembered details: July 1943, the German-Russian fronts near the village of Prokhorovka, south of Kursk. Seven hundred Hausser's SS Panzer Corps tanks rolling through a grassy steppe toward the thatched roofs that marked the village border. A phalanx of might as had never been assembled in history. His father had been a Luftwaffe ground support officer, riding in one of the leading tiger tanks to scan the horizon for Russian planes. The top hatch was wide open. There was a constant rattle and hum; left and right, as far as he could see, silent grasses were crushed beneath the tracks of the heaviest armor in the world.

He spotted what first looked like little square hats strewn in between the folds of the steppe. An illusion. Hundreds of Russian T-34s were rolling toward them. The Tiger tank stopped. Somebody pulled him down inside the turret and closed the hatch. A sharp crack and shudder as the gun fired, the exhaust fans whining at high speed. A burst of heat and the acrid smell of sulfa. Then a sudden tilt, like a ship keeling over. Somebody yelling, "Raus!"

Lying in the grass beside the tank, clawing the soil for cover, he found himself alone. He was near deaf from the crack of gunfire. Black smoke was spewing from between the Tiger's tracks. Grasses burning. Shrapnel kept slashing the sod. What frightened him most was the incredible hiss that a smoldering tank gives off before it explodes. He pressed his face against the soil, which was pounded by thousands of iron wheels. Tanks all around him were crawling through the billowing smoke. A white bird ran in circles jerking her head frantically. A plover maybe, a bird known to flap her wings to draw attention away from her fledglings.

Frank was oddly fascinated by his father's stories but kept them to himself. In later years, he did not want to listen anymore, loathed their repetitiveness. But even then he knew they would stay with him for life.

His first years in high school in the States had been hurtful. His friends never knew how it stung him when they called him Kraut or when they sheepishly inquired if Germans ever had heard of radio or TV. This very taunting taught Frank ways to play lightly on the surface of things to avoid the pain. But the fragments of his father's memory broke through the surface—craggy and cold like ice floes ruptured off the glacier of a burdened past. They raised doubts, demanded corrections, and poisoned him with suspicion.

Lucienne, in one of her angry moments, had once challenged him to name one German father—he could still see her wave her hands—one single one who ever rendered an honest account of his actions and thoughts during the war. His fear that these vivid memories might be soiled by deception was one reason why Frank didn't talk openly about them.

As far back as he could remember, his father had reminisced about WWII—there was always the glee of lost glory in his eyes, and sweat would pearl down his forehead as he strained to hold back his emotions. His stories described great achievements—be it the biggest clash of armor in modern history on the sun-torched fields of Russia, or the flight of a Junkers six-engine plane to within twenty miles of New York City. It always was the glory of war that would fill his father's heart.

The sheen of war's fame had been ardently laid out before him by his father, but as Frank grew older, it would dull. War was boredom interrupted by moments of terror, he learned. And the suspicion began to burden him that the nightly stories about glorious pursuits might have been his father's way to hide the darker truths, the abject deeds of war committed in remote villages, the slaughter of civilians, Jews and gypsies. Deeds not carried out by heroic steel on dry steppes, but in the swamps of Poland, the birch copses of the Ukraine, the sloping seams of small villages. These were the doubts he held close to his heart.

What could he possibly find on this island? Why couldn't he just let it go? Frank's mind kept branching into the threads of his memory until a sense of absurdity overcame him. He covered his ears to drown out the incessant rumble of breaking waves. He felt jailed by the wall of ocean around him and the dread of being condemned onto this island, to live without the comfort of gentle hills or the delight of fractured light, or the joyful recluse of silence. It was as if a cold hand had reached for his heart.

12

LEILA HELD ON TO the languidness lovers feel after making love. And she might have drifted into sleep had it not been for the incessant pounding of waves, which vexed her mind and made her feel as if the sand beneath her was giving way, sliding into the volcanic crater at the island's center. After having spent several nights in a shifting berth, Leila hoped that lying down on solid ground would lull her to sleep, but sleep did not come, and she found herself sitting upright inside the tent.

As the minutes passed, thoughts of Lucienne occupied her mind. Had she betrayed Lucienne? Should she have resisted the temptation to sleep with Frank? She closed her eyes against the weight of childhood memories: the narrow alleys of Montpellier; the oppressive apartment, its windows hung with laundry.

Montpellier in August. Ribbons of heat radiating off the streets. Lucienne and Leila reclining on the living room couch. They were alone. A scatter of bread crumbs on the table. Mother would come home for lunch in those days.

Lucienne got up from the couch, took Leila's hand and led her to the bedroom. She opened a drawer, sliding her fingers with the mastery of a thief among the trinkets that had to be put back in the exact same way: the communion candles, mother's folded wedding veil, mother's first prayer book of black leather with golden cuts and the obligatory red marker band. Finally she worked her fingers into the cracked board and lifted out the envelope with the picture of their father, opened it, and laid it on top of the chest. The slit mouth, *le sourire.*

Leila understood, understood it in a cold way. A whiteness spread across her face like wax, and she ran out of the bedroom and threw herself back on the couch where she kept hitting her face with half open fists. Lucienne walked over, triumphant. Stung by anger, Leila dashed at her sister, pummeled her face, pushed her to the floor and choked her. They fought in silent rage. Lucienne struggled for breath, croaking in such desperation that even decades later remembering that sound would bring back the agony of the fight and shake Leila.

Bathed in sweat, Leila bolted up inside the tent. She unzipped the entrance flap and looked at the fire where Frank was still tending the embers. And as she struggled to tear herself away from the past, she sensed the burden of the present. She yearned to feel the confidence in Frank that came so naturally to Jim. Had Frank been lamed by the shallow life in the suburbs, the life her sister had chosen, a life against which she had always nourished a secret contempt? Leila recalled Lucienne's subtle attempts to put Frank down. Oh, he's so gentle in bed, so considerate, she'd say. But always with a hint at boredom. And more than once, she likened Frank to Charles in *Madame Bovary*, the pedestrian physician who married Emma Bovary to complement his unwitting, dull nature. Leila found her sister's opinion demeaning, but at its core lurked a deadly accuracy that troubled her. Frank made love to her all right, but Jim had a way of pinning her down and making her come until she stammered.

She left the tent and walked to the fire. "I can't get used to the waves pounding," she said.

Frank looked up. "I'm still watching those crabs. They make me feel creepy."

Jim would simply have taken her and fucked her again. But why did she have to think about him now? She hated the lack of real emotion in Jim, but did she really want Frank? Dealing with the two of them on this remote island stirred up a deep conflict inside her, and, with no other distraction, she feared that Clipperton might deprave them of all kindness and compassion.

Leila felt her voice quivering. "I don't see the crabs. They

158

must have left."

"I stared them down." He reached for the wine bottle.

"Thanks. Enough booze for me." She sat down, pulled up her knees and set her chin on her outstretched thumbs.

"Did you have trouble falling asleep?" Frank asked.

"I kept thinking back to the times in Montpellier."

Frank remained quiet. He stared into the fire, unmoving, except once when he shuffled his foot the way animals move when dreaming.

"Jim will soon be here," he finally said.

"He might need another day for repairs."

"I sure hope his mood will be better."

"We can always send him back."

"Yeah! Right." Frank turned and reached into his duffel bag to hand her Jim's small box. "He pulled this from his swim vest."

She set the box down without opening it. Frank pretended to look away and tossed more wood into the fire. The burning embers gave off a dull sepia light, their surface riffled like velvet.

"He handed it to you? To give to me?"

"Weird? Isn't it?"

"I really don't want to open this box."

"That's Jim. Unpredictable!" Frank shrugged his shoulders.

He kept looking into the fire, reaching for indifference, but his anger about Jim's presence kept intruding.

What are we doing? Should she be in Jim's arms? No! It was I who loved her all these years. She's nothing but a toy to Jim. What keeps stopping me from going after her and telling Jim to fuck himself? What's stopping me from making love to her now?

He balanced a smoldering stick atop a mound of sand, and, as if this were a game of childhood roulette, he spun it. Struck by his indecision, one thought burned through him: I have a clipped and wingless life.

He abruptly stood up. Leila reached up to gently pull him down, but Frank resisted and started circling the fire.

"Jim never should have come on this trip," he said.

His words stung her. She should say something, she thought.

But Frank did not pause. "For Jim the world must always seem to be on standby, always available, always laid out and waiting. I have no fucking idea what gives him his feeling of entitlement. I sure don't have it. I come from a fallen nation, fallen dreams...a fallen father...years when everything vanished into oblivion, and what remained was pale."

"Calm down. Come sit beside me," Leila said. But Frank kept circling the fire in silence, occasionally kicking a stick into the embers.

"Lucienne was no great help," she said, and the way he nodded encouraged her to continue.

"I always suspected she wanted to sit pretty in the suburbs and play the social game with people who stuffed their driveways with BMWs. And you had to tag along while she made the party rounds with her colleagues, to hold the wine glass with tipped fingers and make clever remarks about the art scene, graciously dropping names, Ah! The architect who made lots of money. Except that it didn't work out that way. And not because you didn't try, Frank, but because you never had your heart in it. 'Why can't Frank and I afford a house?' she asked me. 'Why does Frank need to fly?' Why? Why? Why? She had you all caged in. You couldn't do right by her."

There it was.

"Lucienne wanted you to melt right in with her suburban shrubs, placid and demure and thrifty, and on the other hand she demanded that you be brilliant and clever and conniving and charming. Hell! She snared you!" Leila started shaking her head. "I'm sorry to be so blunt."

Frank seemed stunned. As if suddenly beaten down, he remained silent.

She wanted Frank to answer. Why didn't he join in and roil

with accusations and resentments? Couldn't he just execute a clean sweep through the past? Instead, he sat there numb and impotent. And they had so few hours until Jim arrived.

"Put the last fronds into the fire," she commanded.

"Why?"

"Throw in all you've got!"

Mechanically Frank obeyed her. As he was fanning the fire, she slid into the bay water. He followed her and swam with slow, measured strokes, lifting beaded strings of water that parted and threaded along his arms. The water was warm and soothing. The sea always relented; its lack of resistance pleased him. Even after the desperate hours in the Long Island Sound, it had never withdrawn its forgiveness.

Leila was swimming at his side. Frank rolled on his back and eased into languorous backstrokes. The whole sky was in his face now. He looked for the Big Dipper, soon realizing he was near the equator and would not see it. Even the sky changed, but never the sea!

Ever since he could remember, he had loved water. Loved to immerse himself and feel its soothing coolness. During his childhood in Munich, he passed many an afternoon at the river Isar, wedging himself against the face of boulders to resist its cold currents. Then he would lie on hot river pebbles and let the heat of the afternoon breathe into his skin. And there were days spent at Lake Chiemsee, south of Munich. When his parents quarreled, he would walk away and slide deep into the lake, and the water would erase his troubles. It was not different now. Cradled by water, the night sky in his face, Frank felt the gentle indifference of the world alongside an overwhelming sense of love. Maybe the deepest secret was that they would go together.

He wanted stillness now, reaching back with his arms so slowly he barely stayed afloat. And in this stillness he could sense the vibrations of Leila's strokes, the patter of her hands.

Frank reached over and held Leila's hand, and they started to tread water together.

The stoked fire kept washing flickers of light across the water, and Frank marveled that it was the only campfire for at least six hundred miles, but it took one light only to overcome the darkness of the world. Leila moved close to him, brushing him with her breast. He touched her while treading water, at times tilting and going under, which made her giggle. She took his hand and swam backward as if to tow him behind her toward the campfire. They made love again, gently; they made love for a long time.

Afterward she lay down at his side, cradling her head in his arms. "I want to fall asleep right here with you," she said.

For that night, Frank knew that Leila felt secure in his arms, that this was possible. And he imagined carving out a lit shelter for her, keeping evil at bay.

13

STILL INSIDE HIS SLEEPIING BAG, Frank spotted Leila
a half-mile to the north. Several boobies stood near her staring
across the bay. Their plumes were tossed across their ice-pick
eyes by the ocean breeze, but the birds did not move. Only when
Leila walked right at them did they waddle away on webbed
feet. Frank hurried to start the coffee and set up a few chairs.

Leila said, "Good morning" and put down an armful of
sages and mosses she had collected on her morning walk. "I'd
better start identifying them."

"Those boobies look like clowns."

"They built the island."

"From shit!"

"No illusions here," she said.

She settled into a folding chair. The breeze fluffed her auburn
hair, and a wad of foam blew in from the surf, slid across her
lips, and quivered in the breeze before it splattered into pieces
and broke off. Frank set a coffee mug into the sand beside the
chair, licked the bubbly trace of foam off her lips, then kissed
her. She closed her eyes and allowed his lips to fold into hers
before she gently took his hand and nudged him away.

"This will be difficult," she finally said.

"Just leave him on the trawler." He suddenly realized that it
didn't come out like a joke. "I'm kidding, of course."

"Not entirely!" Then she said, "Something went wrong in
South America."

"How do you know? Did he say something?"

"No. But he's acting really cagey."

"The night before I left your home in San Diego, there was

a call for Jim."

"Who was it?"

"A man speaking in broken English. Kind of tense. Wanted to know where Jim went."

"You didn't tell him."

"No."

"Are you sure?"

"Sure."

She gave it some thought, setting her chin on her outspread fingers. "Somehow Jim has changed," Leila finally said.

"No need to confront him about it."

"I wasn't planning to, Frank! Not this time."

Frank shook his head as if to fling away his own words. "It seems that I'm getting jinxed by this island." He was irritated. "I made a joke and now we have gotten into this."

She looked into his eyes. "But you do tend to let things drift."

Her words stung, but before he could say anything, Leila hugged him and he felt her breath on his ear. "I am sorry. I didn't mean to offend you, Frank." After a while she let go and whispered, "I'm really sorry."

Frank turned back to the coffee pot and poured two more cups. "Sugar. Dried milk?" he asked. Already, words expressing the small conveniences of ordinary life had begun to sound unfamiliar.

A dozen shots rang out, followed by a pencil-thin line of smoke that rose above the ocean. A bright green light gyrated toward the horizon. It was the agreed upon signal that Jim was ready. After a quick breakfast of dry cereal, chocolate bars and apples, Leila helped push the plane into the bay. Just before Frank turned the key in the ignition, she put her face up to the side window. "I wouldn't bite my nails over all that," she said. She cocked her head, but there was an edge to her smile.

Frank touched down beside the trawler. Close to the hull, Frank noticed several dead frigates. With their heads down in the water, they looked like washrags covered with bloody foam, but Jim kept paddling the dinghy right through the middle of them as if he didn't notice the bloated bodies.

"Why did you shoot them?" Frank called through the window.

"Nasty birds!" Jim yelled.

"What did they do?"

"Don't bother. Start loading." His lips tightened.

Frank could not help looking at the floating bodies that now had washed together close to the hull. It was a tangled mess of dead bodies. His stomach felt queasy.

"Are you done with your job?"

"You bet I am. And that's it for you." Oh, was he ever so subtle, Frank thought. But he couldn't think of a retort, and there was too much noise to have any conversation.

During the next hours, Frank kept threading one flight after the other without leaving the cockpit. Jim would row the dinghy to the plane, open the rear door and toss a couple of bags onto the cabin floor. At noon, Frank and Leila took a break and sat down on top of the low dune to eat some of the sandwiches stored in the trawler's refrigerator. Leila fiddled with the short wave radio.

"What's the forecast?"

"They're predicting a tropical depression. I'll leave the lead containers with the isotopes on the trawler until the storm passes," Leila said.

But for now the sun was still pouring down liquid heat. Leila wore a wide-rimmed hat tightly woven khaki pants and a long-sleeved jacket.

Did she see Jim on this floating coliseum stage staring down Frank, two gladiators ready to fight it out for her favor? Even now, sitting on the dune beside Leila and enjoying what was probably the last fresh food, Frank was obsessed with Jim's dark presence.

"Without Jim joining us we could never have used the trawler, and I couldn't have done my science projects," she said, looking at Frank with an anxious expression. Then her expression changed to one of determination. She stood up, set her hands on her hips and said, "However you two are going to get along, you'd better get used to having a woman with you."

"Gentlemen all the way," he said.

"Yeah! Right!"

"Did you open the little box?" Frank asked.

"Later maybe," she said. Leila took off her hat and turned it in front of her slowly. Her face now was in deep shadow.

"What were the gun shots all about?" she asked.

"The light signal?"

"No. I mean the shots before."

"Jim blasted a couple of frigates."

"He's starting early."

He was ready to ask what she was hinting at but held back. It was obvious that they were in over their heads. Jim's presence gave him a nervous jitter. While refueling the plane from the supply he'd flown over from the trawler, he thought of what to tell Jim: *You sleep with her on the eastern part of the island —I'll sleep with her on the western part? Or maybe: Don't touch her! She's never going to be happy with you! You're just a photographer, and I'm going to be the leading architectural writer on the West Coast?*

What crap! Frank knew he'd never speak up anyway. And as it turned out he didn't have much chance to talk to Jim. Both men kept busy. Three to four large bags per flight added up to quite an impressive pile of supplies, which Leila had begun to spread out near the camp.

About mid-afternoon, Jim yelled through the plane's side window that he would load several cans of aviation gas and they could call it a day. When Frank touched down to pick him up, Jim had already pulled the tarp across the trawler's deck and lowered the anchors. After balancing along the gunwale, tightening the heavy canvas one last time, he stood astern, his muscular body pegged into the scantiest of bikini trunks. He held a bottle in his hand. After donning a swim vest, he slipped down the rope ladder, plopped into the dinghy, then paddled to the plane. It was peculiar that Jim, who had been sailing for decades, was such a poor swimmer. Rick had told Frank once that, as a child, Jim had been caught below a weir and nearly had drowned, but Jim would never explain. All he would say was, "All sailors dislike water; good sailors hate it."

Jim pulled the dinghy stops, but the raft barely deflated. The swim vest inhibited Jim from using his arms efficiently. As hard as he tried, getting more angry by the minute, he still couldn't find a way to deflate the raft enough to fit it through the door of the plane's luggage compartment. The constant prop wash made Jim's efforts look like some clown was wrestling with a dozen rubber ducks in a rainstorm—and the ducks were winning.

"Fuck it!" Jim yelled. He cut his efforts and let the half-deflated dinghy be driven off by the prop wash. He swam to the front, threw off the swim vest, and with his arm slung around the wing strut, yelled through the window, "I bet you can't store it either!"

Frank shrugged and dove out of the plane." After reaching the raft in a few strokes, he lay on top of it and, pulling it under water, made his body weight squeeze out the air. Then he shoved it through the cargo door.

Jim glared at him and revved the engine for takeoff. Frank scrambled to climb onto the copilot's seat.

"Stop that! You've never flown this plane," Frank yelled.

"I can fly a lawn chair."

"You're nuts!"

"Yeah?" The plane was moving already.

And the alpha male was determined to show his superiority. Exhibit One: Jim doing figure eights above of the camping site, pointing the right wing tip at Leila's tent as if guided by invisible wires. Leila watched and swayed her head until Jim finally banked so steeply, Leila spun on her heels.

Exhibit Two: Jim flying low over the lagoon touching the water with one float after another in an alternating fashion, banking in the rhythm of some stupid dance.

Frank yelled, "Watch for reefs! Stay in the zone."

"What zone?" Jim yelled.

"The zone without reefs."

Fear was pushing into Frank's stomach like a cold fist. Damn Jim for running this risk!

Leila was angry. "I warned you of the reefs!" she started shouting even before Jim pulled the plane onto the sandy beach. "That was stupid and reckless. You're lucky if you didn't run a leak. It's no business of yours to fly that plane!"

Taken aback, Jim turned to Frank. "Aren't you helping me?"

"You still think it's a joke," she said. "You almost wrecked the plane and now you're acting like you're ready to give each other high fives."

"Don't pull me into that," Frank said.

"You sat beside him, didn't you?"

It made no sense trying to excuse himself. Leila was upset and rightly so, and she would not calm down until Frank and Jim inspected both floats. They pressurized the floats with a hand pump and then checked to see if they held the air. The procedure took time, and they still had to unpack the duffel bags and erect three permanent tents. Though it was evening and a wind had come up, Jim and Frank were sweating profusely as they worked on the tents.

"She'll get over it," Jim remarked as he looked across one of the canvasses. He was working in his tiny swimming trunks, and Frank felt intimidated and envious. He would have given anything for being able to act half as self-assured as Jim did.

"What you did was stupid," Frank said, glancing at Jim.

"Done and over," Jim said. "But I couldn't help noticing how much Leila got done considering that she was so seasick." His voice sounded clipped.

"Are you worried about the tropical depression?" Frank pointed toward the extra long stakes Jim had been pounding into the ground. But Jim did not even acknowledge the diversion.

"She wants us to put our two tents to her right and left, equidistantly, to express it in architectural terms."

"Whatever you say," Frank said.

"Well! One tent will be empty at night," Jim taunted.

Frank flinched.

"Did you want to say something?" Jim asked. He didn't wait for an answer. "Well, that's that," he added, smirking.

"We'll see," Frank said. Driven by anger and frustration, he resumed pounding stakes into the sand. They barely talked after that, mostly relying on hand signals to finish the job. After the tents were pitched, they stored cans of dried fruits, corned beef, beef jerky, powdered milk, bags of cereal and chocolate bars and built up rows of water jugs. They didn't have to worry about Leila's supplies, since she had decided to leave the lead containers with radioactive sulfur hex fluoride and most of the other scientific equipment on the trawler until the bad weather passed. Eventually Leila announced that dinner was ready, and they sat down on the folding director chairs.

"You chose a good place," Jim commented.

"In 1917 this was the site of the Mexican garrison." Leila seemed eager to explain and move on from the earlier tension. "The location makes sense because it's close to firewood," she said, pointing to the dense stand of coconut trees just fifty yards to the southeast.

"You must have studied the island well," Jim remarked.

"I read Jimmy Skagg's book three times."

Jim took his foil-wrapped steak off the small hibachi grill. "Rare! Just the way I like it."

"You like blood dripping down your fingers?"

"So what, Frank?"

Leila looked up. "Do I hear bickering?"

Jim gave Leila a quick look, his eyes suddenly as small as coal pits. Maybe it was Leila's ironic duplicity, keeping everything in equidistant position, which had begun to irritate him.

"Are we having fun yet?" Frank tried to joke. Jim worked a sly smile onto his face, spread his hands, palms up, then frowned and took to his steak.

The sun was setting fast. Its midday white of heated carbon had yellowed, its rim frayed, and it soon would slice into the horizon like a saw blade.

After eating they cleaned the dishes. Then Leila proposed they go for a swim. She followed Jim to his tent where she opened one of the duffels. Frank could see words were being exchanged.

"What's going on?" Frank asked.

Leila tossed a small bundle at Frank. "Wear these! You're the swimmer."

"These are Jim's trunks," Frank said.

Jim glared at Frank. "How could you be so stupid and not bring swim trunks?"

" I was trying to explain, but you wouldn't let me get a word in. Frank lost his in the mudflats," Leila said.

"How could that happen?"

"Very easy," she said, pretending a tipsy voice.

"Hell! Why would you step into mudflats?" Jim looked at Frank

"Exploring," Frank said.

"On the first day?" Jim looked puzzled.

"Put them on! Go swimming!" Leila said to Frank.

Frank looked over at Jim, who just shook his head and strutted off in disgust.

He knew he should say no, but if Jim could shrink-wrap his privates and show off, then so could he. Besides, it was a way to get Jim's goat. Frank put on the tiny trunks, stared down at the wide rim of untanned skin around his middle, then slipped into the bay reaching out with long, measured strokes. He thought of summers at the Juniata River when he would float on his back and feel the fish nibble his toes, his arms trailing low to stem the drift. Frank would slide into a state of infinite forgetfulness, the river providing a reprieve from Jim's browbeating ways. Whatever the reason was for Jim's fear of water—Rick's stories about Jim almost drowning below a weir had not been consistent—Frank was grateful for his water kingdom where

Jim would never reach him.

Frank swam far into the bay after finding a calm, steady rhythm. Eventually he turned back, heading directly into the low sun that spread an oily palette of red and gold across the water. Halfway back, he saw Leila swimming toward him, her strokes lifting silvery tendrils of water into the glare. They swam silently toward the campsite, the water providing a binding rhythm. Eventually, Jim called to them from the shallow waters, and Leila started to wave.

"I'd better get back. I've ticked him off enough," she said. Frank stayed in the water, enjoying the cool rush of freedom along his bare skin.

When Frank eventually made for the beach, Leila and Jim had already seated themselves around the campfire. The flames were shooting high, throwing tongues of light into the water.

Frank sat down beside Leila. She had given up on the wine and was drinking water.

"Ready to discuss our plans for tomorrow?" Jim inquired.

"You barely went into the water," Frank said.

"I stayed close to the beach. No sense swimming across the bay."

"Whatever!" Leila interrupted. "Just that everybody makes sure not to get near the center of the bay where the extinct volcano is located. Every now and then a plume of sulfa bubbles up and you could suffocate."

Jim turned to Frank. "Ever heard of the carbon monoxide plume that came out of Lake Nyasa and killed hundreds?"

"Where?" Frank asked.

"Kenya," Jim said. "I shot lots of pictures there—"

Leila cut him short. "I say we walk to the rock tomorrow morning, and in the afternoon, we make the trip to the Egg Islands."

"That's a lot for one day," Jim said.

"It's not that far to the rock," Leila explained.

"We can always change our minds if it's too much," Frank said.

Jim shrugged and stared into the fire, his lips tight and his arms crossed. Soon their conversations fizzled. When Frank made a remark about how dark the sky was without the distant glare of city lights, nobody said a word. The first day of adventure and we should be excited, Frank thought. He wondered about the bottle that Jim must have lost during his wrestling match with the half-inflated dinghy.

The palm fronds had fueled a short, intense fire, but now it had shriveled down to a few low flames that crawled among the embers.

Suddenly Jim reached over his head. "Something's in my hair!" he yelled.

Leila jumped up and looked into the sky. "Bats!" she said. "They must live inside Clipperton Rock . . . but there aren't insects on the island."

The night breeze was blowing her hair across her face; she shook her arms at her side and scanned the sky.

"That's it! These are fish-eating bats," she yelled.

"Never heard of them," Frank and Jim said simultaneously.

"That's exactly the type of thing I am looking for," Leila said. "Isn't this fascinating?"

After watching the bats flit around the night sky for a few minutes, they called it a day.

Jim and Frank helped Leila place her cot inside her tent. As if to keep an eye on each other, the cousins decided not to sleep in their tents but to spread out their sleeping bags close to the fire where the sand was soft and dry.

"I see an army of crabs out there," Jim said, preparing to stretch inside his sleeping bag.

"They just hang around."

"Bullshit."

"They were out last night and merely looked us over. They're harmless," Frank insisted.

"I have trouble believing you."

The great explorer has finally shown his nerves, Frank thought. Maybe we are not that different after all. As he was drifting into sleep, Frank tried to conjure up the sense of freedom from his swim. But long after the crabs had retreated into the night, he kept dreaming of columns of plated soldiers piercing his sleeping bag, thousands of claws pinning him down.

14

THE FIRST SIGN OF MORNING was a gray bulge in the horizon. The water Frank splashed into the fire the night before carved black gullies into the embers. A red plastic bag was lying on the sand, looking like a gigantic blister. Soon there will be garbage, Frank thought. He was still in his sleeping bag unwilling to move. His back was aching.

Once everybody was awake, Frank lit the fuel stove, but the instant-coffee granules barely dissolved and left clumps that leached a dirty brown. Jim was watching, his hands cocked on his bare hipbones, a line of contempt between his eyes. "The water isn't hot enough."

Frank turned the stove upside down, blew into the slits and tried to relight it without much success. He overheard Jim tell Leila that the frigates had harried him back at the trawler. "From now on I'll have the shotgun with me at all times," he said.

Frank thought back to his horror at the sight of the crucified albatross and the bloated bodies of the dead frigates floating in the water. Frank wondered what else Jim was capable of.

"I can't believe the frigates attacked you," Leila said.

"It was like a Hitchcock movie." Jim glanced over at his cousin and winked.

What a lying asshole, Frank thought. He eventually blew the dirt out of the stove's head, and they had some coffee with the rest of the sandwiches. Not quite the usual breakfast fare, but Leila insisted that they not waste time preparing food.

They put on cut-off jeans and shirts and then organized their equipment. Leila and Frank each took a knapsack; Jim coiled a climbing rope around his chest and carried the shotgun. They walked on the beach for about a hundred yards until they ran into tree stumps and shifting sand and decided to walk through the stand of coconut trees and the underbrush south east of the camping lot.

What they encountered was a dense tangle of fallen trees, knotted ground vines and matted leaves. Because it was difficult to spot the quicksand, they were repeatedly sucked down to their knees, which made for slow going.

After another hundred yards, the grove began to look like an army junkyard. Sheets of corrugated metal lay in the sand, coiled grotesquely like apple peels dropped off a paring knife. There were remnants of jerry-built huts that seemed to have been crumpled by a giant fist and then smashed into the ground. Burst gasoline drums were filled with rusty, brown water. Scraps of wood with nails rusted brittle stuck out from the filth where the vines did not cover them.

At some point they smelled gasoline. As they started to search for where it originated from, Jim's foot got trapped between the coils of a refrigerator, probably a the remnant of the abandoned WWII American weather station; they had to bend away the metal fins to release his foot. Leila kicked a box full of discarded ammunition. Though they had learned enough about Clipperton to know that the U.S. Navy had temporarily occupied the island during WWII, they didn't expect to find a garbage dump!

Eventually the coconut trees thinned out and the land opened to a puny stretch of beach where they could finally walk on firm sand. Here the slope was riffled and the narrow ledges made them feel like they were running on bleachers. They made good progress until it was Frank's turn to step on some piece of metal. Digging around, they detected it was the wheel of a toppled lorry. The Mexicans had probably used it to load phosphates onto barges for transport across the bay.

"I'll read up on it," Leila said. She bent down for a closer look. "There are lichens growing on the metal, probably *Xanthoria parietina*." She took a pocket knife and scraped some of the coating into a small plastic bag. "Nature makes use of everything."

From a distance Clipperton Rock appeared as a black wall, part of a medieval remnant flattened, hewn and whittled by the shear of storms, its skin prickly as if every raindrop that had ever splashed on it had plucked a spine from its surface. Coming closer, they saw guano splattered all over it. Every inch was dotted with nests that looked like lumps of disheveled wet hair wedged into crevices and crags, plastered on ledges, suspended from every outcrop of this ruined castle with its hundreds of ridges and crevices and soot-blackened spires.

"On the map it's called Pointe du Pouce and Le Rocher," Leila said.

"Why even name this piece of rock?" Jim asked.

"French habit," Frank said.

"Frank at least appreciates the commercial potential," Leila said mockingly.

"Then why doesn't he prepare a lecture?" Jim asked.

At that very moment, they stirred up a bird colony hidden in a tangle of spiny grasses, and a flurry of activity drowned out Jim's quip. Within seconds dozens of boobies and noddies flopped into the air and rained a splatter of white guano onto them while others just waddled in panic across the blowsy clumps of sea grass they used as nests.

A few minutes later, having reached the base of the rock, Jim found dozens more boobies nesting in the eastern face. When he tried to climb into it, the boobies snapped at him from everywhere. They did not even yield when Jim emptied several cartridges into the face of the rock. With all the boobies fluttering about, his khaki jacket became covered with bird shit in no time. Eventually he had to give up, for cosmetic reasons, he claimed. They returned to the western face of the rock where, fifty years ago, a set of stairs had led up to the lighthouse. Now the only remains consisted of a few crumbled cement steps. Jim fired several shots but found there were only a few birds nesting on this side of Clipperton Rock. One thing was certain: Jim was in his element. With the sure grip of a cat, he climbed up while hammering in pitons and hooking in the carabiners through which he threaded his rope.

"How does he do it?" Leila wondered.

She looked at Frank for a comment, but all he could come up with was a lame comment, "Quite good, quite good."

Leila opened her backpack and, while Jim was hammering crimps into the rock, she busied herself collecting lichens and weeds. Frank felt useless. He started walking the rock's circumference. From close up, the rock appeared to tower high although it was a mere ninety feet tall. What appeared from afar as a brittle but uninterrupted wall now looked more like a fence of individual gothic spires soldered together in some ancient fire. There were holes and crevices all through, making this a perfect roosting place for birds and bats.

As Frank kept rounding the rock, his feeling of being superfluous remained. Fact was Frank felt outdone by Jim.

And, of course, Jim rubbed it in when he came down from his mountain, proudly announcing, "Women and children first." But even with the rope in place, it wasn't easy to reach the top. When Leila and Frank eventually stepped through the empty doorframe leading to the floor of the former lighthouse, they had more than a few cuts and bruises, not to mention a good splattering with bird shit.

There wasn't much of Alvarez's infamous lighthouse left. Most of the walls were rubble now—not higher than any of the stone walls crisscrossing the Maine or Connecticut woods—so that the most conspicuous piece turned out to be a free-standing metal door frame still anchored into piles of stones by brittle patches of cement. And the view was boring—sand, dirty green dunes, the eye-blinding tin glaze of the ocean and the faded olive of trees. Only the colors of the trawler's rusty hull and the airplane's red body brought relief from the drabness. In spots where the crumbled wall reached Frank's chest, he could steady the binoculars enough to observe the narrow stretch of land leading from Clipperton Rock northward toward a line of higher dunes across the bay from their camping site. He figured that this would be the right temporal area of the skull shape on the map. It was also the site where the U.S. Navy had tried to force a landing boat through the reef in late 1944. It got stuck of course—almost everything on Clipperton seemed to get stuck somehow—and, forty-five years later, parts of the bridge were still visible.

"On Clipperton, ships either sink or they don't show up," Leila commented.

"Anything more cheerful?" Frank asked.

"The wreck is great for snorkeling," she said. "I plan to do some work there."

They sat down in the rim of the shadow cast by the low wall and started to eat an early lunch. Leila had spread dried fruits, cheese, bread, apples, a bottle of wine, and a jug of water on a cloth she weighed down against the breeze with one of the many pieces of wall that had crumbled and fallen on the floor.

"Enough wine," Leila said. "We have to keep hydrating."

"Watch the birds."

"This is the lighthouse at the end of the world," Frank said.

"I bet the Mexicans stole the lamp for its copper, or maybe the reflector is hanging in some bar," Jim said.

"I'd like to rappel down the side of the rock and find the bat cave," Leila said. "There must be one: where else could bats live?"

"I'll be glad to help you," Jim said. "We've done that before." Jim laid his hand on Leila's knee. Jim's sense of ownership with her sprang like a cold coil in Frank's heart.

Jim turned to Frank. "I bet we have a better chance finding bats than you do finding any of your Nazi stuff."

"It's not my Nazi stuff," Frank said.

"Your old man must have been pretty high up in the ranks to be sent to an island like this. Huh, Frank?" Jim taunted him.

As hard as he tried to ignore him, Frank was irritated by the way Jim plopped each word. And Jim was not going to let go.

"Maybe he came to build a German colony where they

could line up every morning, raise their hands, stump the crabs with their black boots and leave some *Liebfrauenmilch* for the Japs."

Frank sensed his face flushing; it felt like his heart was being bled white.

"Cut it out! Cut it out!" Leila shook her head in disbelief.

"It is my problem to live with that history," Frank said, " not your fucking problem."

He leaned against the wall and closed his eyes trying to feel the ocean breeze pluck his skin. After making love to Leila, he had hoped to share the soothing calm of the ocean with her. But Jim just had to intrude. What a lousy trip this was turning into! Jim's resentment toward his father for being close to Frank was rearing its ugly head again. And the whole thing with Leila. In the past, Jim could never commit to her, but he couldn't let Frank have her either. And now this little box! All of this was enough to make Frank's bile well up.

While Frank was leaning against the wall, Leila and Jim had walked out to the landing—as if nothing had happened—and stood inside the metal frame whose hinges had eroded into what looked like rusted pods of cauliflower. It was the site of the iron door that led to Alvarez's infamous lighthouse.

"They killed him right here," Frank heard Leila say. She acted agitated, repeatedly stepping through the doorframe onto the crumbling slab of cement where in 1917 Alvarez threw Alicia at the feet of Tirza Randon. Leila set one foot on the first rung of the rickety iron stair they just had climbed. "Tirza and the boy and Ramon had to come up these stairs."

"Watch it! It's ninety feet straight down!" Jim called out.

Leila waved at Frank. "Frank, you play Tirza! And Jim, you play Alvarez!" she called.

Frank was baffled. "You want us to recreate the murder?" he asked.

"Yes." Without blinking an eye, she continued, "I can't understand why Alicia would crawl back into the room where Alvarez kept her prisoner."

"Maybe the sunlight blinded her after being kept in a dark room," Jim said.

"What did they do with Alvarez's body?" Frank asked.

"The body was probably still right here when the sailors from the *Yorktown* reached the lighthouse." Leila was pointing to the floor of the ledge.

Frank and Jim contemplated the scene. Perhaps it was the faint awareness of hidden urges to kill or just the thought of Alvarez's murder, but whatever bit of serenity the shrieking birds and the rumble of the waves allowed them was spoiled now.

"Fine! You don't want to do it," Leila said.

"We both could rappel down the rock," Jim said.

"Better done in the evening," she said. "This afternoon we'll go to the Egg Islands, remember Jim?"

She nudged him in a friendly way, but Jim scowled and closed his eyes as if in pain.

"This is my trip," Leila said.

"But we'll come back here."

"Of course. This is the only sightseeing spot on the island."

"I'll leave one shotgun here on top," Jim said as he proceeded to slide it into the tube-like pouch together with some cartridges and minor equipment. "Why carry that stuff every time?"

"It sounds as if you want to move up here with Leila?" Frank said.

"Highest point for 600 miles. Great view."

"And rent free," Leila added. And this time her smile was open and wide, dissipating the tension.

On the way back to the camp in the heat of noon, Frank stopped several times to look back to the rock. The two men had kept silent, mulling over the irritation that had surfaced between them. Maybe it was out of this sense of vexation and dashed expectations that Leila and Frank got into an argument. It seemed to Frank that something about Clipperton had begun to twist their minds.

The argument started when they had almost reached the

stand of coconut trees and a fairy tern burst into the air right in front of them. The tern kept flapping her wings wildly, diving back into the ground only to lift off a second later.

They could have walked as close as they wanted because the bird was trying to protect her chick's life. It barely had pierced the egg's shell, still looking bare and naked, when it was torn apart by several crabs. One had dug its claws into the chick's back trying to pull it away; another had pierced the chick's eye. The mother kept fluttering her wings thrashing up sand, jerking her neck forward like a coiled spring as she was hammering her beak into the crabs' shells. And for a moment, the crabs would release their pinch and retreat, but more crabs were moving in. The chick died with its beak up in the air—her eyes never even opened to see the sky—and still the mother kept picking at the crabs as they were dragging away chunks of flesh. Eventually she took off and circled the site with a shrieking cry.

"Mother Nature is a bitch," Frank said.

"And who's to judge," Leila asked.

"I abhor this fight for survival."

"Get real. Get over it." Leila said it in such a clipped way that it stung Frank.

"In this situation, disgust is the only feeling I can accept."

"Try to take nature as it is."

"Nothing just *is*. We are doomed to interpret," Frank said.

"You're rehashing the stuff they taught you in Catholic school!" Leila turned and started to walk.

Frank and Jim followed, the sun beating on their backs. She kept her eyes turned toward the ground, here and there picking up a shell or pulling a vine. But that wasn't the end of the argument. Several minutes later Leila stopped and bent down to the ground to examine the underside of a large spider with her magnifying glass.

"There are hundreds of larvae wriggling inside this spider." She handed the magnifying glass to Frank, who could easily see the tangle of wriggling worms. "These are wasp larvae," she began to explain. "The female wasp paralyzes the spider with her venom, pierces the skin and deposits her eggs inside. The eggs then hatch and the larvae use the spider as food."

"Are you saying the spider is being eaten alive?"

Leila nodded.

"Does he feel anything?"

"The venom paralyses only the spider's muscles."

"So he still feels pain!" Frank said.

Leila reached for the knapsack, put her finger into the jug of water and let a drop pearl toward the spider's mouth.

"He's drinking. I can see his mouth going," Frank said. "Why can't you come right out and say that this sucks?" he asked.

Why was Leila challenging him? Suddenly Frank was infuriated. He smashed the spider under his heel and ground it into the soil until the sand reached up to his ankle.

"So what did *you* just do?" Leila glowered at Frank.

"I killed out of disgust," Frank said.

"Here you have it! The Good Samaritan at work." Jim said.

What troubled Frank most was the larvae's use of another organism. And in that icy deception there lay something sinister that preempted all meaning. This was different! The larvae's slowly eating the spider alive had a grinding and relentless quality that was unbearable. And it posed a deeper and more unsettling question: Are we all being used? Was nature driven by trillions of tiny genetic machines with no other purpose but to replicate themselves? Could it be that the magician finally had shown his hands and they were empty? Was it for us to see that man is nothing but a puppet, that there is no meaning? *Nichts, nichts, nichts.*

As they walked, Frank's thoughts kept spinning in feverish circles. He barely heard Leila and Jim talking, not that they were talking much. And whatever they said was clipped and breathless. It wasn't until they were threading their way between the overgrown piles of refuse again that he paid any attention to Jim and Leila's presence.

At one point Frank spotted the rusty springs of a mattress

part-way up a coconut tree, evidently washed up there by some flood. "Memories of the U.S. occupation, I'll bet."

"The Germans would have left something more impressive," Jim said.

"What would that be?" Frank asked, regretting it immediately.

"Skulls."

"We should all shut up for now," Leila cut in.

Back at the camping site, Frank ate a few energy bars and hurried to inflate the rubber raft. He was ready to go when Leila and Jim finished their lunch.

"I'll skip my siesta," Jim said. "The sooner we know there's nothing on these Egg Islands the better."

They threw a shovel and a pick into the raft and paddled the half-mile due north, passing the mud flats on their way and keeping parallel to the bay line. As they came closer, the boobies nesting on the Egg Islands began to hop up and down and eventually flew off to sand spits nearby, where they hunched down and stared at the intruders.

Even the largest of the five islands barely deserved the name. It measured roughly sixty-by-twenty feet and never reached higher than three feet above the water. Apart from some dirty-looking mosses, there was no other vegetation. The island was nothing but a dead phosphate rock heaped with guano. Jim slogged across the island several times—setting one foot in front of the other as if measuring the site.

Leila, after stumbling over sharp rocks, trudged around unenthusiastically and seemed at a loss. But soon she called out, "Something here looks man-made!"

She was pointing to a rectangular slab. They knelt down and stared at what seemed to be a hunk of underwater cement. Jim shrugged his shoulders; he wasn't convinced that this would be anything to go on.

"Probably some piece of a loading dock," he commented.

Frank, however, was convinced that it warranted some investigation. From what he remembered reading in Jimmy

Skaggs' book, there never had been a loading dock at this site. He began diving alongside the slab's edge. Leila started to help and, not to be outdone, Jim decided to give a hand.

They loosened some of the underwater corals and guano using the spade in turns. Frank became excited. His face was red and his eyes were burning. With all the force he could muster, he kept wedging the spade into the rock until he had laid bare what appeared to be the top of a metal box about two feet underwater. It took some work to loosen it and pull it onto dry land. It had turned so brittle that Frank could break off thick flakes of rust. Eventually he broke the box open, at first pulling out nothing but layers and layers of oilcloth. He paused when he touched something more substantial; his next yank revealed several Nazi uniforms, boots and bundled tubes which contained tightly wrapped scrolls. He took the first one and spread it on the bottom of the overturned rubber raft.

Meilerlafette fuer Flugzeugabwehrrakete Enzian, he read. April 1944. *Streng geheim.*

"These are Nazi documents!" Frank said. "Blueprints for rockets with Japanese captions at the margin." Frank felt unhinged. He sat down and gazed at the horizon to regain a measure of time and place, but in the glare of day, the seam of land remained uncertain. Was this what he had been looking for?

"Fine. You found it!" Jim said. "Let's get on with business. I want to take Leila to the bat cave today."

"Give me a few minutes." Frank dove three more times and located more containers, but for now there was no use trying to hack them out of their moorings; the dinghy would be nearly overloaded as it was. After they pulled away, the boobies and frigates settled back on the Egg Islands, circling in low spirals and unloading blobs of bird shit that hit the side of the raft with a sharp ping. Frank tried to dodge the attack but took a full hit on his head.

"Getting white on top already?" Leila quipped.

"They are getting back at Frank for the German occupation,"

Jim remarked.

"Here we go again," Leila said.

Back at the campsite, Leila's mind was already on other things. She barely made a remark about the find. She did not offer to help him open more of the tubes but rather kept busy helping Jim pack ropes and carabiners for their trip to the bat cave. And she didn't ask Frank to come along. So be it! If Leila insisted on handling the situation this way—one day with Jim and one day with him—well, what could he do about it? But he could not get out of his mind that smug expression on Jim's face—as if he were saying to her: "Did you really think anything interesting might come from Frank's efforts?" He began to dread the idea that Jim and Leila might consummate everything tonight: a passionate reentry into each other's life, memories of their exotic adventures, great sex.

Bullshit! The heat was getting to him. In recent, Leila hardly ever accompanied Jim on his trips and had barely seen him four weeks out of a year. And Frank knew she had doubts about Jim's lifestyle and his shady friends. She hadn't even opened Jim's gift box. And what could Jim's greatest achievement be tonight? Climbing the highest elevation in a six-hundred mile radius? All ninety feet of it?

"Will you wait for us to come back?" Leila asked.

"I guess."

"You know how to work the lamps." She smudged a kiss onto his cheek and they left.

"Be careful," he called.

Frank watched them disappear in the copse of coconut trees and felt unsettled and restless yet strangely paralyzed. He didn't open the rest of the bundles that he had pulled from the metal container. Was this pathetic heap of Nazi clothes and papers all there was? For weeks he had been anxious to discover what secrets Clipperton held, but now all his inquisitiveness vanished, and Frank felt ridiculous for his pursuit of what seemed like a hopeless quest.

Since their arrival, Frank had observed that the light on

Clipperton did not change, and except for a few magic minutes at sunrise and sunset, the island appeared uniformly bleached by a relentless sun. But now, looking up at the sky, he noticed the light filtering through a high rack of clouds that had drawn across the sky. Bad weather must be coming. For a while, he circled the tents and dug rain trenches, then sat down, drank wine and ate the last of the fresh sandwiches. Eventually he took the binoculars, walked onto a small dune close to the beach and, very slowly, pointed the glasses in the direction of the rock. He spotted Leila and Jim at the base of Clipperton Rock wading through wavering layers of hot air. It looked like they were walking on water.

The sunset ran crimson folds into the clouds. Frank kept watching them from the small dune, a bottle of wine at his side. He wanted to get drunk so he wouldn't feel the sting of Leila and Jim climbing the rock or think about the Nazi scrolls that had been stuck for decades in the metal box which was lying on the sand waiting to be emptied. So much had gone into the preparations for a find that had come so effortlessly and now appeared banal!

The moon rose as a disk, as pale as tin under water, its reflection in the bay momentarily shredded by a breeze. Frank walked into the water and waited for the coolness to wash-over his arms. He swam away from the beach. The ocean could not be corrupted, they said; you could spread your thoughts over it and they would not return. But even the water couldn't comfort him. The scrolls that seemed so banal just minutes ago now struck him as a reminder of something much more ominous, something that had been pushing up silently against the surface of his life and had finally burst onto this deserted spit of soil like boils that would spill out all the unfulfilled promises and the disruption of his father's life. As a child, he had sensed the secret darkness within his father. His mother once told Frank that the Atlantic would separate him from the darkness of a troubled continent, so he dimmed his memories of a father who surrounded himself with orchids and watched blurred TV movies of SS troops parading in Warsaw, their black boots dragging waves across the screen.

Frank kept swimming with steady strokes, parallel to the beach, which was outlined sharply against the red of the sunset. It was a way of losing himself. He was determined not to turn around until he had reached the site where they had dug up the lorry.

When he returned to the camp, he could no longer avoid the scrolls. In the light of two kerosene lamps, he started to get a closer look. The small bundles turned out to be gift packages intended for the Japanese. Each of them contained *Mein Kampf* in Japanese.

Relying on a smooth ride on the German U-boat, they had dared to stuff various delicate items between the clothes. For the Japanese tea ceremony, the Nazis had included a miniature beer stein from Munich with "Greetings from the Octoberfest" plastered on the outside. Decorative plates with scenes from the *Dresdner Zwinger,* eventually pulverized by Allied bombs, had made the voyage intact. The trinkets—among them all sorts of tea and coffee cups—reminded Frank of the kitsch his mother had thrown into the garbage when she left Germany. He also found two neatly wrapped table covers stitched with scenes from the German Alps:

Shepherd boy ogling girl in Dirndl.

Shepherd boy beside outhouse.

Shepherd boy on top of ladder, which leaned against vine-covered wall, properly bending forward to kiss girl through open window.

Man of the house, approaching ladder on flower-rimmed walkway, swinging stick.

Shepherd sitting behind sheep.

It looked like one of the shepherd boy's arms was missing. Frank imagined it was to absolve the artist from stitching in the arm. Well, the lonely shepherd would have to be satisfied with one stolen kiss.

At least the wine is working, Frank thought to himself. As

he became drunk, he began throwing stuff into the dark space around him.

It sobered him slightly to find a sheathed SS dagger and a 9-mm Luger revolver without ammunition. "Nice touch!" he mumbled.

Eventually Frank walked back to the small dune and sat down to drink more wine. How could anybody stay sober looking at that stuff? Witness the glory of the Third Reich—brittle, moldy and utterly forgettable. And this kitsch spread out on the sand was only a minor achievement of the National Socialist movement. Its greatest achievement was the elevation of shit—dealing with repressed discomforts and the silted dirt we close our eyes to. Such as that in any community somebody had to clean up, to take out the refuse. Somebody! The dirty work had to be done; somebody had to kill unflinchingly. Somebody. So let us levitate the task!

The bespectacled SS Fuehrer had pronounced it in a fine way:

"Most of you must know what it means when 100 corpses lay side-by-side, or 500, or 1,000. To have stuck it out and at the same time—apart from exceptions caused by human weakness—to have remained to be decent fellows, that is what has made us hard. This is a page of glory in our history that has never been written and is never to be written.

"So just hold your noses, men, when the stench of rotten bodies gets on your nerves. After all, you looked into the abyss and stayed decent fellows. Never mind that you forgot to ask why the abyss was there in the first place. And why did you not ask? Because nothing gets a German as excited as staring into an abyss—any abyss for that matter—nothing gets him as quickly in line."

Frank felt sick to his stomach. Too much wine and then this crap, he thought. His watch showed eleven and still no sign of Leila or Jim. Even a swim didn't refresh him. Then he began questioning why he was waiting in the first place—was it to see Leila and Jim's victory dance? Hell, no! He decided to light a campfire. His mind eased once he set aside the SS uniforms and the unopened bundles.

He crawled into his tent. The buzz from the wine and the unexpected no-show of the crabs lulled him into sleep.

15

ONLY A FEW PHOTOGRAPHS of Frank's father existed. In the ones taken at his wedding, the flash had bleached all the facial expressions; two others showed his father framed by orchids and among his coworkers at the BMW plant in Munich. The photograph Frank had found in the trunk on the porch, the one picturing his father in German uniform on a hill, was gashed by spidery cracks, one of which ran between his father's eyes. It was as if he didn't want to be remembered.

After having chanced upon the pictures in the trunk, Frank would sometimes try to reconstruct his father's face from memory. He tried to recapture the coarse, angular lines of his jaw, the wide flare of his nostrils, the fleshy lips that conveyed a sense of heaviness. He would imagine his father's face among the orchids in his green house in the hope that his father's eyes might fill in from some repository of the past. But every time the image slipped into the darkness of night, in which would see his father amidst cheap rattan chairs woven by amputees and watercolors painted by veterans who had lost all four limbs. They painted with their mouths, his father would explain. It was as if everything in that green house had been infiltrated by a war that never ended.

Night reigned over his father's films of Nazi parades, cigarette smoke streaming across the cone of light from the lens of an 8-mm projector that reminded Frank of the nozzle of a gun. The sprocket wheel would slip and make the picture jerk. Frank remembered soldiers parading in what they called the whipping step, *Stechschritt*. Their heads would pivot to look toward the Führer, but you couldn't make out their faces because their steel helmets threw shadows across their eyes. The uniforms showed the insignificance of the individual, blurred their faces, hid their eyes.

Some time during the night, Frank heard noises and stumbled to open the tent. Less than twenty yards away stood his father in his Special Services uniform. Frank jerked back and blinked. As the light of the low fire outlined the uniform, Frank could make out the dark gray vest with the triangular pockets, the black collar with oak leaves embroidered on the slender triangles that stood out from it like wings, and the rectangular double-pleated pockets on the side. That was when Frank remembered his father's eyes. The uniform brought it all back, bulging eyes the color of boiled egg white, eyelids tensed across them like the halves of ice cream scoops.

"Papa!" Frank called out, still dazed by sleep.

There was a burst of choked laughter. The figure pulled back into the dark.

Leila's voice hearkened. "Wake up!" There she stood, outside his tent.

He had been tricked! Of course, Jim was behind the prank! Frank's mind was desperately holding on to the moment before being flooded with embarrassment and anger.

"Hey! Just a joke," Jim said, his arms up in the air. He had shuffled back into the light and begun to undress. He'd taken his boots off; the jacket was still on. His Special Services uniform pants were halfway down wrapped tightly around his knees.

"How could you do this?" Frank asked, caught between rage and shame. He dashed forward and pushed Jim, making him hop backward clumsily as his legs were shackled by the pants. Nothing but a few guttural sounds escaped from Jim's throat.

"Trying to be funny," Frank yelled. He pushed again, harder. Jim tumbled backward into the sand, but before Frank could throw himself onto Jim, Leila stepped in front of Frank and yelled with piercing shrillness, "Stop it! Stop it!"

Somewhere in the dark, Jim rolled off like a wounded animal.

Leila turned away. Frank could hear her talking to Jim with an agitated voice. When she came back, she told Frank that Jim was going to sleep. Frank said nothing; there was a better time than two o'clock in the morning to talk things over.

"It was a tasteless joke," she said. "I apologize."

"I feel humiliated," Frank said.

"I am sorry."

Leila and Frank sat down close to the embers for a while, and Frank tried to stir up the bent fire. Leila kept jabbering about the bats. Any talk was better than to sit in silence and let Frank mull over his father's Nazi past.

"So what are those bats feeding on?" Leila kept on talking. "I know of fish-eating bats in Australia." She went on and on. "Didn't the *Kinkora* come from Australia, and couldn't it be possible that bats were on the *Kinkora* when she stranded on Clipperton some time in the 1880s? Couldn't it be possible that the bats stayed on and adapted to eating fish.... Nobody ever had come across anything like it since they found blood sucking finches on Galapagos and snail-sucking cichlids in Lake Nyasa."

Frank hardly listened.

"Any comment?" she asked.

"I might fly back and announce your find at the Scripps," Frank said.

"Oh, no! I don't want Scripps people tramping all over the island. I prefer to do the scientific leg work myself." She kept shaking her head then stood up with hands on her hips, her shoulders squared. "Let's go swimming!"

She undressed and walked knee-deep into the bay. For a moment her body seemed to merely dent the sheet of water. Then she slid slowly inside a circle of hewn ripples. As she swam, her fingers fluttered across the water like struggling fish. Frank swam beside her.

The thought crossed Frank's mind that if Leila and he had swum out together in Biddeford, away from land and away from Jim, he might have had the courage to tell her he loved her.

"What happened back there?" Leila asked.

Back there. Everything happened back there at Biddeford. And nothing happened back there.

"You seemed confused," she clarified.

"Back at the tent! It was half-dream, half-reality," he said.

"Clipperton has made all of us lose our footing." She paused, then added. "It was in bad taste."

Once back on the beach, Frank looked in the direction of Jim, a lifeless clod of gray asleep in his bag.

"Don't leave," Leila pleaded. It jolted him that she had guessed his thoughts.

16

THEY WOKE UP THE NEXT MORNING at sunrise. The sun splayed behind a rack of low clouds and the bay water, which the day before had had the sheen of waxed pewter, had turned a dull brown. Wind fell on the island, riffled the waters and shook the boobies' wings. They knew that it was to be the last day of good weather for now.

Leila prepared a breakfast of flat cakes fried from papad dough that she had sprinkled with tumeric. "We'd better get used to it," she said. "This is basic food that never spoils." Jim was sitting in a foldable chair watching her; he had been the first one to get up and make coffee.

On his way back from a swim, Frank spotted some of the German kitsch he had thrown out the night before. Those miniature steins lay in the sand along with a pair of lederhosen and the SS uniform Jim had tossed into the sand after playing his masquerade. Frank dreaded going back to camp to deal with Jim.

For Leila's sake he would try to put the incident out of his mind and focus on the scrolls. He had barely studied them yet, and he wasn't looking forward to it. He rather wished for the whole kitsch to be buried back on the Egg Islands.

When Frank sat down by the stove, Jim pulled his chair closer. "Leila told me about the dream house you pulled out of the sky," he said.

"I really would like to build one," Frank replied. He hadn't expected Leila to talk to Jim about that.

"I hope it's not one of those claptrap tree houses like my father built!" There was a twinge of rancor in Jim's voice and

Frank, busy with toweling his hair dry, pretended not to hear. "I hope he finally gave up the idea," Jim continued.

"Actually, no. Your father just finished a tree house." Frank put the towel away.

"Why do you always seem to know more about my father than I do?"

"Can I get you more coffee?" Leila asked.

Jim ignored the offer and continued glancing at Frank, sitting beside him. "I guess this is as good a moment as any to congratulate you for the new job," he said. Then, rather abruptly he slapped his knees together and stood up.

"If you haven't figured it out yet, we are drinking coffee out of these classy German porcelain mugs we found in the sand," Jim said. "Here's yours . . . of course we washed it first."

He handed Frank the cup filled with coffee. There was something old-fashioned about the intricate pattern of painted roses winding around the outside of the cup, the golden rim, the bluish thinness of the porcelain. For a moment Frank drifted into the illusion that he was back home on a Sunday morning—the *New York Times* lying bundled on the porch in its plastic pouch, suburban noises drifting through open windows, a dog barking. He conjured up Lucienne in her rocking chair looking out over her flower beds.

He took a few sips before he spotted the swastika at the bottom of the cup through the thin layer of coffee. He didn't have to look up to see the smug look of superiority on Jim's face. He just couldn't quit! Frank fought a throb of humiliation.

Without looking up, he hastily ate the flat cake then turned to Leila. "We are going to dive, aren't we? This is my day." And he got up.

"Why does it have to be right now?" Jim asked.

"I promised Frank," Leila said. She walked to the pile of duffle bags and began to put together the diving equipment. She returned with a folder containing several aerial photographs of the bay. "It's going to take some time to get the stuff together," she told Frank. "In the meantime you might want to check for reef-free areas in the bay so we can use the plane for transportation."

Frank walked down to the plane, opened the cowling flaps, checked the oil and pulled on the engine hoses. Jim followed him and tried some small talk, asking when his new job would start and where he intended to live, but Frank ignored him. All morning, Frank had been fighting the nagging suspicion that this whole stupid adventure was a big joke. He was grateful that the plane provided him a space to flee to.

Frank crossed the bay several times at low altitude. The wind had temporarily eased, and the water had smoothed. He confirmed that several reef-free channels suggested by the aerial photographs were indeed fit for taxiing. At least that part was working out.

After loading the diving equipment and some food, they discussed dropping Jim off at the rock where he intended to drive in more pitons and install an automatic camera near the bat cave. Jim insisted on holding onto the outside of the plane to spot potential reefs while taxiing. After throwing his knapsack and a coil of rope through the rear door, Jim pushed the Cessna off the beach and jumped onto the float. He gave the thumbs-up sign, and while Frank taxied the plane along the bay's coastline, Jim seemed unfazed by the prop wash. Loaded with the knapsack and his metal camera case, he held onto the struts until Frank pulled the plane near a sandbank close to Clipperton Rock. Jim disembarked and yelled, "See you at lunch."

Frank taxied the plane northwest while Leila used the aerial photos to help Frank steer a safe course. They taxied inside the northeast circumference of the bay, a good mile, and let the plane drift onto the beach closest to the shipwreck. They would only have to walk across a narrow tongue of land to reach the area that Leila judged to be best for diving.

After Frank stopped the engine, they climbed on the wing to get a view of the battered remnants of the U.S. Navy landing craft lying shattered just inside ocean reefs on the other side of the narrow strip of land, but one of the taller dunes prevented them from seeing it. A sudden wind kicked up and plowed across the bay. Leila looked into the western sky; it had completely clouded over. "The next couple of days might be rough," she said.

"Last night and this morning were rough enough," Frank said.

"Sometimes I don't know what gets into Jim." She slid off the wing and began to unload the equipment. "Let's start diving before the weather turns." It was clear that she didn't want to talk.

"Are you sure the landing boat is just across?" Frank asked.

Leila ran up the dune and pointed. "Right there!" she yelled.

They dragged both oxygen tanks and some of the scuba equipment across the dunes and dropped them at the open beach. Frank watched as Leila undressed. She wore her string bikini so low Frank could see where she had shaved her pubes. He stepped behind her and helped her put on a buoyancy vest and harness. After closing the latch, he kept his hands lying flat on her belly.

"Jim came up with that idea with the Nazi uniform. Didn't he?"

"Let's forget about it," she said.

"What's going to happen now? Jim and I are barely talking."

"We'll have to clear the air somehow. There's plenty of time," she said.

Frank lifted the tank into the harness. After Leila donned her mask, she slipped into the water. On the way back to fetch the harpoon and the knapsack, Frank stopped on top of the dune to look at the landing craft. The bridge, which had rusted and fallen to pieces and was now perched so precariously, might tumble at any moment. The sight gave him the creeps, and he was relieved to spot the bubbles of air from Leila's underwater breathing.

He sat down in a sand-blown depression and looked out between blades of oat grass. He spotted Leila's head popping up occasionally as she adjusted her mask. At times she looked up to the dune and waved as if to reassure him. They both loved the ocean and seascapes, as if they were images of deep and beautiful terrains of the soul.

Frank's mind reeled back to his childhood. He remembered standing beside his father atop a dune in Normandy as they were looking out over abandoned Atlantic wall bunkers. He was nine then. His father was probably talking about how the Germans gazed through their bunker slits and saw battleships slide across the horizon and thousands of planes crawl across the sky like insects. Too bad he'd never gotten over the war. Frank thought of how joyless his father appeared trudging across those beaches, as if every grain of sand were an irascible reminder of a lost cause.

Frank half-closed his eyes and stared through the windswept sea oats. This, too, was an observation post, of sorts. Assuming that time can build clots around terrible events, then the trick was to concentrate on positive things. But Frank feared that even if time might heal and forgetfulness might numb, history would always fester through the rind and crust of generations.

Leila was coming out of the water. "I'll have your mouthpiece ready soon!" she called. Frank slid down the dune and stepped behind Leila to help her disconnect the oxygen tank from the mouthpiece. At that moment he happened to glance at the sky.

"A plane!" he cried out, pointing in the direction of Clipperton Rock.

Leila followed the speck on the horizon with her eyes. "I can't hear anything."

Just then its engines restarted, and the seaplane sped in and banked steeply right above Clipperton Rock. "They must have spotted Jim," Leila said. "What's going on?"

Then they heard shots. An explosion. Black puffs lifting off the rock. The plane stopped circling and came full throttle to the north, right toward them.

"Into the water!" Leila yelled. Weighed down as she was, she ran off, her lurching steps leaving deep tracks in the sand.

Frank dashed behind her. "How about me?"

"We share."

"What?"

"The mouthpiece."

"I never did that."

"You will now."

Leila was already knee-deep and dove in. Frank wheeled around, catching a glimpse of the plane banking toward them just before he sank through the surface. Everything turned gray. He looked down and saw Leila's face wash toward him out of dim light; he hadn't taken deep enough breaths and had to struggle to the surface. He caught another glimpse of the seaplane as it was landing behind the dunes. He dove back down toward Leila. She handed him something rubbery—the mouthpiece! He was breathing!

They managed to skim the sandy bottom behind the surf line, taking turns breathing from the mouthpiece. For the moment they were safe, and Leila had time to disconnect the fins from the buoyancy vest and slip them on. She shot him a thumbs-up sign.

Suddenly, strings of air bubbles traced through the water. Bullets! Jets of sand kept spouting from the bottom, left and right. Leila pulled Frank toward the reef into the turbid water and brown vegetation, which swiped slimy leaves across their faces. Then solid rock came into view. Finally, they crouched at the base of the reef and shared the tank, holding on tightly so as not to be pulled away by the surges.

All around them loomed a spongy underworld of dark brown cliffs, lined with strange plants whose leaves stretched to thin tentacles in the surges and then billowed back like puffed cheeks. In the murk Leila's body radiated with the gentle glow of ivory and seemed strangely out of place in this world of fawn and green.

They sat still to conserve oxygen until Leila tapped Frank's shoulder and pointed to the pressure indicator, which had dropped close to the red arc. They took some extra deep breaths from the tank and started to swim alongside the reef. Eventually they ascended with knees bent and legs pumping like pistons, surfacing at the same time. Frank flung his head into the air, panting so heavily it took him some time to spot the landing craft several hundred yards to their right. Clipperton Rock was half a mile to their left. He scanned across the low land to the bay; there was no sign of anybody and the sky was clear.

Leila had surfaced just yards away and pulled the mouthpiece out. "What's going on?"

"I don't have a clue."

"We have to run to the rock," Leila said. She was treading water beside him.

"They must have shot at Jim."

"I heard explosions."

There were a few flags of blue sky in the east, but the western sky had turned ink black. A howling wind drove foamy crests across the lagoon waters.

After Leila dumped the equipment, they ran alongside the water line toward the rock as fast as possible, hunching down to keep a low profile. Still a quarter of a mile away from Clipperton Rock, they saw two planes take off to the west. Seconds later Frank's small Cessna turned toward them.

"Damn! They are using my plane."

"They've seen us!" Leila yelled.

Leila kicked up sand as she ran. It made no difference now if they ran on the open crest of land; at least the ground was firmer there. Birds were flitting left and right as Frank and Leila cut through a colony of boobies. Several times Frank's feet got caught in a tangle of vines and he stumbled, fell and got up. A hundred yards more! Twenty yards! He jerked his head around—the plane was behind him. Suddenly dozens of small tongues of sand lifted off beside him, spewing grit into his eyes. He tumbled but kept running until he finally reached the base of the rock where he threw himself to the ground right beside

Leila.

The plane roared through the sky dropping small objects that looked like blackened cauliflower. Smoke billowing. A rain of fragments, sand, rock and metal. A bloodied booby crashed beside them, its wings still beating the ground.

"They'll kill us!" Leila shrieked.

Frank heard the engines being throttled. It seemed they were setting up for a landing close by. "Run to the steps!"

They dashed around the base of Clipperton Rock. As Frank clutched the first hold, ready to climb into the rock, he turned around and looked toward the bay. The Cessna landed and was now racing toward a sandy stretch near the rock with such speed that the floats were slicing frothy flags out of the whitecaps. They were close enough to shoot.

"Get going, Frank!" Leila urged.

But he stepped away from the rock and pulled Leila. "Go ahead of me!"

She started to make her way up the wet rope—barely noticing that it had begun to rain—flinging her body from one foothold to the next. "I just hope Jim fixed it the whole way," Frank yelled. Jim's improvements to the stairs had seemed superfluous this morning, but now their fate depended on them. Frank struggled to keep up with Leila, who snaked her way up with the limberness of a contortionist. Looking back over his shoulder, he spotted a stocky man beside the plane pointing a rifle. Seconds later, the first bullet hit the rock with the clang of metal wires snapping. Wet dust slapped Frank's face.

With no time to spare, Leila rolled across the landing at the base of the iron ladder. She was out of the line of fire. Frank got shot at several times before he could throw himself onto the landing. He crashed beside Leila with such force that his forehead burst open.

"Thank God, you're safe!" Her voice was shaking.

Frank stayed motionless, his face pressed against the rough slab of cement, incredulous that he had not been hit. When he looked up, he saw that Leila's face was crusted with dust.

Raindrops driven by the wind had whipped white rills into it.

"This was close," Leila stammered.

Now only the ladder was between them and the floor of the former lighthouse. Though the rungs were out of the direct line of fire, they had to crawl up to avoid the bullets that kept ricocheting off the ledge.

Jim sat crouched up against the wall of the lighthouse holding his leg. "They shot me," he stammered.

Leila crawled to the knapsack, took a can of Coke, and handed it to Jim.

"Who are these bastards?" Frank asked.

Jim put the can down. "I never thought they would come after me."

"Don't tell me you know them!"

"No time for that now!" Leila's voice choked with panic.

Frank looked at her. "Do you understand what this is all about?"

"I don't."

A bullet chipped the top of the wall, splattering fragments on the cement floor. Frank turned and cautiously peered over the wall.

"How many are there?" he asked Jim.

"My bet is three!"

There had to be two pilots. Frank could make out the white fuselage of the twin-engine plane at their camping place, where one of them must have taxied it.

"Can you see them?" Leila asked. She handed him the binoculars. As he adjusted the focus, he hoped against all reason that an orderly world would emerge, but instead he saw an island raked by rain and wind. Two men, one stocky, the other lanky and tall, hunkered down behind thin brushwork about two hundred yards to the west. They had set aside their two rifles and were waiting.

What could he do? Luckily, Jim had left his shotgun at the lighthouse. It crossed Frank's mind that Jim might have anticipated the attack. As for the rock, it was impossible to climb it without ropes, and so the attackers would have to come by way of the footholds. Good! But all he had was a shotgun. How could he get within short range of these bastards who could spray him with bullets from hundreds of yards? Frank sat down against the low wall. Leila squatted beside him and closed her eyes, rocking her head into the cradle of her knees.

"We're dead," she whispered.

Frank slung his arms around her, holding her tightly. Long rolls of black cloud carpets raced across the sky, and rain poured in from all sides.

"At least they can't drop the grenades from the air in this weather," Frank said. Leila stopped shaking and looked up at him. The wind had slapped strings of sopped hairs across her brow. The white of her eyes was spidery red.

"If they manage to climb even halfway up the rock, they can toss a grenade up here," she said. With sudden resolve in her voice, she turned to Jim. "They are looking for you."

"Bastards!" Jim said.

"Can we try to negotiate?"

"I'll do anything to get you both off the hook," Jim said.

"What do they want from you? Money?"

"So they *are* looking for you!" Frank cut in.

Jim cringed as he tried to change his position; Leila bent down to help him straighten his leg. "I doubt they want money," he finally said.

"Did some Colombians double-cross you?" Leila asked.

"Bullshit!" Frank refrained from jumping up, realizing that action could be deadly. "Let's hear it. Who are those fucking guys?"

"Mexicans. They're only after me," Jim said. A rind of dry spittle had formed around his lips.

"Drug dealers. I'm not stupid. And goddamn you, you made them angry and then were stupid enough to leave tracks so they could follow you to this shit place." Frank's voice was choked with anger. "I bet they know your San Diego address and rummaged through the house. They must know we have no rifles."

But Jim didn't answer.

"Find out what they are up to, Frank!" Leila hissed. "Don't waste time."

"We'll get to the bottom of this." Frank set the binoculars on top of the wall where it was low. In the mist that had begun to shroud the island, it took time to center the two men in the glasses' narrow field. The good news was that they were still sitting there waiting. But what were they planning? When Frank had finished observing them, he saw Leila examining Jim's flesh wound. "It was a shrapnel from the grenades," she explained. "It looks deep, and there could be bone damage."

"Well, you can't chase these guys across the island," Frank said. "Not in your condition."

"Maybe we could talk to them. Negotiate," Leila said. Jim nodded in approval.

"Oh great, Jim! And in what language? And what can you possibly offer them. Your head on a platter? Would that make those bastards happy?"

"But it's my problem," Jim said.

"Oh fuck it is! For God's sake, they shot at us when we were in the water," Frank was in a rage. "They risk nothing if they kill us all. Sharks don't talk."

"Jim wants to get us out of this," Leila said.

"Shit he does." Frank gave a hoarse laugh. "You don't know the first thing about what Jim did or didn't do, and now you already have a plan to negotiate. That's absurd."

Frank crawled to the side and looked across the top of the wall to find out if anything had changed. One of the two men was trying to anchor the airplane against the stiffening wind, but what worried Frank was seeing him pull a large duffle bag from the cargo door. Leila could be right—they might attack with grenades!

As he was straining his eyes to keep the men in focus, Jim and Leila started to quarrel. He could hear Jim defending himself. "I didn't take money…. I was like a prisoner."

And in between, the cut of Leila's angry voice: "They follow their own code of honor. How could you be so stupid?"

Their conversation surprised and angered him, but something more urgent entered Frank's mind: The day before, he had noted a crevice halfway up in the rock's northern face that he thought might be wide enough to hide in. Frank took cover behind the wall and crawled back inside.

Jim was yelling, "Fuck the Mexicans!" and slapping the wet cement floor.

There was no time to figure it all out. No time for arguing. "We have to do something right now!" he shouted as loud as he could.

"Are they coming?" Leila turned toward Frank, getting up on her knees.

"Stay down! One of them is carrying a bag with grenades. They'll be here in a minute."

"What are we going to do?"

"Listen! I'll take the shotgun to a ledge halfway down the rock and hide there."

"You haven't a chance."

"It's a good cover."

"I don't thin —" she started to say.

"You have a better idea?" His voice was shrill and hoarse. He grabbed her shoulders and shook her. "Someone has to do something now!"

Leila was shaking. She struggled to get hold of herself. "You better wear Jim's hiking shoes," she finally said. Frank took off his sneakers and bent down. His face was so close to Jim's, he could see where the rain had washed dried spittle off his lips, leaving a slimy trail. Jim's face looked ashen.

"I screwed up," Jim stammered.

"Fuck you!" Frank spit on the floor, just missing Jim's face. He stepped back and jerked both shoes off Jim's feet, making him flinch. Holding Jim's ankles gave him a strange sense of power. Maybe it was the feeling of taking over. Or maybe it was that Jim was down and he could get back at him for all the humiliations. Frank caught himself. In an hour they all might be dead—*krepiert*—as his father liked to say.

After he told Leila what he was planning to do, Frank hastily stuffed some cartridges into his swimming trunks, grabbed the rope and rolled over the crest of the wall. Leila had already tied the rope to an iron hook that had been driven into the outside wall about three feet from the crest. The rope was slippery, and Frank spiraled down fast, scraping the rock's face. Luckily this side was angled away from the sight of the two Mexicans, although he had to stay close for cover. Eventually he reached the ledge and pushed himself into a wide crevice, then scooted to the front where the fissure opened toward the path to the top. As intensely as he was staring through the gap, wedging his face into the opening, all he could see were a few footholds.

After a minute he heard a scraping sound. Leila had tied the shotgun to the rope and was lowering it. He scooted backward, reached behind his back, grabbed the barrel then untied the knot and worked the gun alongside his body into the fissure. As he slid his fingers alongside the double barrel, Frank felt a strange and unexpected reassurance.

A dead booby, killed by the Mexicans' grenade attack, had fallen onto a nearby crag. Its sodden feathers were folded so smoothly; they appeared like wet silver until the wind came drilling powerfully into them, exposing the bloody shear of shrapnel. Strangely, the feathers shook in the wind as if the booby had been given back a measure of life. It died an ordinary death. In the final reckoning, all dying was ordinary.

Frank pushed his forehead against the rock and glanced at the sky where clouds were rolled tightly and hung like black snakes. The wind had eased and had changed direction from north to south. There was a sucking hiss in the air as if Clipperton Rock were in the swirl of a baneful eddy. Struggling to fly back to their nesting places, frightened boobies perched on the rock. One of them came too close, and a downdraft speared it on a stony spire in front of Frank's eyes. It shrieked like a slaughtered pig.

Fuck Jim! Frank pounded the rock slab with his fist. It had

to be some drug deal gone wrong! Suddenly, bullets started hitting the rock above, ricocheted with a twang. Frank feared a bullet would fly through the gap and hit his eyes. He couldn't get the image out of his mind—eyes leaking fluid, pieces of brain splattered, life oozing away. It is not death we fear, Frank thought, it is violence and agony. And that was what threatened to paralyze him now. He bit his tongue to keep his teeth from chattering. *Retreat! Retreat!* a voice inside ordered. But he stayed and pushed his face against the fissure, looking out into a senseless landscape of desolate rocks and sheets of rain and waiting for the Mexicans to come.

It was a long wait. First, a face slid around a rock ledge below, then a raised hand tossed something. Frank pulled both triggers. The recoil slammed the shotgun against his belly. Somewhere above there was an explosion. Smoke bit his eyes. A taste of sulfur choked him.

Frank reloaded, pressed his face against the fissure and waited. Nothing was happening.

"You could never have done it." He could still hear his father's voice tell him this over and over. No more! He was tired of being ruled by the voice of a dead man. There were no rules on this freak island. Clipperton was an abnormality, an evil miscreation. What was the chance of getting attacked by hoodlums in the middle of a water desert?

But it was happening. The anger kept him alert, helped him forget the exhaustion creeping into his bones. He kept staring intently at the few rungs that were visible. If his body had been slightly less contorted inside the crevice, he would have fallen asleep. His eyes were tearing from the strain of gazing into the fading light; they felt like two fists burnt into his face. After what seemed like an eternity, Leila shouted with a loud voice and, though it was difficult to make out what she said, he eventually understood that the two men had left and he could leave his hideout.

After Frank pulled himself back up to the top in the piercing rain, Leila explained that he must have shot at least one of the

Mexicans because she'd spotted him limping away. Both men had left for now, but the sheets of rain, as dense as milk glass, prohibited her making out details. She was, however, able to see them taxi the Cessna back to the camping area where the other plane was anchored.

Leila pulled up the rope and the shotgun, and they put the weapon and the remaining cartridges back inside the plastic pouch. Her voice was hoarse and she was shivering as she told Frank that Jim had been drifting in and out of sleep. Though night had fallen, there was still enough light for Frank to see that her face was as pale as chalk. He put his arms around Leila, the warmth of their closeness bringing a momentary reprieve.

After a while, Frank knelt down beside Jim and, with the flashlight, tried to examine the shrapnel wound. There was already a faint fetid smell. Leila had torn off a piece of Jim's shirt and kept it draped over the wound.

"Keeping it moist is the trick." Leila instructed.

Jim stirred. "I'm cold." He was shaking and could barely open his eyes.

"You have a fever," Frank said.

"They're going to kill me," Jim stammered. He tried to say more, but the words were garbled inside his mouth. As suddenly as it had come, Jim's shaking stopped.

Leila pulled Frank aside. "By now they must have rifled through the stuff at our camp."

"Did you get any more information out of Jim?"

"Down in Columbia, Jim got detained by some drug lord to fly wooden airplanes smuggling contraband."

"Don't they have pilots in South America?"

"The drug smugglers had bought several wooden planes that couldn't be picked up by radar. They were Czech models that were difficult to fly. And, true to form, Jim was stupid enough to brag about how experienced a pilot he is."

Frank asked, "Why did he get involved with them?" But Leila just shrugged her shoulders. "For money?"

"When I told him on the phone that we were planning to

come to Clipperton, Jim wanted to get out— "

"To join us!" Frank interjected. "And did he get out of the deal?"

"He thought he could get out of it by dropping the plane off at a remote airstrip in the Amazon."

"He just walked away?"

"I think so."

"And took the drugs?"

"No."

"Money?"

"No."

"There's nothing for Jim to negotiate."

"I fear so," Leila said.

Frank expected to feel angry, but he didn't. The rush of adrenalin had burnt away, leaving a leaden heaviness. All he wanted to do now was lean against the wall and fall asleep, but that would have to wait. They needed to make an inventory of Jim's knapsack.

Leila laid out the contents: two sandwiches, four chocolate bars, one Swiss army knife, a second flashlight, several pens, a notebook, two pairs of sunglasses, gloves, a hat, Jim's 35-mm camera with accessories, a book and several packs of cartridges. In addition, they had the shotgun, ropes, a foldable spade and two small tarpaulins Jim had left the day before. They spread the tarpaulin over Jim's lower body and slid the additional cartridges into the plastic pouch. He barely stirred.

"I just can't do it anymore," Frank said. "I have to sleep."

"They won't try anything during the night. Not in this weather."

Frank proposed that whoever woke up throughout the night should take a turn keeping guard and changing Jim's dressing, then set the alarm button on the watch and leave the watch at the other's side. That was as far as his thoughts would go. Total exhaustion had set in. They both fell asleep at the base of the wall, resting their heads on the coiled ropes. The wind was ferocious, driving raindrops into their skin like ice picks. Frank slept restlessly. When he woke up the first time, it was 12:30. He must have slept through the alarm he had set for midnight. He got up and took the binoculars to screen the horizon. These were powerful glasses designed for night conditions, but as hard as he tried, he couldn't even see the copse of coconut trees. A roiling mass of clouds and driven rain obliterated his view, making observation impossible.

Frank bent down to change Jim's dressing, but Jim tapped his hand. "Leila just changed it," he said. His voice was weak and gravelly.

"How much pain?" Frank asked.

"I can handle it," Jim said, then he added, "Are you listening?"

"Sure."

"I never imagined they would hunt me down," Jim said.

"How could you leave that plane down in South America and walk away?"

"I called them and left them a message."

"Federal agents could have been listening. Did you consider that?" But Jim seemed unfazed. "You were incredibly stupid," Frank added.

"I had to see Leila," Jim said.

Frank did not respond. He already loathed what he knew was to follow.

"I had to leave for South America to realize that I love Leila." Jim's words pounded Frank's mind.

"Well. We'll see." Frank had no idea what to say. How many times had Jim gone to South America over a couple of decades? And now he decides he loves Leila? It didn't matter.

Frank walked away abruptly, crossed to the other side and lay down beside her again. Jim's real engagement gift was passionate, reckless abandon for love's sake! Did he actually think that risking his life in order to be with her would convince her to marry him?

Frank's thoughts kept speeding along and, despite his exhaustion, he couldn't rest. What sleep he was able to drift into was interrupted by rages of jealousy. *We'll see. We'll see.* These words ran through his head like a mantra. Memories of the icy morning at the Juniata River returned; suspended above the river and tangled in the trees together, if either he or Jim had made one false move, the other would have slid off the branches to certain death.

Frank woke at 1:30 a.m. with a fear so crushing he couldn't move. He opened his mouth and sucked in the swirling air, but couldn't get enough. They would all die. Daylight was only hours away, and they hadn't a shred of a plan. But what could they do with a shotgun against planes and rifles and hand grenades? Frank's ideas spun away from reality—maelstroms of melting hopes. He fell back into tattered sleep, woke up, then fell asleep again. It was about three a.m. when it struck him that there might be a chance to marshal help from the outside.

Leila had just changed Jim's dressing. "You're awake?" she asked.

Frank took her hand, and she sat down beside him. "Jim's wound is smelling," she said. "It is getting worse."

"I have antibiotics stashed away in the plane."

"Where?"

"Inside the floats."

"You can't get to the plane. It's impossible," Leila said. She started to shake her head. Frank turned and grabbed her by her shoulders. "Listen! There is a more important reason! The plane has an emergency locator transmitter—an electronic beacon that goes off in a crash—but it can also be triggered by hand. I can sneak up to the plane and switch it on, and the Navy will look for us in no time."

But Leila still didn't want to hear of it. She pulled up her legs and cowered at the base of the wall. The driving rain had swept tattered hair into her face. Even in the gloom of the rain-drenched night, the white of her bare skin shimmered like porcelain.

"I have to," Frank said.

She started to cry. "I don't want you to leave."

Frank said "I love you" and put his arms around her. Overwhelmed with fear, she began to shiver. She wedged her head between her knees to keep herself from shaking, and though the roar of the storm blotted out her crying, Frank could feel her shoulders heaving from her sobs. Frank wanted to relieve her anguish, but in the pitch-dark night, his own despair came close to breaking his resolve, and he started to sob until a new strength driven by fear rose inside his heart. It was to be this fear of not being able to act—of succumbing passively and cowardly to certain death—that eventually made him get on with his plan.

Frank hugged Leila reassuringly; then he stood up and walked to the stairs. As he stepped onto the upper rungs, he held his head up and kept watching Leila until the white of her body disappeared into the soot of the night.

The moment his feet touched the ground at the base of the rock, he felt the island shaking. Froth balls the size of fists kept swiping his face. The wind was raw with salt. He crouched low and moved cautiously. The wide band of sand they had walked on the day before had been pinched into a narrow strip by the surging waters; not even two hundred yards away from Clipperton Rock, the ocean had already broken through the land. Frank tied the pocketknife to his swimming trunks and drifted into the bay.

17

FRANK SWAM CLOSE to the shore keeping the coconut trees between him and the camp. He had used Jim's binoculars before he left the rock to make sure that his Cessna was still anchored near their campsite. As Frank swam toward it, he contemplated the irony of the situation. As carefully as they had tried to plan, there would have been no way to prepare for these bizarre events. The weather bureau had forecast a mild tropical depression and then clear weather for most of the trip, and while Jim's presence had intruded on his fantasy trip with Leila—considering the threat to their lives—this now seemed merely a matter of inconvenience.

This unanticipated storm may have threatened their safety, but they would have found a way to survive it. But to be battling this storm on a two-bit island in the Pacific while hiding from vengeful drug dealers who wanted to kill them because of Jim's irresponsibility was purely insane. Obviously the Mexicans hadn't expected to blunder into this storm. Events had gone wrong for these bastards, too—this rotten island screwed them all! Strangely, the thought made Frank feel more confident, as if the storm and the island helped to even the playing field.

The storm was wreaking havoc to the coconut trees, hurling snapped branches like darts and blowing sheets of corrugated metal into the air where they unfolded like the wings of gigantic birds. When branches hit the water close by, Frank decided to swim away from land, even if it meant being tossed about in the open bay. As he was fighting the storm-driven waves, water jetting up his nostrils, he felt the familiar reassurance of his arms slicing the water.

Soon Frank could make out the tents and three men. Swimming closer, he realized that they had pulled out the tie-downs of the Cessna and were hooking them up to their own plane. But without any tie-downs, the Cessna would be carried into the air — it was already jerking up with each gust, rocking precariously. Time was running out. Frank swam toward the plane as fast as he could, threw himself on top of the float and grabbed the cargo door. As he pulled himself into the cabin, the whole plane began to rock. He fingered the switch for the locator transmitter, but as he clutched the casing, he felt a hollow space. Damn! They had removed the battery!

That moment everything tilted, and Frank flew out through the open cargo door. The plane tossed about in the air above him. He was upside down under the water, twisted by the shear of torrid currents. Suddenly his head popped to the surface. The waves looked like rolls of black slime sliding across the sand. Frank panicked—Clipperton was going under! He started to pant, sucking air into his lungs. The water pulled him down into a fetal position. He choked on brine. His body was stretched and twisted. He was breathing water and drinking air in swirling darkness.

Eventually he was washed into some calmer region where he could tread water. Still terrified that the currents might pull him under again, Frank gulped air and tried to orient himself. What had washed so violently across the island? Maybe the men had drowned? A feeling of hope wedged itself between his exhaustion and the bitterness of dashed expectations. To his right the dark form of Clipperton Rock loomed in the distance, and to his left one of the Egg Islands appeared between the waves; he had been swept into the most northern part of the bay. Land was close, but when his feet finally touched the sandy bottom, all strength drained from him. He crawled ashore and sucked water from rain puddles. Then he hid below a cover of creeping vines where he fell asleep in wind and drenching rain.

The next morning Frank could barely identify anything in the gray seeping light. He looked around but didn't dare stand up for fear of being detected. Unable to make out the whereabouts of the planes, he had no idea what had happened during the night. On one hand, he was hopeless and dejected, unable to see a way out. Yet having escaped death gave him a sense of oneness so complete it made him shiver. He tried to retain this momentary bliss, but as much as he tried, his awareness would coil back to his bodily pains, his burning eyes, the hunger and the wrenching realization that they were marooned.

Suddenly shots fired somewhere near Clipperton Rock startled Frank. Automatic gunfire echoed from the water. The Mexicans had survived! Despair raked Frank, and he slid his hands into the sand and hugged the soil. When everything leaves you, you still have the earth, his father would tell him, but there was no relief. Clipperton gave no solace. This forsaken island was no part of this earth; it was territory beyond.

The Mexicans would murder Jim, they would rape Leila then kill her, and then they would search for him. But as much as he tried to come up with a plan, he could find no way of coming to their rescue. As long as there was light, his only option was to remain in the cover of vines.

Frank tried to ease his hunger by chewing the bark of the stems. After he managed to scrape out a shallow trench to shelter himself against the wind, he collapsed into a fitful sleep. During his waking moments, he would mull over a few possibilities, figuring that he could stay where he was and look for crabs at night and find booby eggs and rain water. He could survive beneath those vines. With some luck the Mexicans might assume he had drowned. Whatever the details, there would probably be some sort of rescue eventually. But one thought unhinged him: If he did nothing, Leila and Jim would die. Selfish betrayal.

He had betrayed Lucienne when he swam away from the floating plane that night in the Long Island Sound. The expression on Lucienne's face before she turned her head away—this last look of despair—could not be extinguished; it seeped into his sleep, his dreams and his heart.

In moments when reality and dreams mingled, he would

find himself back on Clipperton Rock hearing Leila's voice. "Don't go, don't go!"

He had to make it back to the rock.

It was about noon when he first spotted a metal case washed ashore about thirty yards away, apparently loosened from its moorings on the Egg Islands. Crawling low on both elbows, his cheeks scraping the sand, he inched toward it. But from the edge of the vines, he still had several yards across open beach. So he kept hoping that one of the low scud clouds might obscure Clipperton Rock for a moment. When a cloud finally drifted across, he scurried out and dragged the metal case into the vines. He used his knife to pry open the soldered case. After peeling off endless covers of oilcloth, Frank saw a type of rifle he had never seen nor heard of before. Attached to its side were two clips of ammunition and a handbook titled *Deutsches Krummgewehr*, but no explanation was necessary. The barrel bent almost ninety degrees. It was obvious he was holding a gun designed to fire around the corner. Krummgewehr was probably the last flash of German brilliance to help the Japanese with house-to-house fighting. Maybe a whole arsenal had washed ashore, Frank thought, but though he kept looking out all afternoon, he didn't see any further flotsam.

Finally dusk set in and another line of scud clouds drifted in front of Clipperton Rock. Frank said the hell with it and triggered the gun. It worked. Like Woody Allen starting that Volkswagen in a cave. How strange he would think about that movie now. Eventually he wove a basket of vines to make it resemble the small floats of tangled vines that bobbed about in the bay then crawled out from under his cover. Frank imagined that he made quite an unconventional sight. In order to keep the bullets dry he pulled Jim's bikini pants over his head. Stark naked, he slid into the water and waded around the northern corner of Clipperton, keeping his head under the vines and the crooked rifle straight above his head.

But nothing seemed ordinary on Clipperton, the island of fish-eating bats, the loneliest rock in the world, where a German descendant in search of some remnant of a father was now making his stealthy way. For Frank, this was one way to satisfy what his father always had wanted him to be—his German soldier. He could do it. Frank proceeded as a one-man Nazi commando fifty years after World War II, wearing bikini pants on his head, holding the most crooked device German ingenuity had come up with.

The night was lit by a quartering moon that broke through the clouds. Any light was bad, and so it was slow going. Frank's head chafed against the vines, and water splashed into his nostrils. He learned to bob up and down with the sudden surges while keeping the basket above his head. About halfway, after having spent hours in the water, he crawled out and hid behind a low dune. When the moon had set, he wrapped the bikini pants over his head, rearranged the vines and Krummgewehr above his head and slid back into the water. As he came closer to the rock, he slowed down and, when he was sure that he couldn't be seen, he threw himself at its base, clutching the sand as if his life depended on it. The rock's northern face rose like a huge mass of gutted black candles. Cold and untouchable, a sintered hell. They reminded him of the dark candles at the confession booth back in Catholic High; they reminded him of years filled with doubts; they reminded him of his prayer: "Father I do not have the calling. Why do I not feel the fire?"

He dozed off and woke to a slate-colored light. No time to give in to exhaustion. Frank picked up the crooked gun and put on Jim's bikini. Staying close to the base and following the sound of screeching birds, he detected a wide fissure; he wedged himself into it so forcefully that something gave.

Suddenly, he found himself inside a cave. First he didn't dare move, but after his eyes adapted to the faint light sifting through openings in the ceiling, he started to walk alongside the walls. He found a water-filled trough that seemed to have been chiseled into the rock, and then he stumbled onto something wooden on the sandy ground. As Frank started scraping off the dirt, he realized he was digging up the staves of a barrel whose metal bands had rusted away. Evidently, the cave had served as a shelter before; you would not die of thirst here, simply—press your lips against the wall and suck the water that, with all the rain, came down in rivulets and collected in gullies. But how could he survive without food? Luckily, he found crabs in crevices close to the entrance. He smashed them and forced himself to suck out the thready flesh, though all he could stomach was the claw meat. Eventually he might have to swallow all of the slimy flesh, but for now he couldn't face the abominable thought.

The sun rose higher and more light filtered in through the ceiling, which resembled a sieve, maybe fifty feet above his head. What was beyond it only God knew. As Frank looked around, he found a recess in the wall lit by the sun where clay and sand, soaked by a constant drip of guano, had mixed into a fertile soil favoring the growth of algae and ferns. It formed a ledge wide enough for a man to hide behind the plants and rest. Frank laid down his crooked gun and slept from exhaustion.

When Frank awoke, he found the cave still lit by shafts of sunrays that threw a slatted light of ever-changing patterns. Around him grew ferns with deeply split fronds and odd plants with puffed-up blades that looked so primitive, he felt like he was intruding on a prehistoric world. He noted a sandy area where the ferns hadn't taken hold, leaving room for a few pale-pink flowers. He gently lifted one and studied the oval leaves on its stem, holding its head between his fingers where a pink hood reached over a single white, lip-shaped leaf. Something tugged at his heart, and he held still in the half-dark of the cave, drawn back to memories and forgotten enchantments.

These were orchids!

Frank started combing the sand with his fingers. He loosened the soil and found several broken glass flasks. He remembered that back in Munich his father had used similar flasks to grow seedlings on sugar agar. And now the seedlings had grown into orchids. Unbelievable! Loosening the soil further, he found a tin box roughly five inches square that impressed him as well crafted with even soldering lines and folded edges. Then, with a jolt of affliction, he recognized a swastika molded into the lid. Left over by the Nazi landing party, Frank thought. He began to sieve the sand and found tiny balls resembling wax drops and a few seedpods. All this looked oddly familiar.

Frank walked to the center of the cave and held the box in a slant of light.

He rubbed it clean with sand until he could read the monogram in stenciled letters. H.H. Hans Herrmann. This was his father's box! His father's orchids! Now he remembered the waxy clumps of pollen and the pods his father kept in the tin box on a table in his greenhouse, where he spent most of his time tending to his precious orchids.

Frank sat down, stricken by memories of that winter night back in Munich when bricks shattered the ceiling of the greenhouse. It had been a frigid night; snowflakes came spiraling in through the hole, silently settling among thousands of glass crystals scattered on the floor. Frank remembered his father stumbling about in the glass house, grabbing the closest orchid pots and carrying them to the living room, mumbling, "My God, My God!" The orchids had to be carried immediately into the living room and set near the potbelly stove, their only source of heat.

Orchids were his father's life. Frank's mother, however, never shared his love or even tried to understand it. Frank remembered his mother calling an appraiser to establish the value of the orchid collection several days after the incident. Frank's father flew into a rage when he learned about this.

"They'll never take them from me!" he yelled.

"It's your turn at the *Kristallnacht*," she shouted back. The night of the crystals when German mobs attacked Jewish shops and broke their windows.

It always had struck Frank as a strange response, thinking back about it.

That night his father came down to Frank's bed after he had stopped fighting with his wife in the upstairs bedroom. Frank had heard thumps and was frightened. But soon he was listening to his father's gentle steps as he filed his way between the many orchid pots on the floor. The alcohol might have worn off, or maybe he had become concerned that his son might all too well remember the yelling and fighting. He sat down on Frank's bed.

"Remember not to step on the orchids. They are my soul!"

Frank fell asleep that night peacefully and kept dreaming of all the moist muzzles breathing through thick-lipped openings in the dark beside him. All these decades later, he remembered this tin box on a small antique table in the corner of the greenhouse full of orchids.

What if Frank's mother had understood the delicate beauty of his orchids and had not rejected his obsession? Would his father have spent all those nights alone in his greenhouse, drinking and watching reel after reel of Hitler parades?

Eventually, hunger pains pulled Frank back into the present. He crawled into the entrance, but the crabs had disappeared and he could catch two only. This time he would have to stomach whatever he could rip off their skeletons! He watched his hands break the skeleton and rip out the raw flesh, as if these hands were not his.

All pretense was gone. Frank knew he would have to kill. There was a chance he could save Leila and Jim if the rope was still hanging from the hook in the wall, but he would have to climb up at night. And the night was passing quickly.

18

SARGE, THE TALLER ONE of the two Mexicans, stepped out on the landing. When he turned his back, Leila reached for a dead fish, ripped open its guts with her fingernails and smeared the milty innards between her legs as Tirza had done it to repulse Alvarez in 1917. As she was frightened by the replaying of those events, her senses sharpened by two long days of terror, every word in Jimmy Skaggs' book came back to her vividly.

Leila avoided looking at either Sarge or Slink, a stumpy half-breed, who for the last hour had been sitting on top of the wall scanning the island for Frank. Slink would come down to get out of the wind and rain on occasion and walk the floor of the lighthouse—twenty strides from one wall to the other, seventeen or eighteen when he was agitated. Then he would pace furiously, swinging his rifle. On those occasions he would stare at her with dark eyes that looked like leaches, and the fear of being raped overtook Leila so strongly it sucked her heart into her bones.

Sarge came walking back through the tilted frame, and she held her breath. Leila glimpsed at his Mayan features, the bulge of his genitals. His brooding hate permeated his being.

Sarge picked up a dead fish and threw it into her face. It slapped her cheek then fell onto the wet floor. "Pick it up, slut!" The broken English came out with a whistle that shook his slackened cheeks. A nervous twitch crossed his face. He'd been sitting for most of the morning with his back against the wall in drenching rain balancing a switchblade in his palm.

Sarge bent down and stuck his face in front of hers. "You want to smooch?"

A rank odor of putrid slime escaped from somewhere between his teeth. He pushed her head back against the wall, laughed, and then let go; straightening up, he stood swaying his hips with a grin on his face. Leila tucked her head in between her bent knees.

"Cook those fucking fish," he yelled.

Leila started to crawl across the floor of the lighthouse. "I wanna see you wiggle your ass, bitch," Sarge called out with a hoarse laugh.

Leila crouched down and started stuffing shredded coconut fronds into a small hearth made from a pile of loose stones.

Sarge flung another fish at her. "Fucking dead fish all over the place," he yelled. She lit the match he handed her, but its flame died after a short hiss, barely singeing the wet fronds. Sarge kicked Leila's side, throwing her into the wall.

"Take it easy!" The short half-breed with the tar-colored eyes jumped down from the wall and put himself between Sarge and Leila. Then he took the fronds, rubbed them between his hands, shredded them into small pieces and struck another match. Still the quick flame collapsed without even a curl of smoke. Sarge grabbed a fish and smashed it into the stones, splattering its guts. "Fuck! Fuck!" he yelled.

Leila flinched. She ran her hands down her swollen cheeks where this morning he had hit her with a fist as hard as a ball of iron. She still could taste blood in her mouth.

Sarge fingered a cigarette but realized he shouldn't waste one of their few matches. "Try the goddamn cartridge," he yelled.

Slink set two shotgun cartridges on the floor, knifed them open and spilled the powder onto the pile of shredded coconut leaves.

"Excitement for you, honey! Light the powder!" Slink said. He twisted his moustache. "Hold match right into pile, nice and easy." He grinned. Leila lit a match and held it toward the pile of powder and leaves. Though she jerked her hand back immediately, the flame singed her badly, and all she could do was roll her body over the burnt hand to ease the pain.

Sarge kicked her again. "Are you waiting for the Red Cross? We are hungry!"

Using her good hand, Leila started to wrap fish in wet coconut leaves and laid them across the low fire. The men didn't wait long; they grabbed the half-cooked fish and pulled the meat. They kept laughing, spitting mouthfuls of slop.

"The slut is good for something," Sarge said.

Eventually, Slink positioned himself back on top of the wall with the shotgun and binoculars at his side. The rain had eased and the clouds had thinned, hovering like thin, brass-colored scarves in the evening light.

Only two nights before, Sarge and Slink had fought their way up the stairs. Jim's shotgun had been no contest against the Mexicans' rifles and hand grenades. And now they had the shotgun, too. Escape seemed impossible, but Leila couldn't stop thinking of the rope hidden in the face of the rock. After Leila and Frank had pulled the shotgun up to the lighthouse—just before Frank left to retrieve the antibiotics from the plane— Leila dropped the rope down into the face of the rock again; could she use the dark of night to climb over the wall, slide down the rope, then hide in some cave?

"Out on the landing," Sarge ordered Leila. She walked out. "Sit down!" She sat with her back against the edge of the ninety-foot cliff. Sarge wore shriveled blue jeans that clung to his calves. His jacket was torn and some of the pockets had lost their buttons. Looming in front of her, he placed the nozzle of his rifle against Leila's breastbone. "Back!" He advanced the nozzle. "Back, you bitch! Back!" She felt the edge of the landing cut into her buttocks. "I sneeze—you fall." His hoarse laugh escaped through his sneering grin.

"Now you tell truth." He paused then spoke slowly and deliberately. "Where is other man?"

"He left the rock two days ago," she said.

"And now?"

"He drowned."

"You're goddamn lying." Sarge dug the rifle into her breastbone.

Leila tried not to shake for fear of slipping off the edge. Her heart raced as she held on. "He drowned," she gasped.

"You see him drown? Did you?"

"No."

"You want to die? One more time. Why he leave the rock?"

"He wanted to switch the transmitter in the plane on."

"Good. You tell me truth. We see him try . . . Why did you come here?"

"Research. Please." Leila pleaded, "You want Jim, not me or Frank—"

"Shut up! Why did this Frank come?" Sarge pushed the nozzle. "The truth!"

"During World War II, Frank's father was a Nazi. When the war was lost, the Nazis tried to ship gold and secret weapons to the Japanese. In 1944 Frank's father was in a German submarine that landed on Clipperton."

"Where is this German stuff?" The cold metal of the rifle pressed hard against her skin.

"I'll lead you there."

The nerve in Sarge's face twitched again. "Spill it!"

Leila closed her eyes. "I'll lead you there if you want me to. But please let me go. I beg you."

Sarge pulled the nozzle away abruptly. "Go back." He followed her and spat tobacco into Jim's face. He was lying with his back against the wall beside the entrance. Hours earlier, Sarge had beaten Jim, but now he seemed uninterested in him. Sarge talked in Spanish with Slink for a few minutes and then walked back out on the landing.

Leila waited for dark to fall, and when she was sure Sarge was asleep on the landing, she pushed her fears aside and crawled across the floor, shoving scraps of half-cooked fish into her mouth. She knew Slink was watching her. How far could she go?

In the two nights since Frank had left the rock and the Mexicans had shot their way up to the lighthouse, it had become obvious that Sarge was the ruthless leader and Slink, who'd merely been the pilot, was afraid of Sarge's rage and, showing some compassion for Jim and Leila, acted as the appeaser. With both planes destroyed and washed away, Sarge didn't need Slink any more. He might kill them all in one of his rages. Leila understood Spanish well enough to figure that they were talking about when the other Mexicans would arrive: "*Dos dias, tres dias.*"

Leila waited for dusk. There was still no sun, but the cover of clouds had thinned.

"I'm going to redo Jim's dressing," she said in a low voice.

"Try talking to him and you'll lose more teeth," Slink said.

Leila touched Jim's forehead; he had no fever, but she could smell ammonia coming from his leg wound. She took his hand and spat the chewed fish into his palm. He closed his hand as quick as a clam. Thank God, he was alert.

She unwrapped the dressing very slowly, waiting for a swell in the surf. "I faked a story of Nazi gold." This was all she dared to whisper before she returned and cowered opposite the rusted doorframe. Leila cradled her scorched hand into her groin then tucked herself into the corner to find sleep. But she couldn't shake the image of Frank's face sinking behind the iron ladder, his eyes wide open despite the whipping rain. As he disappeared into a wall of rain, his skin looked glazed as if a ray of light had touched his half-naked body.

"Get over here," Slink called. Leila came across and squatted down at the base of the wall beneath him.

"How did you get mixed up with that worthless ass?" he asked. The question jarred her. "There's no Nazi treasure on this piece-of-shit island," he continued with a tongue as heavy as a bell clapper. He's tired and wants to keep himself awake by talking to me, she thought.

"The Germans stole loads of gold coins from the bank of Prague. They are missing to this day," she said.

"You made the story up," he said.

"No," Leila insisted. "It's all true."

"So where's the gold?" he asked.

"I'll show you. Take me there."

"You want to save your ass. That's all."

"I have lost everything already," she said.

"The other guy—your lover, huh?" He continued mumbling. "This Jim—he's finished. Moving to the bottom of the food chain."

Leila started sobbing.

"Shut up! You want Sarge to kill you?"

She pulled her knees up tightly. She yearned for sleep. She would give anything right now to wake up with the horizon of her childhood in her eyes, to look toward Maguelone again as she had done so many times from the mansard window in the Montpellier farmhouse she shared with her mother and Lucienne. To put her face into the wind, sweeping in from the Mediterranean waters where it lifted white cusps from the waves, a wind that tumbled clods of red clay around her garden, ran up the cypress trees like an invisible hand, fluffing tufts of grass into a spray of green.

She dreaded what Sarge might do next. He had beaten Jim brutally, swung the butt of his rifle into Jim's leg and kicked his stomach, screaming, "Bastard, gringo." He might have killed Jim if Slink hadn't suddenly called out, "There's this other guy." And Sarge stomped to the wall. "Where? Damn, I don't see anything."

"Sorry. Sarge. Maybe just birds in those vines." As if on cue, a group of boobies went screeching by.

Leila drifted in and out of a restless sleep. When she woke up, she heard Jim ask for water. "Go ahead!" Slink said. "But keep quiet."

Leila stood up and walked toward a small stone basin filled with rainwater. She had arranged the stones and lined the small reservoir with canvas. After Jim gulped down the several cups of water that Leila had scooped out, she moistened his dressing.

Pus was smeared all over the wound opening.

After a short time, Slink called her away. Now that it was night, he was very cautious, and this was as far as he would let her go.

Every time Leila thought about their circumstances, she found herself running through the same hopeless sequence. She wasn't expected to be back in San Diego for another three weeks. Nobody would look for them, and now that the storm had sunk the trawler and shattered both planes, there was no escape. To make things worse, Sarge was becoming more and more unstable. She dreaded seeing him walk through the doorframe. "Is that piece of shit still alive?" he would ask. He had come close to shooting Jim several times.

Half asleep, Jim slouched against the wall across from Leila, whimpering. The streaks of pus on his leg glistened like resin oozing from a dying tree.

Leila remembered one evening a month after Lucienne's death. They were on the way to the airport in Jim's car, the neon lights of Manhattan washing a purple sheen into Jim's face.

"Do you ever think of death?" she asked him.

"Would that make me a better person?" It was a strange response.

"Why do you say that?"

"Look at Frank," he said. "I know you think I'm shallow compared to him."

"You're not shallow."

"He makes me feel like it," Jim said. "He's wearing *Weltschmertz* on his sleeves. Poor fatherless fellow, forever maimed by his Catholic upbringing. Oh, oh! All that pathetic bullshit."

He caught himself then and jerked away from the festering resentment. That evening, more clearly than ever, she'd seen Jim as troubled and afflicted. Perhaps he was right and she did judge him as shallow. But that evening, she caught a glimpse of a deeper side to Jim, one that he struggled to hide with all his bravado.

Leila tried to stretch out on the stony floor, but it was uneven and cold. She tossed about in half-sleep into the wee hours of the morning. Though she had told Sarge that Frank was dead, she prayed he had survived. But now fear for Frank's life began to weigh heavily on her. Was there a chance that he was still alive? Would he ever build her a house again?

19

WHEN FRANK WOKE UP, the cave was in total darkness. Through the din of screeching birds, he sensed the strange tug of hollow spaces above him. He felt numb. Something fell from the cave's ceiling and hit with a thump. Maybe a dead bird tumbling from the void. Only the clap of cresting waves and the swish of waters jolted his mind with the pang of reality.

The fear returned. A cold terror as shapeless as slime weighed him down until it hardened and held him in a grip of iron. His mind kept racing away to think how this would end. It could all turn out well, he tried to tell himself. But the possibilities had long been closing themselves out. His only hope, for now, seemed to be in a rock, a rope, a crooked rifle, a knife—and fear.

He touched the nozzle of the Krummgewehr and ran his fingers along the steely bend. Then he fondled the sand, poking around to caress the orchids and feel their delicate softness; his mind was going through the bends. Minutes later, stumbling through the dark, he kept talking to himself in a fear-wired voice: *You can do it. Climb onto the rock, edge the nozzle across the wall of the lighthouse and kill the Mexicans! It can be done. There can be an ending!*

But as he squeezed out through the narrow exit, his teeth began to chatter. He imagined how they might stab him, bind his body, snap back his head and torture him.

Frank looked into the sky where a tin-foil moon cast a cold light. A sudden breeze chilled his bare skin. He smelled seaweed. The trick was to think clearly and reach the rope without being detected.

At the first sign of light, Frank prepared to climb to the top. He rubbed dirt on his skin, slung the rifle crosswise over his back and tied the knife to his trunks. Using the footholds, he worked his way up close to the cave from which, two days before, he had fought off the attack. Eventually he left the area that was secured with pitons and crossed over onto the rock's face. Now the rope hung no further away than twenty yards, but the spiny outcrops cut his arms and legs, streaking them with blood. The wind, now blowing to the north, made him shiver; he looked up into the cliff, and it seemed to come toward him like a fall of ice. Cowering on a ledge, he waited for the faint bulge of light in the eastern horizon. He struggled to take the measure of his situation, to pull his nightmare back into a scalable world, but the universe had shrunk to fifty feet of precipitous crags in a mountain of frozen lava with nothing around it for hundreds of miles—on an island alien to anything human. An evil kingdom of murder.

Frank's thoughts wandered, and he remembered waiting for the sun to rise on Easter morning back in his childhood. *Lumen Christi!* The recollection gave him no comfort.

When a sickle of light swelled the horizon, he tied the rifle to the rope and, bracing his feet against the rock, began to pull himself up. Racing against the rising sun, Frank struggled to calm his wheezing breath and bear the torment of his scuffed skin. For a long time, he saw nothing but black rocks, until a sliver of sky moved in against which he could make out the crest of the lighthouse wall. But his advance was slow because he had to rest at every ledge to calm his breathing for fear the Mexicans might hear him panting. His numb hands kept shaking even after he finally reached the single crimp that had been driven into the rock just below the top. Clutching crimp and rope, he steadied himself and probed the crevices and crags in the remaining four feet of rock wall that separated him from the top. Eventually he felt a ledge wide enough to support his knees while holding on to the rope. This would allow him to rest the rifle's bent part on top, then slowly lift his head above the crest. He kept listening for a human voice, but heard nothing. He couldn't wait. Once the Mexicans had started to walk about, anything might happen!

Without untying it from the rope, Frank pulled the rifle over his head. His right hand on the trigger, he lifted and turned the rifle, laying the bent muzzle on top of the wall. He moved his face above the rim, his eyes just inches away from the muzzle. There was a man perched on top of the opposite wall right in the line of the muzzle. Below him, Frank spotted the white of Leila's face. The second Frank turned his head to look for Jim, the man jerked his head. Forced to act, Frank pointed the muzzle and pulled the trigger. Dust and rock fragments stabbed his eyes. The burst deafened his ears and the explosive force jerked the rifle out of his hand, slicing the muzzle open. Frank tumbled backward and spiraled onto the face of the rock. He struggled to keep a grip on the rope, desperately reaching for some hold to stop the gyration. When he finally steadied his feet against the rock, it was the very rope he had been clutching that tempted him to escape. He could rappel down in seconds, reach the cave and rethink everything—but what would happen to Leila and Jim? He still had the knife. Clenching his teeth, he started to pull himself up again, fighting off the cowardly instincts his body kept unleashing against his renewed determination.

He cautiously lifted his head above the rim of the wall and glimpsed Leila. She stood in the middle of the lighthouse floor pointing a rifle at a man sprawled on the floor. Even in the dim light, he could see that pieces of flesh had burst off the man's face, which ran dark with blood. Leila must have shot him because the other Mexican lay splayed out on top of the opposite wall. But were they dead?

Frank dropped down, ran a few steps and jerked the gun off the Mexican on the floor. It was Jim's shotgun! He spotted Jim from the corner of his eye. Jim was yelling something, but the explosion of the Krummgewehr had triggered a hissing mess in Frank's ears. As he pulled at the shotgun, the Mexican rolled over flat on his back, exposing a chest shredded by bullets so violently that pieces of his shirt had been sucked into the wounds.

Frank looked up as Leila dropped her rifle. They immediately turned toward the man who had collapsed on top of the wall. Leila walked over and put her ear close to his mouth. Was she holding his hand? Frank yelled, "I killed him." Stunned momentarily when he could barely hear his own voice, he yelled again. The dying Mexican must have gotten out a few words, because as Frank stepped closer, he could see an occasional bubble of air rise through blood pooled in his mouth. Leila kept listening, a gesture that touched Frank by its simple decency amidst the terror.

An unexpected calmness settled in his mind. At that moment he knew they were safe. Years later he would remember the feeling of trespass that assailed him when he frisked Slink's pockets and found Jim's watch, matches and a pack of cigarettes, a pocketknife, two candy bars and at the bottom of the pocket some folded papers that looked very familiar.

Jim was trying to drag himself toward them until Leila and Frank lifted him up and seated him against the wall.

"He's okay!" Leila yelled, but Frank barely could hear her. She showed Frank two fingers and then the cutthroat sign. Two Mexicans, both dead!

"You have to yell!" He pointed toward his ears.

She put her arms around Frank.

"You did it!" she cried into his ear so loudly it would have jerked a dead man out of his grave.

"Are you hurt?"

She drew back and lifted her arms above her head in a gesture as if to say, "Here I am in my red bikini." At some other time, it might have made Frank laugh.

"How did you shoot them?" she shouted.

"A German gun."

"What?"

"I'll explain later," he said. "My hearing isn't back yet."

But he could not help asking one more question. "What happened to the trawler?"

"It sank," she yelled, lowering her hand in a diving motion. Frank felt a cold fist clutch his throat.

"We'll talk later." She pointed toward Jim.

A quick inspection of Jim's leg wound showed that it was draining green pus.

They took turns drinking from the rain-filled canvas, using empty Coke cans. At first, the light of dawn was reassuring, but soon the sun lit the corpses starkly. Sarge looked riveted to the ground by Leila's shots, and Slink hung on the wall, a limp bundle of torn flesh.

Frank unfolded the sheets of paper he had retrieved from Slink's pocket. These were the typewritten pages they had drawn up in San Diego as a reminder of things they needed to carry to the island. Leila nodded in recognition. Frank handed the papers to Jim, who dropped his head. It was obvious that Jim understood, but he caught himself, quickly smoothed over his initial gesture of disgust and started sliding both arms upward. *Mea culpa*, it said. "What do you want me to do?"

"They searched my house!" Leila shouted so loudly that even Frank—half deaf as he was—recoiled. He pulled the papers from Jim's hand and gestured Leila toward the doorframe.

"I need to know what happened after I left," he said.

Once they were on the landing, she told Frank that after the trawler sank, the Mexicans' plane crashed and the Cessna tumbled into the ocean. She pointed to the east where he spotted a wing sticking up from the reef. Leila's gesture of resignation said it all.

"We can't get to it," Frank said. He was beginning to hear his own voice again, but it was more like words rumbling about in some hollow spaces inside his head.

"Those bastards did their homework," he said. Leila nodded.

"Jim probably gave them the idea for a new drug route," he added.

She crossed her hands in front of her face, signaling that she did not want to deal with that suspicion now, then pointed at

Frank's chest, arms and legs. Frank had been so caught up in the moment that he hadn't noticed his bruises and gashes. Leila was not bleeding openly, but she was covered with bruises. The worst circled one of her eyes. Frank gently lifted her eyelid, which was so swollen it resembled the bloated body of a jellyfish— pale color, bluish veins and all. The white of her eye was pooled with blood. When Frank touched her battered jaw, she winced. Then she took his hand, folded it into a fist, and guided it to her jaw. Coming from one who had been beaten so brutally, it was a strangely disarming gesture.

In a few sentences Frank told her how he'd failed to trigger the Cessna's emergency locator, been washed into the bay, found the Krummgewehr, slept in the cave, then climbed his way up the rock and shot Slink.

Leila filled in the rest. "Luckily Sarge was sleeping outside on the landing. After you shot Slink, Sarge rushed through the doorframe. Jim threw himself across and jerked Sarge's legs right out from under him. I got hold of his rifle and pulled the trigger. God! I don't know how I did it. I was so frightened I couldn't stop shooting into his body."

"This bastard had two guns on him," Frank said.

"The rifle and our shotgun."

"What happened to the third Mexican?"

"He drowned."

"How do you know?"

"They told us that he's dead, and I believe them."

"What else did they say?"

"Jim messed them up, they said. They called him a traitor. Some of their amigos died in a government raid, and they held Jim responsible."

"Those amigos might come after us."

"I can only guess. You'd better ask Jim."

Once back on the lighthouse floor, they noticed that Jim had managed to make his way to the rope and pull up the German Krummgewehr. Now it lay on the floor, its crooked barrel spliced open like a peeled banana.

"Kaput! Isn't that what your folks call it?" Jim commented. Still the old acid confidence even though his leg was seriously wounded and his breathing was a mere shuffled wheeze.

"You're not in any condition to move around," Frank said.

"I can use that impotent thing as a crutch."

"You have an infected wound. Stay put!" Leila said.

"But it's draining, Leila! Those bastards opened it up when they beat me with the rifle butt," Jim said. "I didn't know they had the therapeutic touch."

They pulled Jim back against the wall and set the Krummgewehr beside him. Using his T-shirt, Leila laid a wet dressing on the wound, which was glued over with pus. At least for now, the drainage gave Jim some relief.

"I couldn't retrieve the antibiotics from the plane," Frank said.

"Oh, well. I guessed that."

"Who would have imagined such a storm," Leila interjected.

"You were lucky that I was awake when you shot Slink," Jim said.

"How's that?"

"If I hadn't grabbed Sarge, he would've killed all of us."

"What are you saying?"

"Your banana gun." Jim burst into a hoarse laugh. "What a harebrained idea!"

"I did test fire it."

"Oh, well. But look what happened to it."

"I killed the bastard. That's what I see."

"You're just lucky. Sarge could easily have finished us off."

Did Jim actually have the nerve to think that he was the hero?

Where have you been since the first shot, Frank? Bumbling around? Hanging in the face of the rock? Was that what Jim thought?

Frank felt his blood rushing to his head. He bent down. "Let me clear the air!" He jerked the Krummgewehr out of Jim's hand and threw it back over his head with such force that it slithered across the lighthouse floor and hit the opposite wall.

"Your goddamn shady deals! You screw up big time just because you so urgently need to come back to the States, and all these crooks south of the equator are after you. And you have the gall to rake me over the coals for trying to get us out of a mess that you're responsible for!"

He flung out his right hand to silence Jim.

"Shut up! I could have hidden on the island and waited. I could have watched them beat you both to a pulp. I could have hidden in the cave while you were rotting away. But by God. I didn't." Frank stood up still shaking his head in disgust. "You are despicable. Don't tell me that I have nothing to do with saving you! What arrogance. What crap!"

Frank turned abruptly, lifted Sarge's body by his shoulders, dragged the corpse out on the landing, stripped away the pants and khaki shirt, and pushed Sarge off the cliff. Then he pulled Slink down from the wall and dragged the corpse back out on the blood-smeared landing to kick him off too.

Jim's insults kept repeating themselves inside his head like a stuck needle on a record player. No matter how much he tried to tell himself that Jim had a life-threatening wound or that Jim was down on his luck, his anger kept boiling. He felt like throwing up, getting rid of this misery with one big retching of his soul.

Once he was back on the floor of the lighthouse, Leila handed Frank his share of a piece of chocolate bar. He let it melt inside his mouth to make the flavor linger, but he had knocked out a few teeth when he had fallen, and the sweetness gave soon way to the tart taste of blood. They sat along the wall to stay in the thin shadow it cast, their thoughts immersed in separate worlds of exhaustion and despair. Eventually Leila sidled over and whispered into Frank's ear

"I know you have a right to be angry, but this is no time to quarrel," she said.

"How did Jim get us into this mess?"

"Would it really help us to know?"

"Their cronies might come after us."

"And what could we do about it?" Leila asked.

She hadn't slept the night before and was too tired to think straight, so she rested her head on Frank's legs and dozed off. Frank's thoughts kept spinning questions. Why was Jim never short of money? What really happened during a visit to Chappaqua when one of Jim's shady friends had drawn a knife? Why was Jim always flying in unexpectedly from some foreign country? But worn to a frazzle, Frank soon gave in to sleep.

They drowsed in the shadows by the wall all morning. When the full sun began to beat on them, Frank covered Jim with Sarge's jacket even though it was stained with blood, although first he had to shake out pieces of flesh blown off by the bullets Leila had shot into Sarge's body. Jim avoided looking at Frank, and neither said a word.

It was almost noon when Frank, assisting Leila with a dressing, noted that Jim's eyes were tinged yellow and veined with red streaks. For a second, without intending to, he found himself holding Jim's hand. It felt limp and spongy, drained of all life.

"Maybe you won't talk to me, but at least try to listen." Jim's voice was shaky. He looked up at Frank's face. "I've been thinking about this. It's best that I stay up here and Leila and you hide in the cave." Small curds of spit clung to the corners of his mouth; Leila made him drink from the cola can.

"Are you proposing that we leave you up here?" Frank asked. Jim didn't answer. "Well?"

"You just said it."

"Out of the question!"

Jim looked at Leila, who kept shaking her head. "Frank is right," she said.

"They are only after me, and this gives both of you a chance to hide."

"No!" Frank said. "You got us into this mess, but now we

are in it together." He turned to Leila, his voice firm and crisp. "They would know that in his condition, Jim could only have survived with help from somebody else on the island."

"Hopefully nobody else will come after us."

"When these bastards don't return, their buddies will come looking for them," Jim said.

Frank shook his head in disgust. "And what in God's name will keep them from killing all of us? They'll throw us to the sharks—we'll disappear without a trace!"

"If you hide they might not find you. And you can arm yourselves," Jim spoke in a weak, reedy voice.

"They'll flush us out. Clipperton just isn't a good place to hide in the first place. We're in this together—whether you deserve it or not."

It was reassuring to claim the higher moral ground, to speak with resolve and to hold back anger. But doubts kept nagging Frank. He knew too well that there was a way to hide in the cave, and that he and Leila would be able to take food to Jim at night. This would be a compromise to abandoning Jim. If they could survive this, it might give way to something better. Somehow, Frank trusted that they would eventually cross that threshold. But after Jim belittled Frank's part of the rescue in such a sarcastic way, Frank had felt denigrated and humiliated. Each of Jim's words kept grating him. At times in the past, there had been an occasional sense of closeness, but all that was left now was the galling dance of jealousy and resentment. He would no longer ignore it

"So how come the Mexicans had our shotgun?" Frank asked.

Jim looked up.

"What? Didn't you figure the shotgun was no match against their rifles, that you couldn't use it anyway because you were injured?" Frank didn't wait for a response. "Why didn't you drop the shotgun back down the face of the rock once you knew you couldn't possibly defend yourself? I knew where to find it and could have used it for a surprise attack."

"I thought it a good idea but I didn't insist," Leila said.

"Because Jim talked you out of it?"

"What is that supposed to mean?" Leila had a pained expression in her face.

Frank was in no mood to let the argument drift off. "Jim has been telling you for a long time that you can't count on me, hasn't he?"

"Don't answer," Jim said. His voice was gravelly.

Leila stepped back, stunned and surprised. Beating her fists together, she started shouting, "I can't stand what you are doing. Both of you! Both of you."

Frank wanted to touch her shoulder, but expected her to brush his hand away, so he refrained. "Leila! Listen to me! I know that Jim has been telling you that you can't count on me."

"I told her that there won't ever be much going on with you," Jim said with such vicious defiance, the very emotion seemed to cut rills into his face.

"I hate to disappoint you, but you're wrong," Frank hissed.

He walked out on the landing and propped himself against where the outside wall cast a sliver of shadow. He hoped for some ocean spray, but since it was close to noon, the light breeze barely took the spray off the surf. For an hour, they each cowered against some part of the lighthouse wall, separate and silent. They appeared lifeless, their contours reduced like drawings of chalk on old bricks.

Eventually Leila joined him out on the landing. She wore Sarge's oversized jacket draped around her body, its bloody hood pulled over her head as protection against the sun. She handed Frank Sarge's hat and one of the Mexican men's undershirts.

Frank had moved to the ledge to catch the cooling updraft. His legs were dangling across the ridge, and he had to avoid looking straight down so he would not become dizzy. Ninety feet below, waves washed in and out, tracing a swirling pattern between the outcrops of the rock.

"Sit beside me!" he told her. She shook her head. "Sarge

forced me at gun point to sit right where you are now and then kept questioning me while he pushed toward the edge."

"What did he want?"

"He kept asking about you."

"You told him I was dead."

"Yes," she said.

"That's when he beat you?"

"I was afraid for my life."

"And did you believe I was dead?"

"It was a terrible storm," she said.

Frank moved several feet back from the edge, Leila folding her legs quite easily next to him. Even with all her bruises and cuts, she's still limber, Frank thought. He tried to see her face, but it was covered by the jacket's hood.

"You were right to set Jim straight," she said.

"I get so pissed that I bring up the past, and I don't want to go there."

"You might have to."

"All that crap from so far back."

"Everything starts with childhood," she said, nodding her head. The hood went up and down and, in a bizarre way, reminded him of Catholic confession, the priest's measured gesture of approval, reluctant and contingent, yet so powerful.

"Frank, we owe our lives to you…. I will never forget," she said. Slowly pulling back the hood, Leila showed her face and looked straight at Frank. "I want to ask you a question…. That day back in Biddeford you told me you were cold in the eyes of God. Was Jim the reason you held back telling me how you felt?"

"Jim has intimidated me all my life," Frank said.

"I always sensed you were in a mode of perpetual waiting."

"I was hoping…" Frank's voice started wavering, "hoping for something to unhinge my life, a passion to burn deep down to my roots."

"It has happened," she said. She took his hand and her lips

brushed his cheek lightly.

"And Jim?" he asked.

"For now, bury the past," Leila said. She put one finger across his lips in a soothing gesture. "Right now the question is how to survive."

"I can't argue."

"Any ideas?"

"First we need food, so we should hunt for crabs."

Frank started to lay out a plan. They would let down the rope—there was enough length to reach the ground—then leave the rock, use the spade to kill crabs, boil them, and finally load them into the backpack which they would tie to the rope and pull up. They also could fill the two Coke cans with water and stick them into the backpack with the crabs. Some drinking water would spill, but they could pull up as often as necessary to fill a canvas reservoir.

"We have to do it now," Leila explained. "After the storm, the bay water is as low in salt as it ever will be. If we wait, the water will become saltier, and drinking that brine will make us throw up."

"Can we add more cloth to widen the reservoir?" Frank asked.

"We don't have enough to wear as protection against the sun as it is."

"What can we use for fish hooks?"

"I'll pull the wire out of my bikini top."

"Clever."

"And for vitamins we can use any kelp that's brown. Those aren't toxic. They don't taste great, but . . . "

"The only usable fruits I can think of are coconuts. But how can I climb trees with razor trunks?" Frank asked. "I'll bleed like a pig."

"I could wrap you in rope to protect your skin and make you look like one of those Michelin tire advertisements. But you might not have to climb because we should find some fallen trees to pluck the coconuts from. And there are other possibilities. I identified the *Strongylodon* species of drift moss, which must have been washed over from Indonesia. It's edible, as is the aquatic *phanerogram,* Ruppia maritime, which we can scrape from rocks just below the water line."

They walked back through the doorframe. Leila removed the backpack that Jim had been using as support and tossed in a knife and the flashlight; Frank soaked Jim's dressing in silence, leaving it to Leila to fill Jim in on their plans.

Once off the footholds at the base of the rock, Leila and Frank sat down in the rock's shadow. Frank reached over to examine Leila's eye again. Encouragingly, her vision seemed mostly intact. "If you have retinal bleeding, you'd better not do anything strenuous," he said.

He kissed her gently on her forehead and eased her into his arms. But she couldn't relax. Trembling, she gasped, "We're going to die, Frank We're not going to make it."

"We will get through it," Frank whispered reassuringly. He held her until her quivers settled to an occasional heave of her chest. After he let go, she said firmly, "I don't want soothing words, Frank. No lies!"

"I'll tell you some more of my ideas once we've had something to eat," Frank said. Expecting that the crabs would stay in the shadows, he began to look for them on the northeastern side of the rock where he had found them before. But no matter how often or how far he put his hands into the gaps or how thoroughly he swiped palm fronds through even the most minor crevices, he could not flush out any crabs. Not knowing what else to do, he headed for the rock's sun-exposed southern flank. He had barely rounded the corner when the sight of Sarge and Slink's bodies jolted him. The naked corpses were teeming with crabs that had pierced the eyes, releasing a slimy fluid that covered the Mexicans' faces like a pale mask. Fighting for a place to dig into the torn flesh, the crabs had ripped deep gashes into the bullet holes. Several crabs were pulling a lip off a face, stretching it into a bizarre grin. Wherever flesh was exposed, a crab had dug its claws in, tearing away bloody pieces with scurrying feet and cold, unmoving eyes.

Will this be the end? Is this what everything will come down to? Frank wondered. He had promised Leila that they would survive this nightmare, but he wasn't so sure. Driven by anger and raw disgust, Frank threw rocks at the crabs, but the creatures held their ground. He started thwacking them with sticks, flinging them off left and right, but they kept fighting their way back.

What was the sense of it all? Soon they might be corpses being ripped apart and eaten. Not even the grace of being rendered to dust, as the Bible says. He sat down and tried to calm his disgust. They had no choice but to eat these corpse-devouring crabs!

Once back at the rock, he told Leila that the Mexican corpses were swarming with crabs. "I want you to be prepared," he warned her.

"I'll join you," she said.

A few yards away from the bodies, Frank dug a deep pit that he stacked with the wood Leila had been collecting from a stand of palm trees a few hundred feet off where the storm had washed broken fronds and branches into the sand. He began hitting the crabs with rocks and tossing them into the pit by the dozens. As most of them had merely been stunned, the pit was soon filled with a wriggling mass of claws and armored bodies. They had begun biting each other and struggling up the walls. A few reached the rim and charged with convulsing claws at the Mexicans' boots that Leila and Frank had put on.

Frank threw a match. Through the column of hot air that rose from the fire, as if looking through disturbed glass, Frank saw piles of crabs scuffling toward the walls. Soon, sheets of fire engulfed them; a hissing noise filled the air as the heat drew bubbles from their scalding armor. Some seemed to kneel in prayer. Suddenly this mass execution gave Frank a chill. One of the burning crabs almost reached the rim then fell back, her eyes scorched down to stumps of hellish pain. The crabs were writhing everywhere—between the palm fronds, alongside the walls, on top of each other. As the flames spread to the pit walls, they scrambled toward the center, ramming each other with their grotesquely large claws. They struggled to climb but became knotted into a tangle of plates and legs and claws and burning eyes, building up such a mass of blistered bodies that, even in their despair, they still seemed to be reaching for something higher. Anything. They kept piling on top of each other, using their claws like picks, hacking each other in such despair that they would stay entangled long after their last convulsion.

Frank and Leila pulled the crabs out in chains, tore them open quickly, scraped out the steaming flesh and gulped down the slimy pieces. They tasted like rotten fish. Refrying helped some, as did dangling the stringy slops into their throats then swallowing as fast as possible to get them past their taste buds.

What followed their wolfing down the slops was nausea so vicious, it threw them onto their knees. Bent over like drunken sailors, they twisted their fists into their stomachs so as not to lose all the food. It took a long time before their retching ended and they could find some release in the rock's shadow. When Leila took off her jacket, undressing down to her red bikini, Frank was startled to see how battered she was. She had been kicked in her buttocks. There were bruises on her lower rib cages and her elbows. Her knees were chafed; the skin over her shinbones opened with sores.

They waded into the bay to cool down, and Frank stretched into a few strokes to regain, if only for a moment, the expansive feel of water and sky. But nothing came of it. Nature appeared more hostile and impenetrable than ever.

When Frank left the water, Leila was waiting for him at the bottom of the rock where she had already tied the backpack to the lowered rope.

"How long can Jim hold on with a flesh wound like his?" she asked.

"President Garfield had a bullet in his side for two months."

"But he died from it."

"We'll be out of here in a few days."

Leila stared into the sand. "The Scripps Institute won't start searching for us for weeks."

"We can hold out that long."

"The Mexicans might arrive first and kill us," Leila said.

"Those thugs probably don't care a damn about their missing comrades. They may never come here, or they might come after we've been rescued." Frank didn't want to give her any time for objections. "And maybe we'll find a bunch of German weapons and take them down. And if this doesn't work we can hold them off with some tall stories about Nazi treasures!"

What stupid ideas! It was idiotic! Didn't he still have to bury the corpses, and wasn't the blood on the lighthouse floor screaming "murder"? How could he forget?

"I'm trying to believe you, Frank. I'm really trying," Leila said.

He was relieved that Leila had decided not to rip apart his optimistic outlook. And a new thought had begun to chafe him: the Mexicans' twin-engine plane had probably flown close to its range unless they had added auxiliary tanks, but Frank did not remember spotting any. This could only mean that the Mexicans intended to bring in a fuel supply by boat, which might already be on its way. He'd better come up with some ideas soon!

"Just before we left the lighthouse, Jim insisted again that we hide somewhere on the island," Leila said.

"My answer is no. How would we take care of him?"

She looked into his eyes. "I knew you would say no." Leila jerked the rope several times as a signal for Jim to pull up.

The first ascent of the backpack worked out as planned. Jim let the rope down with a slip of paper saying that the two Coke cans spilled water. Even after Leila had woven palm fronds into a nest to hold the cans upright, Jim kept sending the dreaded message: spilled. Eventually, Frank found a solution by filling the bottom of the backpack with sand and setting the Coke cans upright into it. But Jim had tired of pulling the loads and sent a note asking to stop.

"In the future one of us has to do the pulling up," Leila said.

"At least he has food now."

Leila and Frank sat down in the rock's shadow and somehow managed to doze in the stupefying heat.

Frank drifted into a dream in which he was still a child living in his parent's house in Munich, much as he remembered it in the 1950s, except the floorboards in the living room had been ripped out. Frank had started to dig a tunnel away from the center of the room, working inside a ditch, his hips already below floor level, shoveling dirt over his head onto the floor. His father kept shouting from somewhere: "Dig! Dig! *Graben! Graben!*" But every time Frank would reach one of the walls, his father would yell: "Kehr um! Kehr um!" Eventually, he found himself buried in the center of the room with nowhere to go.

Frank jumped up when Leila poked his ribs. "You were mumbling in German."

"Something about my father," he said. His memory kept working into the fringes, mixing shredded impressions from his dream and images of burning crabs scurrying toward the center of a pit.

Frank shook his head to separate dream and reality.

"I want to show you the cave." Frank stood up and took the spade and flashlight.

"I'd rather climb on top and help pull up water," Leila said.

"I found orchids my father must have grown here in 1944."

"Orchids?"

It did seem impossible. But, of course, this was Clipperton where anything could turn real: dregs of war and secret weapons and sand stained with the blood of children and a lighthouse built for ships that would never arrive. Why not orchids?

"Sometime in 1944, my father must have visited this cave," Frank explained. "He left behind his tin box with orchid pods and glass flasks which must have broken and spilled. Believe me! There are orchids growing in the cave."

"You found a tin box," she asked, "but how do you know it

is your father's?"

"It has his monogram and the swastika."

Orchids on Clipperton! Leila pulled on the jacket and squeezed into the cave behind Frank. The cooler air offered comfort, but the din of birds assaulted their ears, and Leila kept wiping her eyes, irritated by the ammonia. They waited somewhere in the center of the cavern for the outlines of sintered walls and ceilings to emerge from the murk.

"How many ways are there to get in here?" she asked in a loud voice, her face close to Frank's ear.

"As far as I know only the way we came."

"This wasn't more than a crack in the rock, and it's hard to see."

"I was lucky to find it!"

"We could actually hide inside this cave."

"No," he said. "We have to stay on top of the rock."

"Frank! This actually is a good place to hide."

Her face drew close to Frank's. "There's bad blood between you and Jim." Despite the noise, Frank could hear her voice tremble.

"I won't betray him. Enough!" He turned and started to make his way to where he had found the orchids the day before.

But Leila wouldn't be diverted. "This cave is our best bet." When he didn't answer, she continued, "You're being unreasonable!" She shouted to make herself be heard against the birds' racket.

Frank turned around. "Doesn't take much to change your mind, does it?"

"You need to prove something to Jim, don't you?"

"I have already! Stop it, Leila. I just want to show you my father's orchids." Frank crawled halfway into the wall recess and pointed at the orchids.

Leila just stood there for a few minutes. Finally she followed him and crawled past him. Frank heard her gasp at the discovery of orchids at such an improbable location. Leila cradled the flowers in her hands, examining them closely.

"Don't cut yourself. Watch for broken flasks!" Frank warned her. He pulled the tin box from the sand and wiped it clean to point out the stenciled monogram. Leila removed a shriveled seedpod and gently rolled it into the hollow of her hand.

Inside the recess, the noise was muted, and they could finally talk with voices less strained. "Your father must have tried to grow orchids seedlings in those flasks," she said. "I guess he had to leave suddenly."

"He lived for his orchids."

"He might have been hiding other things."

"It crossed my mind, but I didn't have time to look around."

She crawled deeper into the recess, using the flashlight as it turned darker, eventually turning onto her back like a miner would when working toward the face of a coal seam. Frank wedged in beside her as well as he could. They kept digging into the ground, Frank holding the flashlight and Leila pushing the spade into the mixture of clay and sand. Suddenly the spade hit something metallic.

They pulled a rough box out of the sand and carried it outside. Handling it very gingerly, Frank pried off the top and found a notebook. After wiping the cover, he read aloud, "*Schulenheft.*" God! It was his father's diary! Frank lifted the cover and found the date 16.2.1942 inscribed on the first page. They were surprised to find the writing preserved and wondered if the guano may have prevented molds from invading. However, most pages were gummed together, and blowing on them and shaking them only loosened a few.

As much as Frank wanted to start reading it, a sense of dread tinged with shame struck him and held him back. He slid the diary into the large pocket of Slink's jacket. When he pulled his hands out—he noticed blood on them.

"Why don't you look at the diary?" Leila asked impatiently.

"Later."

"Why would your father hide his diary in such a forlorn

place?" Leila asked.

"Haven't you figured it out, he had to leave suddenly?"

She backed off when she heard the irritation in Frank's voice. "Just wondering," she said.

They rested for a while with their backs against a smooth part of the cliff. An irksome silence had fallen between them. With every minute passing, the diary inside the jacket seemed to weigh more, pull heavier, almost become an affliction. Frank finally set it down between them. Leila picked it up, weighing it in her hand.

"It is heavy."

The burden of history, Frank thought. Whatever else he might learn from the diary, these truths he already knew: that he had lost his father to history long before his birth and that he would never unshackle his conscience from Germany's. Such were the poisoned headwaters of his nation's past.

He listened to the surf. To Frank the indifferent heave and pound of the sea rendered the disquiet of human history absurd. But the repulsion that filled him at the thought of this very absurdity and relentless indifference did not bring him despair; rather, he sensed an opening to new depths and felt the sting of a righteous shame that offered redemption.

Leila guessed his thoughts. "This diary is what you came for."

"But I didn't ask for all hell to break loose."

She looked at Frank with an anxious expression carved darkly by her bruises. He added, " If they attack, we can save ourselves by some ruse. It's just that I have to find a way to hide somewhere with a rifle."

"Where?"

"Maybe outside the wall or under a pile of stones, if we can loosen enough of them…. I don't know yet."

"And where's Jim going to be?"

Frank shook his head. "There is no way of getting Jim down into the cave safely."

"This would be one way to make him disappear. Wouldn't

it?"

"What are you getting at?"

"I say that Jim's presence got us into this mess in the first place," she said.

"We both know that."

"If they find the two of us up at the lighthouse and we tell them that Jim and their Mexican pals have drowned and we are the only survivors they might just leave us alone."

"Or more probably throw us to the sharks."

"But maybe."

"It won't work! Anyway, we can't get Jim into the cave."

They started to discuss how they might reach the twin-engine plane that had been blown into the reef, only to come up with no solution. The notion of finding usable Nazi weapons seemed farfetched at best. Books, maybe, or some ridiculous Christmas gifts for the Japanese, or even another Krummgewehr. But nothing that could match the hand grenades or heavy weapons the Mexicans would use.

"I'll try to find weapons tomorrow," Frank said.

"Forget about fighting. They might not show up. First try to collect coconuts."

On the climb back up to the top of the rock, they felt weak and disoriented by the glare of sky and sea. It took much longer than they expected—thirst, hunger and the lack of sleep had begun to take their toll.

20

FOR SOME TIME Jim had been leaning across the top of the wall retching like a horse. Just looking at the slops of burnt crabs would trigger a spasm. To make things worse, the strain of pulling up the backpack had further injured his leg. He let himself down on the floor, drank from the canvas and moistened his dressing, then tried to scoot backward out to the landing for a few prickles of salt spray. But even moving a few yards exhausted him, and he felt the chills of his fever coming back.

When his thoughts drifted back to his childhood, he fought them at first, but the fever lifted Jim into a floating world strangely pleasant and removed, conjuring up memories of his hometown, of the attic room in the house at the river when all was still well, of watching his father come home from the night shift in the steelworks as he crossed the tram lines, his bent figure outlined against the yellow glow of blast furnaces so that his father seemed to be stepping through gilded rain puddles, in one hand always his Thermos bottle, always oddly tilted up the way all the steelworkers seemed to carry them. There was that same spot where his father would lift his head and look up to the house, and always with a smile.

That was before he came into money, before he entered the zone of flighty ideas, before all the drinking and the beating. Strange that, even after all these years, remembering his father crossing the silvery net of tramway tracks beneath that spider web of electric feeder lines could give him so much comfort.

The fever chills had brought on a peculiar indifference, a reprieve from a dismal present, but with the falling curve of fever, Jim's thoughts reeled back to South America. He should have listened to O'Reilly, a drunkard for sure, but one with good judgment. He had smelled whiskey on O'Reilly's breath the first time he met him at the airport in Cuzco. "May I introduce myself: Irish, touch of Hemingway, do my best work with a bottle on my desk." He was a drunkard, yes, but one who knew.

"I always can smell a rat," he told Jim. "Don't get involved with Carlos," he had advised him at the end.

It was the second rush of fever that would again loosen Jim's thoughts and instill in his mind moments of transparency. Gazing up into the boiling sky, he felt as if he were looking again through the rectangle of his attic window in the house on the Stonycreek. And for a moment he conjured up lights in a circle around him and ice buckets with beer and cakes, yellow roses and the lines of electric lanterns his mother had strung around the small garden's perimeter. He closed his eyes and let himself float inside the tide of voices of those who had gathered for the celebration of his first communion. For weeks he would wake in the wee hours of the morning, sneak down to the back porch, light the lanterns and sit marveling at the magic rectangle suddenly lifted out from all the dark neighborhood gardens. What he would give now to sit one more time beneath those lights!

He had been happy in the small house that straddled the Stonycreek River, feeling solace in the predictable, the clink and thump each morning as the paperboy slid the paper into the mailbox, the wait for the school bus and his mother waving from the doorstep as he made his way to the back seat. He had found comfort in the mellow bustle of the small town, familiar lights washing into his room in the evenings, the same slanting blue from the neon sign across the street and the thin chirping sound it made.

Once when visiting his father, Jim had experienced total darkness inside the cave above the Juniata River, and he remembered the terror that had struck him then. Jim still could hear his father's excited voice: "One day this cave will be a world-famous tourist attraction!"

His father spewed words about all these projects, none of them ever to be completed. He remembered that his father fell silent and switched off the lamp then. The darkness was as sudden as a flash. Struck by night and silence, he reached for his father's hand, which hung limp and warm like a fleshy leaf somewhere in the dark. But why, after so many years, was he still embarrassed that he had reached for his father's hand? Was it pride or arrogance, or was it the price he had to pay for shunning fear? He had allowed his father to slip away!

Leila nudged Jim, snapping him away from his memories. "We're back," she said.

"The crabs made me sick," Jim mumbled.

"They're food from hell." She glanced at Jim's leg, then laid her hand on his forehead. But there was furtiveness in her gesture.

"Did you scout the cave?" Jim asked.

"We talked of getting you down into the cave," Leila said. She was holding the Coke can filled with water.

"It was Leila's idea, not mine," Frank said.

"Don't bother thinking about it. I wouldn't go," Jim said.

"Great! Finally each of us has a different plan." Frank was irritated that Leila had so openly added yet another idea onto a pile of pathetic losers.

"So what's your plan?" Jim asked.

"You stay!" Frank shrugged his shoulders, turned away, then pulled up the backpack in which he had placed the tin box and the diary. He didn't care to tell Jim the story. Why the hell should he try to explain his past to somebody as sardonic as Jim?

Frank sat down at the base of the wall where the sun cast some shadow and removed the diary. This was the first time he really touched the paper. He gently lifted the few pages he could separate. They were coarse, with dull sepia margins as if a dull brownish fluid had seeped in from the rim. Frank's father had written in Gothic German, putting down the sharply peaked old German notations in tilted pen strokes. All his father's exactitude was evident on these pages, but Frank knew nothing of Gothic German letters; it would take days to decipher these runes. By probing further he was able to loosen additional pages: one with pen drawings of flowers, one and one with sketches of willows lining the River Vistula (annotated in italic letters) and, so it seemed, a rough map of a primitive airfield. It was the name Vistula that made him think first of Poland – then, finally, Auschwitz. German history would come down to that.

Running his thumb across the notebook's outer edge, he felt some ridges. He suspected they were protrusions of thicker pages and when he finally pried them loose with the knife, he found out that his father had glued typewritten notes onto them. Some of the ink had been lifted off the pages or smeared, and some sheets he could not peel apart completely, but most importantly, the type was in Roman letters.

3.1.1943

Himmler will watch the gassings tomorrow at 0900. Brand's adjutant helped me find soldiers to watch the Heinkel during the night. (Since Heydrich's death, Himmler is even more cautious.) It was the only way I could leave the plane in Krakau and accept Hoess's invitation. My room is splendid. I can see the Sola River but it is too dark to take a walk. I'd like to go down to the river and search for orchids but this would be possible only with guards. Dr. Korherr from Koenigsberg has the room next to me. Tells me he keeps statistics for Himmler. We eat in the officers' club, which is almost empty at this time, and afterward Korherr opens a bottle of champagne in his room. Told me that Auschwitz is the testing ground for the superior race of the future untouched by morals but spirited by a sense of transcendence. He's drunk and can't stop talking. He knows I'll be leaving next day and I wonder why he confides that much in me or maybe that is the very reason. I get the impression he tests me.

"Will you be at a selection?" he asked. It is the insider question but I avoid an answer and tell him that Himmler has time for the gassing only.

"To have seen it and lived through it and experienced it and still have stayed clean . . ."

(I was in Posen the time he gave the speech.)

Frank looked up from the page, realizing Leila was tugging on it.

"I am talking to you," she said.

Frank turned the notebook toward her, and Leila sat down beside him and began to study the open page. "I had a few years of German in school," she said. Speaking slowly, "*Und dann oeffnet Herr Korherr eine Flasche Wein fuer mich in seinem Zimmer. Er sagt mir dass Auschwitz....*" Leila stopped and turned her head and looked at Frank

"My father was Himmler's pilot."

"You didn't know?"

Frank shook his head.

The heat of the afternoon lay on them like a burning fleece. Leila did not know what to do. She wanted to put her arms around Frank, but at the same time she wanted to tell him to find some food, think of a way to collect coconuts, do something. What she eventually said, after sitting beside him in silence, was simply, "I am sorry." Then she stood up and walked away to give him the privacy to continue reading.

4.1.1943

We have vanilla cobbler and real coffee. Himmler has been getting into a discussion with Hedwig Hoess, which leads to a delay.

Nobody dares to interrupt them. The party leaves at 0945. I take a Kuebelwagen two cars behind Himmler's Mercedes. I am concerned about the delay because I have received a call that the landing lights on the Heinkel cannot be replaced on short notice and I have to avoid a night flight if Himmler decides to take the plane from Krakow. There are about 80 people packed in front of the crematorium's observation window. Two SS men salute and the lieutenant apologizes for the turmoil and crying inside the building. I can hear fists thumping against the walls. Himmler peeps through the round observation window and lifts his hand. After several minutes he turns back, pleased. Hoess offers him a cigarette and lights it.

"Why are they climbing on top of each other?" Himmler asked.

"Cyclon B is heavier than air – all these Jews try to overtake each other . . . Himmler shakes his head. "Good," he said. I have rarely seen him that relaxed.

About 50 feet behind Himmler, two female inmates dressed in skirts had laid out a table with small bunches of fresh flowers that they handed to the few women who were in the group of visitors. Some of them were drunk; the rest did not pay attention. Only two or three took the small arrangements. When I came close to the two inmates, one of them thrust a flower arrangement into my hand. I didn't know what to do; it came so unexpectedly. The woman's face was swollen; she was blonde, maybe one of the inmates who had arrived by rail from Holland the week before. I don't know what made me take the flowers. I stuffed them into my pocket, more embarrassed and annoyed than anything else. Back at the room, in the presence of Korherr, a small note fell out from between the stalks. I had nothing to hide and spread it out:

Call Red Cross. Thousands murdered each day.

Korherr, looking over my shoulder, was incensed. He called the compound adjutant and told him to notify Hoess immediately. After several minutes the floor telephone rang. Korherr did the talking. An hour later two Gestapo officers interrogated me. Had I ever seen her before? Had I ever been in a hostile or neutral country? As if they didn't already know that!

I told them that I was to fly Himmler that very afternoon, but they informed me that the interrogation had been cleared with him. That afternoon they made me watch the execution of the woman. I had to wait standing alone in the middle of the yard near the gallows. I'm sure Himmler knew about it. They hanged her wrapped in a sack. I could see her pointed knees through the cloth. When her neck snapped she wet herself, which is what haunts me most, that spot on the cloth as it widened and darkened.

I should never have accepted the flowers.

Frank screened the following page but found recipes only: how to stretch the yield of coffee beans by mixing them with ground tubers, how to broil sauerbraten and thicken cabbage soup. His father's writing picked up the events three pages later. There the notes were written in slightly different ink, but the glare of the sun onto the paper made this difficult to discern.

5.1.1943

Korherr gloats when he sees me returning ruffled. He offers me some of his Landjaeger. He himself is a vegetarian, he says, looking at me with such cold eyes they rip me open. I feel naked, embarrassed. We SS men stay clean, he says. There is nothing personal in our doing. We are for the first time in history embarking on an ideology that is driven by ideas, nothing else, no sloth, no greed and no ideals but those of our race.

The communication officer calls at eight to say Krakau commando has called, they expect me to report in two days. Himmler has already made his way to Warsaw. They do not tell me if he has been flown or driven. I call the airport and tell the ground crew that the Heinkel will not be needed for two days. But they had orders already. I do not know who gave them.

Severa...night officer knocked at my door... telegram...Panzerdivison

The letters after this fragment had been sheared off the page, rendering the message unreadable. Frank, still holding the book in his hand, closed his eyes.

These were the headwaters he had been searching for. This was where the river began. And as rivers flow they branch into eddies; they stretch into smooth runs; they fold into ripples and fall; and then there are rivers that enter a chute that forever will define their destiny. And there are chutes that lead to perdition.

Frank put the notebook beside the tin box on the slab, fighting a visceral terror about what he had learned. He set his hand on the top cover as if to push it back into the cave never to be dug up again. His thoughts rushed forward to the present, and it angered him that he had perforated the sides of the tin container that otherwise could have been used to carry water.

He got up and walked to the opposite side of the lighthouse floor, leaned over the tarpaulin, drank water from his cupped hands and swallowed a few slimy pieces of crabmeat. Eventually they would have to come around to eating the slops. There was no choice.

Soon Leila dozed. If she was aware that Frank had gotten up and was walking about, she did not show it. Frank lifted the dressing off Jim's leg; it was covered with green pus. He wrung out the dressing, reapplied it and moistened the cotton strip, dripping water onto it from a can.

"We have to change the dressing more often," Frank told Jim.

"Sit down beside me," Jim said. Frank remained standing. "I know that you lost your father," Jim said without waiting, "but my father was soon to replace yours. I have never gotten over the hurt in seeing that my own father preferred you."

Frank felt as if he were being choked; he felt the cold clutch these memories of his adolescent years still exerted. Some cautionary inner voice held him back from responding.

Jim never had brought that up; he never would admit a loss.

"It split us apart," he heard Jim say.

Jim wants me to admit I have taken his father from him. He needs me to feel guilty so we can patch things up. And how often in the past had he complied! How often had he paled his own feelings of rage and resentment, searched for the hidden poison in his own soul so he could blunt the insults? No more!

"You should be talking to your father, not me," Frank said.

"He might not listen."

"You level with him and tell it straight."

"And you have nothing to do with it?" Jim's voice was straining with sarcasm, his lips sharpened into razor blades.

Frank bent down. "You got that right. I have nothing to do with it," he said.

"You always were a conniving coward," Jim said.

"I was your doormat. But I'm not anymore! . . What counts now is that I'll get you out of here and that's it." Frank felt like hitting Jim's face, felt like knocking that rotten, sarcastic smile back into his throat.

"You are a drug-dealing punk," he said, already turning. He walked across the lighthouse floor and sat down. But anger kept roiling in him no matter how forcefully he closed his eyes; it kept toppling the small, artificial world of peace and repose he tried to regain.

This was no time for tepid remorse, but eventually Frank did walk back over to Jim, who barely looked up.

"I meant what I said," Frank said. "But you should know that your father might have changed his mind about rejecting you."

"How come?" Jim asked with a vaguely inviting nod of his head. Frank remained standing.

"You did the photograph of the airplane in Tanzania. The one that crashed into the Serengeti, the one with grass grown around it leaving the pattern of a cross. You titled the picture 'The Cross on Naabi Hill.'"

"I received three awards for it," Jim said.

"It's an impressive photograph."

"What about it?"

"Before I headed west I visited your father and spent the night in his new treehouse." The very word seemed to trigger a hard pinching anger in Jim's face.

"Listen!" Frank continued, "He had your photo of Naabi Hill enlarged. It's now hung in the top room, and I also remember your catechism from First Communion laid out in the open. Maybe there is a message."

"He always ignored my work," Jim said.

"It's all up to you," Frank said and started walking away. He fought the thought that Jim might not have the chance to see his father again, but what frightened him even more was the insight that deep inside his heart he wished Jim dead.

Meanwhile Leila had awakened and started searching between the stones in the rubble behind the primitive stove the Mexicans had forced her to build.

"I stashed away a few scraps of crab," she explained. Frank shrugged his shoulders and started to help move some of the stones. Besides some pieces of burnt crabs, they found nothing until a metal blade stuck in a crevice drew their attention. It was a piece of a pick loosely inserted in what might have once been a wooden handle that had rotted down to a brittle stump.

"It's the pick Alicia drove into Alvarez's back," Leila said.

"How many people have died already on this rock," Frank said. He lifted the pick and kept sliding the rusted blade between his fingers as if looking for traces of blood that even decades of rain might not have washed off. Maybe he could loosen some stones, pile them into a defensive wall then hide with a gun and shoot the intruders? Leila judged the plan hopeless; nevertheless, he began whacking at the wall to pry off stones, loosening only one or two before giving up.

There didn't seem to be any way out. They were all ghosts now, he thought: Jim, his face parched thin, cheeks carved into ridges, surviving on arrogance; and Leila, crouching away from the sun under her jacket, bruised, with one eye swollen black. In the last reckoning, it wouldn't make any difference what they chose to do. But heat and exhaustion soon dulled his despair and replaced it with a stupor and indifference that were almost pleasant. For a while he stretched out alongside the wall, let the sun flit across his closed lids and slipped into a mindless state.

21

LATE IN THE AFTERNOON the hunger wrenched them, and Leila and Frank started picking at pieces of burnt crabs while talking about food and nothing much else. Should they use the few rounds left to shoot boobies? Was it worth it to leave the rock now and try to fish or look for seaweed? Leila doffed her bikini top and took out the wire, then bent it into a primitive fishhook, something that had turned out to be impossible to make with the brittle pieces of iron Frank had pried off the doorframe. While talking they kept pinching their noses to make the slops of slimy crabmeat bypass their taste buds. Jim had drifted off in a fever, and even frequent changes of his dressings woke him no further than to mumble a few words.

Leila stretched out in the shadow the wall was casting, baring her endless flat stomach, her firm little breasts. As if suddenly aware of her nakedness, she pulled on her bikini. Then, resigning herself, she let her hand rest where her minuscule suit crossed her pubes. Frank felt a cut in his breathing as he remembered holding Leila in his arms. It had been but a few days ago, yet it seemed a lifetime had passed since he had caressed her breasts, kissed her lips.

"How long can Jim tolerate this fever?" Leila was whispering although they were out of Jim's range of hearing. She slowly sat up and pushed her fist against her stomach. "My stomach cramps are coming back."

"We'll be out of here before Jim's in real trouble."

"Before what?" Leila coiled herself beside him.

"Surely before his leg has to be amputated," Frank said.

"And what makes you think so?"

"We'll blow the island up," Frank said. The idea had struck him just minutes ago, and though it came with a rush of clarity, he would have preferred to hold back and give it more thought. But here it was!

"Oh! Great." Leila snapped.

"You remember the smell of gas on the very first day when we walked from our camp to the rock? Among the coconut trees! We got distracted because Jim stepped on a refrigerator."

"Great insight: There are junked refrigerators on this island. But where's the gasoline?"

"I tried to put the pieces together," Frank said. "I suspect the Nazis sent a submarine to Clipperton to bury gasoline, drums to refuel Japanese aircraft."

"I have trouble believing that."

"They might have landed off Mexico, crossed the land and commandeered a fishing vessel to Clipperton. Something like that."

Leila seemed to give it some thought. "I remember the smell but I haven't seen any drums, and after all these years the fuel would be mixed with water."

Frank knew he was on to something now and kept spinning out the possibilities. "If there is gasoline we can burn the palm trees and make them fall and reach the fruits. But more importantly, we'll have a gigantic fire in the middle of the Pacific! Some airliner or satellite will pick up the glare, and they'll look for us in a matter of hours."

Leila eventually agreed to help searching for gasoline. In order for the fire to be seen, they would have to burn the trees at night, and it was already evening. Frank hastily stuffed a flashlight, matches, the spade, some burnt crabs, even a pencil and a writing tablet into the rucksack while Leila tried to penetrate Jim's fever fog to explain what they were trying to do. She filled the two Coke cans and the tin box with water, then instructed Jim to keep the dressing moist. She left scraps of crabs and the remaining bars of chocolate in easy reach. That was all she could do for him.

After Leila had made sure there was enough water left in the canvas, they hurried down the rock in long daring reaches and started walking west toward the palm tree grove. The gashes the ocean had cut through the stretches of sand had begun to silt, and although the loose fill made it difficult to breach them quickly, it took less than half an hour to reach the first palm trees. They felt weak, but a wild anticipation had whipped into their bodies an unexpected strength. Frank kept scurrying between the trunks of palm trees, using the spade to lift the mat of old leaves, grass and crab-eaten moss in search of anything that looked like metal.

He stumbled over pieces of broken-off roof covers, picking up an occasional empty can of some war ration. Suddenly the slanting evening light put something into relief: The top of a gasoline drum!

He called for Leila before he even felt the rush of adrenalin. "I found one! I found one!"

They hastily dug around the rim. The smell of gas was undeniable, and it was not hard to imagine how the top of a buried gasoline drum might have been freed of sand by the storm they had lived through. The land had been washed away almost everywhere, and even the lorry that they had passed on their way had been turned upside down, stuck in the open, clearly visible. But daylight was fading fast, so Leila and Frank decided to hunt for more fuel and leave prying the drum open for later.

It was tough going as the cove had turned into a tumbled mess of fronds, sticks and tousled mosses. But they couldn't care less—they smelled gasoline again! Leila sniffed the air and tried to find her bearings. The ground was a rotten sod of leaves and mosses that not even the flood had been able to wash away. Crabs were everywhere. After several minutes, Leila stopped and pointed to a puddle of water lit by the very last reflections in the sky; it was glistening with the rainbow sheen of gasoline that had spilled through the rusted top of a fuel drum tilted on its side. Now they had the second one!

"Hurry! There must be more," she called.

Racing against the night, they worked farther into the

thicket, looking for anything sticking out of the ground, barely feeling the cuts on their arms and legs as they sliced through the underbrush. But it was dark already and the mat of leaves, branches and tilted trees camouflaged everything and dispersed the rapidly dimming shine of their flashlight. Maybe, just maybe they could make all these barrels explode and light up the night! But where should they look in that muck? Leila was ready to give up and try again in the morning when Frank, convinced the drums might have been placed in a straight line, insisted on one last try. Two small fires, one at the site of each drum, would serve as landmarks, define a straight line and be guides to search between. Fortunately, the second drum had rusted sufficiently to allow them to pierce it, and Leila immediately started a small fire with sticks she had dipped into the gasoline. Frank grabbed some gasoline-soaked branches and took off into the underbrush to start the fire on the other end.

But the two fires were nothing but piddly specks of light in a dark, endless waste of ocean, all too easily confused with lights on fishing boats. They had to do much better to achieve the raging inferno they needed to attract attention from satellites and jet planes!

But once the small fires were burning, Frank had some guide to look for additional gasoline drums. He kept stumbling over branches, sinking in to his knees as crabs scurried into his groin. It took Frank an hour to locate the third drum, but at least then he knew he was right. It was one o'clock when he located the fourth, about two o'clock for the fifth, but he hadn't pried any open yet. Leila, who had found a sixth drum, was waiting at the fire for him to return. When he arrived, his skin was glistening with sweat, his knees shaking.

"I filched some chocolate for you." She handed him one of the bars.

"I'll make these woods burn like cinder." Frank said. He broke the bar in two and gave half to Leila, then drank water from the bay and waited until the shakes had left his legs.

"Keep soaking whatever sticks you can find with gas,"

he told Leila. Then he took the spade and went back into the underbrush, where he started to ram the blade into the tops of the drums. Leila had already started to throw down a line of gasoline-soaked branches and sticks. The trick was to move quickly, to connect the drums with a line of fire and pry them open just enough to let the flames penetrate.

Frank worked feverishly while Leila called out the time. At three o'clock all drums had been pierced; the main task was now to finish connecting the six drums with gasoline-soaked branches. At four o'clock, daylight was close, and they had to ignite.

They fell into each other's arms. So much depended on it! Frank pulled a burning frond from the small fire, shook some flames out of it, then started toward the woods. As he ran between the trees with the burning frond, the eyes of hundreds of crabs lit up. He tossed the flaming frond onto the first drum and dashed off. The force of the explosion took him by surprise. Although the gasoline-soaked branches caught fire almost immediately, the flames were somehow interrupted and did not connect to the second drum. He relit the line with a burning frond, and the second drum exploded so violently he felt air being sucked away from under his feet. For a second it felt like levitation. A sudden exhilaration flooded him; all fear had left and, as if in a dauntless dream, he continued stepping between the widening pockets of fire even after he had finished exploding the rest of the drums.

He heard Leila calling, and somewhere to his side, he saw the red of her bikini flash through the trees: she was dashing toward the bay. Eventually a hiss rose from the woods, and flaming branches floated down on Frank, forcing him to dive into the bay. He spotted Leila swimming toward him with long strokes, pulling the knapsack and clothes, which she had tied into a bundle on a short rope behind her. When she got close, she began treading water and pointing toward the flames still whipping into the crowns of the trees. She yelled, "By God, you pulled it off."

Curling smoke wove between the trees; fire-lit scarves of strange beauty wafted sensually in the haze. Frank felt pangs of exhilaration. The burning fronds kept swaying, snakelike, before they burst off the trunks in a brightness that pricked Frank's eyes, but he could not make himself look away. Even as he put his head underwater, he still felt drawn in by thousands of writhing reflections penetrating the dark.

They kept treading water, slowly drifting toward the rock as the fires dulled from a fierce white to yellow and then velvet crimson, wrapping the trunks that split open, baring a red-hot center, which seemed to spill from the very core of hell. But the hiss of the fires was finally easing into a low hum, less and less interrupted by the crack of bursting branches. Somewhere in the weak light of dawn, thick smoke drifted across the bay.

They stumbled ashore halfway between the rock and the burning woods and threw themselves on a spit of sand. Though a watery gray rim had already oozed into the eastern horizon, Leila's skin still reflected the western fires and shone golden like the hide of certain salamanders. She lay still with exhaustion, eyes shut.

"Somebody has to detect this fire," Frank said.

"What if you hadn't thought of it?" Leila mumbled.

"They might even come for us today," Frank said. He had visions of helicopters and gray warships on the horizon. A torrent of feelings surged through him: anger toward Jim, who had put them in this mess, but also exhilaration from lighting the fire and relief at the thought of rescue.

And then the sight of Leila's red bikini suit, so skimpy it cut across her pubic hair, aroused him and overtook all the emotions. He felt the urge to slide his fingers across her bared pubes. She let him pass his fingers across her stomach and didn't move. A tingle fingered into his groin. He circled his fingertips up to her breasts, lifting her nipples into hardening cherries. She sighed, giving him the smallest of encouragements. His fingertips felt her shiver. He slid his hand into her slip and felt for the cleft of her vulva, spreading it and releasing, spreading and releasing.

Then, hooking the tip of his small finger, he fleshed the clitoris, rubbing it gently against her pubic bone. She did not move, affecting exhaustion and sleep, but he could feel her body tensing into a reed strung taut by her lust and submission to his slow seduction. She lifted her buttocks just enough for him to slip off her string, then spread her leg ever so slightly; never had he been so much in tune with a woman's body. He kept rubbing her clitoris, throwing ripples across her skin. Again and again he would stir her into shivers and almost imperceptible lifts of her body. And still she pretended to be half asleep. So was he, lying almost still with his eyes closed while his hand kept probing her wetness until she groaned and finally turned sideways, her fingers now circling his erection. In a wild turn he swung toward her and slid into her writhing body. She came with a loud yell, her body heaving before it fell back onto the sand.

Afterward they stayed in a deep embrace. Frank wanted to express something about their love, but Leila laid a finger across his lips.

"Soon the sun will rise," she said.

Frank let himself sink back into the sand. It felt as if pebbles weighed his eyelids with a heft he couldn't resist. For some time they kept lying on the beach holding hands, sometimes close, sometimes with outstretched arms like two children playing snow angels.

When Frank opened his eyes the sun had already cut through the horizon. He looked west toward the burnt woods, where the first rays lit a pink sheet of thin smoke across the bay. Becoming stronger, they sent bright shafts in between gloomy billows in a spectacle of gothic light that lifted Frank's mind into a pleasant state that for some time would hold off the cold grip of reality.

But the recognition that they were still marooned on a forlorn island lost in a wasted sea eventually pierced all this softness. Frank walked down to the bay, fighting the fear that maybe the fire had gone unnoticed. He ladled some brackish water into his hollowed hands and, though the salty taste sickened him, he kept drinking. After all, the Mexican garrison had subsisted for months on bay water only.

They untied the bundle Leila had towed behind her and ate what was left of the burnt pieces of crab. This time they were able to stomach the crabs, and they felt strengthened; the early sunshine was pleasing and a short swim in the bay quickened their spirits. There were now only a few open fires. With all the branches charred, the flames had begun to penetrate the ground, working into tree stumps and roots, searing the soil. Off and on they could hear the crackle of exploding ammunition, probably rounds of bullets the Americans had left in 1945, and it was even possible that some undetected drums of gasoline blew up and shot flares into the sky. For the first time they had reason to hope for a timely rescue. Leila was elated.

"You saved our lives," she said.

"I had something to do with it."

Leila stood in front of him looking at him straight. "You talked about the fire that would burn down to your roots," she said. A slight tremble in her voice told him to keep silent. "The one you've waited for all your life." She slowly put her arms around him and hugged him.

So she had been listening, he thought, and had not forgotten. She had understood all along. What he had done for her and Jim had changed everything. It occurred to Frank that what was lost in his life could be regained. Jim was now far away. Frank had proven himself, and the burden of the void that had weighed on him all his life, the life-draining sense of emptiness, had finally lifted.

Leila slowly moved away, still holding Frank's hands. "What do you plan to do now?"

"Jim needs only one of us," Frank said.

"I can take care of him."

"Are you sure there's enough water in the canvas?"

"The tarp was half-full the last time I looked," she said.

"I'll scout the beaches," Frank said. "I might find some German supplies washed up."

"Maybe a pair of lederhosen."

"Well! The Krummgewehr was of some help. Wasn't it?"

"I haven't forgotten," Leila said. Her voice was serene now. "Maybe you should look for seaweed first, and you might be able to reach a few coconuts."

"Except that, for the time being, I'd burn myself walking across hot cinders."

"A few trees might topple into the bay and you could dive for the coconuts."

For a while, they sat on the sand watching the smoldering embers. Another round of discarded ammo blew. Then a tree fell, the crown hitting the bay with a thumping sound.

"Voila!" Leila exclaimed. "Time to go!" She opened the knapsack and Frank looked through it again, finding the knife, the lighter, the foldable spade, paper and pencil and two more bars of chocolate.

"Jim needs to gain strength, so the last bars of chocolate should be for him," he said.

"And what's on your menu?"

"Clipperton trout with a light salad of seaweed and roasted coconut as dessert."

Frank realized that she intended to smile, but she was stifled by a sudden pain in her bruised eye.

"Try for something better than slops of crab," she added, then told him briefly what she knew about coconuts, where to pierce the fruit and how to float it in the water.

"You have to keep still," he told her. "Any straining is bad for your eye. You've put yourself out too much already."

"I had no choice," she said.

"Take it easy on the way up to the lighthouse," Frank advised.

She started to walk away, off and on looking over her shoulder at the fading fires as if she too couldn't stop asking the question, "What if nobody noticed the burning trees?"

22

THE WIND HAD PICKED UP, blowing ashes across the bay; it rippled the surface and, wherever it spread cinders, the water appeared like old skin. Frank followed the beach alongside the smoldering fires, swimming into the bay only where the fires were burning too hot.

Collecting coconuts turned out easier than expected; two palm trees had toppled such that their crowns had fallen into the bay, and he could dive for the fruits. He cut them loose, pierced them at the site of the largest of three round scars as Leila had instructed him and eventually chanced upon one with milk. After slurping the milk down with abandon, he smashed the fruit with the spade and used the knife to scrape out the hollow; eating the pulp, however, knotted his stomach into cramps again. He rubbed his skin with pieces from the rind and walked on.

He could see no trace of their former camping site: all that remained were washed-over sandbanks. Having appeased his hunger, he felt stronger and his thoughts were more lucid. First order of business was to supply Jim and Leila with food; everything else could wait! He walked back to the fallen coconut trees and cut off a dozen of the pods with their fruits. Frank floated the fruits in the bay, keeping them in front of him as he swam back toward the rock. The coconuts kept bouncing against each other, and occasionally one would drift off, but in general he was doing quite well. Frank started to wonder why the approach of his exceptional supply convoy hadn't drawn any attention on top of the rock. Didn't they realize that starvation was over? But nobody was waving; no shirt was fluttering in the wind.

Suddenly the chop of rotors broke into his thoughts and, almost simultaneously, two helicopters burst into the sky, one on either side of the rock. One hovered briefly then landed a hundred yards away between Frank and the rock. Several heavily armed Marines jumped out even before the blades hung limp. Propelled by overwhelming relief, Frank threw his body into powerful strokes toward land, leaving the coconuts behind him clacking in the water. Just as Frank reached the shore, two soldiers came running over and introduced themselves as HM3 Collins and Sgt. Davis.

"Do you need medical attention, sir?" Collins asked. He unzipped his medical bag.

"There are three of us . . . the other two are on top of the rock, and one of them has a badly infected leg wound," Frank said, surprised about how succinctly he had squeezed the words through a throat choked by happiness. "I can guide you up there," he added. But Sgt. Davis had already walked off toward the rock. Only a blind man could have missed a woman frantically waving a jacket and wearing a red bikini.

Frank started to follow the sergeant. "Stay, sir! I need to take your vitals," the corpsman commanded. "You come back! Lie down!" Frank reluctantly permitted the examination, but he would rather have shared this moment with Leila.

"When did you last eat?"

"Three days, no four . . . five," Frank said.

"How about water?" He didn't wait for the answer. "You are severely dehydrated; your blood pressure is low." Nasal chatter came through the microphone. Another Marine joined them and set a backpack down beside HM3 Collins.

In this interval of assured rescue, when the gods take over, when all is fine and grace suffuses every fiber of your soul, Frank understood he had recast his life. He had reached his headwaters. He saw it clearly now: Jim could no longer hobble him with the burden of a familiar dread. There would be no more!

The Marine who had joined them knelt down beside Frank. "What are you doing here?" he asked.

"Leila, she's the woman waving the jacket up on the rock . . . she's been doing research for the Scripps Institute. I accompanied her . . . the third person is my cousin Jim. He's the one who got injured. We were attacked by three Mexicans and killed two of them in self-defense. The third died in the storm."

"Don't move," Collins ordered. "Extend your right arm. I'll start an intravenous line."

"Jim needs the help. Not me."

"You may need more help than you realize. Listen to Collins," the Marine said. "Why did the Mexicans come here?"

"Drug runners."

An expression of disbelief crossed the Marines' faces.

"Go on!"

"The short version is that they flew onto the island and tried to kill us, but we retreated to the rock. Shrapnel hit Jim in the leg."

"They used grenades?" the sergeant interrupted.

Frank nodded his head and continued. "I left the rock trying to retrieve antibiotics I had stashed in the airplane and hoping to set off the emergency locator transmitter, but the storm washed me into the bay. In the meantime two of the Mexicans, both armed, climbed to the top and took Jim and Leila prisoner. I was in hiding on the other side of the island when I found a German rifle from the Second World War. Yesterday morning, I climbed to the top of the rock and shot one of the Mexicans. Leila killed the other."

"You used a German World War II weapon?"

"A Krummgewehr."

"What?"

"A gun that shoots around the corner."

He shook his head. "Did you fly to Clipperton?"

"Yes. So did the Mexicans."

"Where is your plane? Hell! . . Where is the Mexicans' plane?"

"Sunk by the storm." Then Frank added, "There's stuff from World War II all over the island."

The man's mouth dropped open. Collins laughed at him and quipped, "That's the one we won."

"I'll call the lieutenant," the Marine said. He unhooked the microphone from his shoulder pad and started to talk. Turning back to Collins, he said, "The lieutenant wants you to get your ass up that hill right now."

"Told you," Frank said.

After Collins rushed off to the rock with his medical case, the Marine was left holding the bag with the intravenous solution.

"This is going to infiltrate. Isn't it?" Frank said, and with a sudden jerk he pulled the catheter out, making the intravenous line drop into the sand. "Too bad!"

"You better know what you are doing!" the Marine yelled.

"I'm not going to roast in the sun here doing nothing," Frank said. "I know how hot it gets."

"You'd have a bad time in the Marine Corps," the sergeant hissed.

"My name is Frank Herrmann."

"Sergeant Willard."

He looks like he came from the heartland, Frank thought. His upturned nose rimmed by puffy cheeks gave him the appearance of somebody benign and homely.

"Why waste time here?" Frank asked. "We'd better get back to the rock."

"Can you walk?"

"I just set the whole island on fire. What do you think?"

Willard kept pace beside Frank, giving him a hand for the first minute to keep Frank from stumbling in the rills cut by the storm. But when they had to slush through a wash-over, Frank forded it so easily that Willard realized he would be fine and rushed ahead to give the lieutenant a heads-up.

Marines were scurrying to and from the helicopters, unloading small canisters, boxes and bags, with the center of activity at the base of the rock, where the antenna of the lieutenant's radio stuck into the sky. By the time Frank arrived, the lieutenant had already climbed to the top of the rock, leaving a small group of Marines at the bottom awaiting orders. After Frank instructed them on the use of the pull-up rope, they made a few radio calls and repacked some of the equipment, and it was pulled to the top.

The news about Jim was grave. He was in septic shock and needed immediate medical attention; all Collins could provide him for now was intravenous infusion, antibiotics and drugs to stabilize his blood pressure. The concern was that Jim might be developing respiratory distress syndrome. Willard conducted all the radio communications, and Frank stayed close to hear what was going on.

"The lieutenant is thinking of belting Jim onto a stretcher and then letting him down."

"I have to talk him out of it!" Frank said.

Willard activated the microphone. "The other man we found wants to talk to you." He handed Frank the mike.

"Sir! I don't think Jim can be transported down on a stretcher," Frank advised. "This rock is literally spiked."

"Whom am I speaking with?"

"Frank Herrmann."

"Frank. I'm Lieutenant Kaminski. We are not able to lift stretchers into the type of copters we have."

"I understand, sir, but I don't think it can be done. May I come up? I have some important personal belongings," Frank said.

There was a pause. "Things are complicated. The island has been declared a crime scene. We have to leave everything the way it is," the lieutenant stated. "Are they taking care of you? You need to start eating—but very, very slowly!" Leaving no pause for any further objections, he added, "Hand the mike back to the sergeant."

Frank sensed a deepening entanglement; it occurred to him that he had not given much thought to where the helicopters had come from. After Willard had finished taking orders from the lieutenant, Frank asked how they happened to come to the island. He explained that a U.S. aircraft carrier happened to be conducting exercises nearby; the fire had been picked up by satellite, and the Navy had ordered a flight over the island.

"Right now they are rigging up a copter with a crane to lift the stretcher," Willard informed Frank, "and then they'll send down the woman."

They offered Frank more bottled water, and a Marine brought beef broth. "Orders from the lieutenant that you drink the broth first."

It was so delicious, so nurturing, that Frank swore he would never forget the contentment and satiation that came with every spoonful.

Finally Leila came down. Frank held her in his arms and they hugged with silent tears of relief. Leila sat down in the shadow beside Frank.

When a Marine handed them large cups of broth, Leila commented, "Thank you—as long as it's not crab soup." They drank slowly lest their jittery stomachs act up again. Leila told Frank that Jim had turned for the worse in the last hour she had been on top of the rock, and that the medic had had trouble finding a vein for intravenous access. "At one time they couldn't measure any blood pressure."

"What about this being a crime scene?"

"Oh? That explains why they didn't let me collect my belongings."

"I saw them carry around cameras."

"They took pictures on top."

Leila cut her conversation short when a Marine approached and replaced their mugs of broth with bowls of soup. Real food. With each spoonful, they felt life's energy returning to their weary bodies.

Sgt. Willard approached them once they had emptied their bowls of soup and asked for a brief timeline of events. "Whatever you say cannot be used against you," he joked.

One look at the faces of Leila and Frank told him that they weren't amused.

"Okay. This is not a formal interrogation, so relax. First, tell me what you know about the Mexicans."

Leila glanced at Frank with a worried look in her eyes.

"What's the commotion, sergeant?" Frank asked.

"From what I understand, this is becoming an FBI investigation. Eventually, they will interview you."

"Do we have to stay on this rotten island?"

"We'll get you out tomorrow," he clarified. "Is it all right if I call you by your first name, Leila?"

She nodded.

"You will be interviewed in the presence of an official of the French consulate."

"What will happen to Jim?"

"We'll get him off this island, stat. But first I need to know more about the Mexicans."

Frank and Leila repeated the story about the attack, Frank's rescue and the killings, what weapons they had and what plane they had flown.

"You are sure it was related to drugs?" Willard asked. But distracted by an urgent radio message, he didn't wait for the answer. He turned away, talking with an urgent voice. "20 miles north. On radar . . . a plane."

"These are the Mexicans. They're coming for us," Frank said.

"Advise not to intercept, do not intercept!" they heard him repeat into the microphone.

"You stay put!" Willard ordered them. "There's going to be some action."

The two copters had been restarted and the cluster of Marines thinned as several boarded the copters. Willard stayed with Leila and Frank but maintained ongoing communication on the microphone. The copters took off and hovered 30 feet above the sand spit, their violent backwash rippling the bay waters.

"They'll probably fly right out of the sun," Frank yelled at Willard.

As the seaplane touched down, the two copters dove out from under the shadow of the rock. Willard informed them later that the Marines took four Mexicans into custody and were detaining them at the former campsite until Mexican authorities could be flown in.

When the radio died down, Willard turned to Frank and Leila and asked, "Did you know that the FBI is looking for your friend?"

Frank felt an icy chill run through him. Leila dropped her head into her hands.

"What do you know?" Willard asked firmly.

"He visited Peru and Colombia on some photography assignment. Then he rushed back to the States to join us," Leila said.

"Well! He must have found time to screw up big," Willard said in such a curt tone that Frank and Leila dared not ask questions. Frank lifted his soup closer and played with the chunks of meat in the bowl.

When Willard stepped away, Leila nudged closer to Frank. "Jim's in trouble."

"How could he slide from one life to another so smoothly?"

"It seems so obvious to me now," Leila said. One of the Marines removed the empty soup bowls and gave each of them a plate of stew. "If this is too much for you to chew, we'll bring more soup," he said.

"I had a few teeth knocked out and Leila's face hurts even worse from the beatings," Frank commented. "But we'll give it a try."

The stew eventually began to ease their hunger; they tried their best to chew but ended up swallowing most pieces whole.

When the sergeant returned, he asked everybody to move away from the rock to avoid the rotor wash of the large copter, which would be arriving soon. Leila and Frank sat down on the western sand spit about fifty yards away. The twin-rotor copter was huge, appearing even wider than the rock in the featureless splay of light. The angry howl of the copter's revving engines and the rotors chopping whipped the air into their ears such that they could not even hear the waves ramming into the reef. As the copter hovered into position, air rushed down onto the rock and scoured the stones, spiraling into crevices where birds were hiding, tearing off guano, purging ancient lava. The straw of boobies' nests was blown away with splintering force, and the birds were tossed against the slopes. A cloud of sand particles, dried grasses, broken nests and guano dust swirled away from the rock then raced across the sandbar, filling Frank's and Leila's eyes with tears. They could only glance up to the top of Clipperton Rock for brief moments to watch the stretcher being let down from the cargo door. It sank smoothly inside the silent core of a maelstrom. After Jim was heaved up, the copter slowly turned away, and the noise died into a distant chop. The clouds settled and the sky turned blue again. The Marines shook sand off their uniforms and started to gather into small groups; somebody played "American Pie" on the radio. Some deep cleansing had occurred with Jim's departure.

"Drove my Chevy to the levee," Leila began to sing, making her swollen cheeks bulge out like a bullfrog's, which made Frank laugh.

"Not quite up to speed yet," Leila said.

"I'd spit out some teeth just trying."

The lieutenant came down from the lighthouse with two Marines who had packed Frank's and Leila's belongings into two plastic bags. They asked Leila and Frank to briefly identify what belonged to each of them. Frank wanted to take the diary, but the request was denied. "Sorry, sir, we're just following procedures."

Frank started to argue but the lieutenant cut in, "Did they give you enough to eat?"

"Yes, thank you," Leila responded. "But what is Jim's condition?"

"We noted sloughing tissue that looked like gangrene. He also developed bleeding into the skin, which made it urgent to get him back to the aircraft carrier. "

"And from there?"

"A twin-engine Medevac will fly him back to San Diego."

"Why is the FBI looking for him?"

Frank saw an expression of surprise in the lieutenant's face, but his voice did not give it away. "Something that happened in Peru or Colombia. . . . I can't answer any more questions."

Activities had slowed down. Some of the Marines boarded a helicopter and took off. The lieutenant stayed behind. Leila and Frank learned more in bits and pieces: The Mexicans had been handcuffed and chained to the palm trees at the former campsite. According to one of the Marines who kept supplying Leila and Frank with water and chocolate, they planned to leave guards.

"The island is a crime scene now," the lieutenant repeated.

"It has been for decades," Frank said. "More souls have been killed on its miserable soil than have returned from it. "

Unsettled, the lieutenant wrenched his lips. "I'm here to do what needs to be done," he finally said. "We'll provide each of you with a sleeping bag. I can see they brought you fresh jackets and pants. I'll tell them to apply some antiseptic to your bruises and cuts."

"We can do that ourselves," Frank said.

"First brief me on some details and draw a map of Clipperton. I intend to do an air sweep to search for the third Mexican's body and have a closer look at the crashed planes."

Leila and Frank leaned over the lieutenant's clipboard and drew the map. Leila pointed out their camping site; Frank explained where he had been washed into the bay and took the occasion to talk about the Egg Islands, the cave inside the rock and his father's diary.

"Jim tried to explain something about a diary, but we couldn't understand him," the lieutenant said. "I figured it was some document. Don't worry. We have all items in plastic bags, and I'll see to it that your father's diary is handled with extra care." He got up, took the clipboard and stood there for a second, shaking his head. "Hard to believe the Nazis were here," he mumbled.

Two Marines brought them sleeping bags, bottles of antiseptic solution, gauze, jugs of water and a tray of Chinese chicken chow mein. Leila and Frank sat down on the sleeping bags and ate and drank while watching the Marines prepare the helicopter. Leila took off her jacket and pants so Frank could clean her cuts and bruises with puffs of cotton he had soaked in antiseptic solution.

Once the copter departed, its chop growing more and more distant, the gentle tug of the senses came back to Frank. He heard the rhythmic roll and trundle of waves, the hoarse cry of boobies, and felt again the gritty rub of sand on his toes. He kept daubing Leila's cuts and gashes gently. The world restated itself, and, in so doing, brought the promise of immeasurable depth in simple tending.

"We never had a chance to take care of each other during this ordeal," Leila said.

"We can do that now," Frank responded.

"We wouldn't even be here now if it weren't for your courage," she said.

He nodded and kept painting her wounds with the amber colored antiseptic, which made her look bronzed in the slanting light. Some of the gashes were deep and circular as if drawn by knives twisted into her flesh; others were superficial scrapes from being dragged alongside piercing rocks. Frank knew he couldn't fathom what Leila had suffered through; there hadn't been time to think about her hell and despair. But as he was cleaning her wounds, with each cut he dabbed and each stab he soaked, the promise of healing lifted his heart. It was as if the simple task of tending to her was drawing him back to a reality anchored in hope.

When it was Leila's turn, she, too, kept paying attention to each of Frank's scratches with the gentlest of hands.

The evening light flowed into the horizon and formed a thinning lens of a brief brightness below the darkening sky.

"It feels like our first evening on Clipperton," Leila said, looking at Frank. "Why did Jim come between us?"

"It wasn't your fault that he moved heaven and earth to get here."

"I should have told him I didn't want him to come, but . . . oh, Frank, it was all so complicated."

When the helicopter returned, a Marine sergeant walked over again, brought one more tin of food, and reported that the Marines had received a radio message that Jim's condition been stabilized as he was being flown back to San Diego.

"I'm leaving a flashlight, and in case you need us, we'll be just yards away. Good night! . . . Of course, you may sleep in the copter. . . ." He was waiting.

"We'll watch the stars come out," Frank said. "Thank you."

The next morning they woke before sunrise to watch the pilots load the copter that was to leave first. Soon it was their turn; they sat down on the narrow seats and fastened their belts. The helicopter lifted, then turned away from the island, making it dissolve in the glare of the morning sun like a bad dream.

"It's an odd feeling not to have anything, to know we don't carry anything with us," Leila remarked.

"We are free," Frank said.

"I do have something," she said.

She reached into her jacket, lifted one hand toward Frank, then slowly opened her palm. Frank cupped his hand below hers. "One of your father's orchid pods," she explained. "Finally released."

A dust of golden seeds drifted down into his open hand.

ABOUT THE AUTHOR

Photo by Chuck Mamula

Karl Berger, a native of Germany, is a practicing pediatrician in Johnstown, Pa. He is an active member of the Loyalhanna Writers Association and has been published in the *Loyalhanna Review*. Dr. Berger is working on his second novel.

To order copies of *Clipperton* as well as other titles from Harbor House, visit our Web site:

www.harborhousebooks.com.